Paint

ME A CRIME

A ROSE SHORE MYSTERY

HOLLY YEW

Relax. Read. Repeat.

PAINT ME A CRIME
(A Rose Shore Mystery, Book 1)
By Holly Yew
Published by TouchPoint Press
Brookland, AR 72417
www.touchpointpress.com

Softcover ISBN: 978-1-956851-62-5

Editor: Kimberly Coghlan
Cover Design: ColbieMyles.com
Cover images: Adobe Stock

Visit the author's website at www.hollyyew.com

 @hollyyewauthor   @hollyyew   @holly.yew.author

First Edition

Library of Congress Control Number: 2023933196

Printed in the United States of America.

For Samuel, for replying "Why not?" when I asked if he thought I could write a book one day.

Chapter One

Tranquil, painted to represent the ocean's own choreographed rhythm of dancing bright blues and deep greens, had to be one of the most beautiful pieces of artwork Jessamine Rhodes had ever witnessed.

And she still couldn't believe it was right there on display as the center showpiece in her brand-new community art center for their opening day. Even better, *Tranquil* would soon be joined by the talented artist who painted it.

"Are you just going to stare at it all day? You know those mason jars aren't going to fill themselves with water." Emilia's teasing snapped Jessamine back to reality.

"Right, those. I was secretly hoping Andrew would do it if I left them long enough." Jessamine slowly drew her eyes away from *Tranquil*. If time allowed, she could gaze at that gorgeous painting all day. It had a way of instantly transporting her to some tropical beach; she could almost feel the warm kiss of the sun. She was glad the painting had arrived early that morning, long before the day's festivities so she had some extra time to admire it. But Emilia Kent, her friend and caterer, was right. There was still work to get done before that afternoon's event.

"I still can't believe you were able to get Gabriella Everhart to teach your first art class. She's such a well-known and respected artist around here."

"Not just here—around the world! Her portfolio is amazing. *Tranquil* alone is worth ten thousand dollars." Jessamine's voice sped up with excitement. "That piece has been featured in art shows in San Francisco, London, and even Rome. I first met Gabriella at the art show in San Francisco, where *Tranquil* debuted."

"I heard a rumor she's finally going to sell it. Has anyone talked to you about buying it?"

"A few people have shown interest, not that I really have anything to do with buying and selling artwork anymore. I'm more interested in testing out a potential relationship between the art center and Gabriella today, but she did mention she's already promised *Tranquil* to a local art collector named Victor Carlisle and will be selling it to him after the watercolor class." Jessamine paused for a moment. "But if you wouldn't mind, keep that to yourself. I mean, you're technically part of my staff today, so it's all right if you know, but we don't want word getting out until the deal has gone through."

"Of course. I'll keep it quiet." Emilia made a playful motion like she was zipping her lips. "And I'm sure a relationship with Gabriella will work out. My perfectly blended tea and raspberry dark chocolate teacakes are sure to win anyone over."

Jessamine smiled in appreciation. "I'm feeling so anxious about today. It means so much to me to host the perfect opening. I really want to impress the Rose Shore community."

"Don't stress about it. Everyone here is nice, and lots of residents are thankful you're reopening the art center. People have good memories of this place."

Jessamine knew her friend's words were supposed to be comforting, but they made her even more anxious about making a good impression. Both she and Emilia had similar stories; they'd both left behind the big-city life to settle in the small town of Rose Shore in the Okanagan Valley in B.C. Jessamine had recently moved from Vancouver to purchase the community art center, which closed a few months ago and had only recently been put up for sale, and Emilia had moved from London, England, to open her own tea shop. The Secret Garden Tea Shop specialized in brunches and afternoon teas and was getting its start in the catering world.

"That's what I hear." Jessamine turned the tap back on to finish filling the mason jars. "And thanks again for catering. From what I've sampled, it's all delicious."

"Everything Miss Emilia Kent makes is delicious." Andrew Marsh, Jessamine's administrative assistant, came over with his cheeks puffed out and telltale cookie crumbs on the collar of his shirt.

"Hey! You haven't broken into my catering containers, have you, Marsh?" Emilia placed a hand on her hip, even though her big brown eyes showed amusement. "And you only think everything is so delicious because you're not cultured enough to have sampled any other fine teas and delicacies."

Andrew gave her a mock look of hurt. "Hey! I consider pizza to be a fine delicacy, and I've had plenty of that."

Jessamine rolled her eyes and ignored the bantering between Andrew and Emilia to turn her focus on finishing tasks for the upcoming watercolor painting class.

Once the last of the mason jars were filled with water and set out along the tables, two per spot as Gabriella's instructions specified, she looked over her printed to-do list. There wasn't too much more to complete, but she wanted everything to be absolutely perfect. Giving up her job as an art curator at an extravagant gallery in the heart of downtown Vancouver for a career change and long-distance move had been a tough decision. Owning an art center was a great way for her to share her love of painting and creating with her new community, and she was excited to work with many of the local artists of the surrounding Okanagan area. She needed the new pace of a simpler life, but it was still hard to let go of the Go-Go-Go stride she was so used to.

Wandering over to her one in-house teacher to go over the guest list one last time, she found that Molly Williams had already spread out the list over the front table in the foyer in her usual, organized fashion.

"Hey, Molly, how does the guest list look?"

Molly looked up from behind her wire-framed glasses and tucked a loose strand of ash blond hair back into her low ponytail. "Excellent, Ms. Rhodes. There aren't any mistakes on the guest list, and I have it organized for Andrew to check guests in as they arrive for the watercolor class."

"Perfect. Thank you again for doing this."

"It's part of my job, Ms. Rhodes." Molly nodded at Jessamine and started to turn back to the guest list.

"You know you're welcome to call me Jessamine."

Molly looked uncomfortable for a moment. "I—I will see. I have always thought of work to be a place for formalities."

"Well, whatever makes you comfortable is fine with me."

Molly nodded again and turned back to her task.

Jessamine smiled to herself as she walked away. She'd never been one for formalities, but she did appreciate Molly's strong work ethic and knowledge of art. She had also appreciated Molly's knowledge of the people of Rose Shore. Since Jessamine barely knew anyone in her new town, she trusted

Molly with deciding on whom to invite to their special first class. That afternoon would give her a chance to properly launch her new business *and* get to know her fellow Rose Shore residents.

Gabriella's painting with watercolors art class was supposed to have started ten minutes ago, but Jessamine couldn't find the teacher anywhere. The main classroom of the art center was filled with eager guests, and Jessamine tried to smooth over any impatience as she scurried around greeting everyone while simultaneously keeping one eye on the door for Gabriella.

"Well? What are you thinking we should do?" Andrew caught Jessamine's elbow and led her out into the hallway. "Molly tried calling Gabriella again, but there was no answer."

"Where is she? People are getting restless." Jessamine blew out a breath in frustration. "All right, let's get Emilia to start serving the refreshments. We were going to put them out after the class, but maybe that'll buy us some time. I'll go make a little welcome speech while you help Emilia."

"Sounds like a plan. Good luck." Andrew gave her a good-natured salute.

Jessamine split off from Andrew and headed toward the front of the classroom. She felt a strong case of the nerves, and she was definitely not looking forward to potentially having to cancel her opening art class. She or Molly could possibly try to wing it and teach the class themselves, but it wouldn't be the same. She took a moment to smooth out her royal blue wrap dress that swished just below her knees, a dress she picked out because Emilia had insisted the color perfectly brought out the highlights in her nutmeg French twist and matched her bright blue-green eyes. Now Jessamine took in a deep breath, looked out into the crowd, and caught her friend's gaze. Emilia gave a reassuring nod from the refreshment table, and it was all the extra courage she needed.

"Hello. Could I please have everyone's attention? I'm so sorry about the delay, but I'm sure Gabriella will—"

Her speech was interrupted as Gabriella Everhart burst through the doorway of the classroom and hurried right up to the front next to Jessamine. She heard a few murmurs of excitement.

Gabriella placed her large messenger bag on the table and whispered so only Jessamine could hear. "I apologize for running late. Please give me a few moments to set up, and then we'll be good to start the class."

Jessamine nodded and turned back to the class. "Again, thank you so much for your patience. We'll begin the class in just a few short minutes, but, in the meantime, I wanted to thank everyone for attending today. I'm so excited to be working here at the Rose Shore Community Art Center." Jessamine took the time to share her hopes and visions for the art center until Gabriella gave her a nod. "And it looks like we're ready to start. It's my pleasure to introduce our very first guest teacher, Gabriella Everhart!"

The full classroom clapped and cheered as Gabriella took center stage and got started. With magnets, she put up large photographs of various sunrises and sunsets on the whiteboard for inspiration.

"Hello, everyone! Welcome to the Rose Shore Community Art Center. Today I'll be showing you the basics of painting with watercolors. Now, everyone should have two mason jars filled with water. No, one is not to drink."

A small laugh murmured through the crowd.

"One is for rinsing your paintbrush, and the other is for painting with. You don't want to be using the same jar for both, or your painting will eventually turn into one mucky brown color."

She started off by showing different strokes and techniques and then walked around to give one-on-one tips to everyone in the class. Gabriella was an amazing teacher, and besides getting started late, Jessamine was happy with how the first class was going. She had a good feeling her art center would be a success.

As the late afternoon light turned into dusk, the painting class neared its end, and Jessamine snuck off to make sure Emilia was ready for the guests to spend some time munching and mingling. She noticed during the hour Gabriella had spent talking about color charts, paintbrushes, and watercolor techniques, the back of the classroom had filled with curious guests who'd been invited but hadn't wanted to actively participate in the class, possibly only wanting to check out the newly reopened art center or meet the famous painter.

Jessamine nodded appreciatively at everyone as she walked to the refreshment table. Before she got there, a hand reached out and grabbed hers, shaking it in a greeting before she could even look up to see who it belonged to.

"Ms. Rhodes, might we introduce ourselves?" a handsome gentleman with styled silver hair asked in a low voice. "My name is Victor Carlisle, and this is my wife, Madeleine."

"Oh, Mr. Carlisle, Mrs. Carlisle. Yes, of course. I've heard so much about you and your art collections. It's such a pleasure to meet you both." Jessamine looked into his intense blue eyes and enthusiastically returned his handshake before shaking Mrs. Carlisle's hand.

"Please call me Victor." He was dressed very formally for a community art center in a black suit and bright-blue bow tie.

"And call me Madeleine." She looked to be a couple of years younger than her husband, her hair still more blond than gray.

"Then you must call me Jessamine. Welcome to the Rose Shore Community Art Center. Did you just arrive?"

"Yes. Just in time to catch Gabriella when she's done with her class, I hope. I've visited this art center a few times over the years, and I'm ecstatic to see what you'll do now with the place. Great things, I'm sure." Victor was very charismatic.

"Do you collect art as well?" Jessamine asked Madeleine.

"Oh no. I leave that passion all to my husband. I don't usually tag along on his art trips, but we have a vacation home here along the lake, and I love visiting Rose Shore."

"I'm glad you could join us today. Did you get to see any of the painting class?"

"I did. Gabriella is a wonderful artist and a great teacher. And I must get the contact for your caterer. I tried a few goodies; I hope you don't mind. Everything is so delectable."

"Not at all. I'm glad you helped yourself. It was all done by Emilia's Secret Garden Tea Shop. She's my new go-to for any event like this. Have you tried the mini quiche Lorraine? Those are my favorite."

"Yes, delicious."

"I must have gobbled up half the serving dish," Victor exaggerated. "Now, I must thank you for putting together such an event for Gabriella and myself, and oh, it looks like Gabriella's class is just finishing. Please excuse us."

"Uh, sure. Nice talking to you . . ."

Victor had already moved on from their conversation. He rushed after Gabriella as the artist packed up her supplies and greeted her like an old friend. Madeleine gave a quick apologetic smile before turning to catch up with her husband.

Jessamine thought about his odd comment about the event. Why would it be put together for him and Gabriella? She stood there perplexed for a minute before heading over to where Emilia was refilling some of the serving dishes at the refreshment table. Andrew stood nearby chatting with a few guests.

"I just met Victor and Madeleine Carlisle. They're very nice, but he seems to think this whole event was arranged for him and Gabriella," Jessamine said.

"Oh, I'm sure he's just excited." Emilia fidgeted with the knot at the back of her small, lace apron, which covered a lilac dress that looked fabulous against her dark skin.

"Do you need help with anything?" Jessamine asked.

"I've got it!" Andrew stepped in to help.

Jessamine had to stifle a laugh at his obvious ploy to impress her friend.

"It's okay, Andrew. I don't really need help," Emilia said with exasperation as he practically tripped over himself to assist with the catering.

Before Andrew could convince Emilia otherwise, a bright camera flash temporarily blinded the three of them.

"Ms. Rhodes, care to give me a few words about this afternoon's event?" asked a short, young man with a sandy flop of hair and a rather obnoxious way of drawing out her name in a dramatic fashion. He held a large camera in one hand and a notebook in the other.

"Um, who are you?" Jessamine raised her eyebrows as she looked down to meet his gaze.

"Name's Howard 'Click' McCoy. I own and write for Click's Journal, a blog that keeps everyone informed with the happenings in Rose Shore." Howard handed her his business card.

"Oh, well, it's certainly nice to meet you, but I—"

"Now, what made you want to purchase the community art center? Are you running away from something? Why did you leave the big city?" Howard interrupted with a string of questions.

"That really is none of—"

"And how did you convince Gabriella Everhart to teach a class for your opening? How much are you paying her?" Howard's inappropriate questions continued.

"Howard," Jessamine held up her hands to get him to stop talking. "I don't seem to remember issuing you an invitation. How did you get in?"

"I flashed my press pass at the front door, easy peasy."

Jessamine inwardly groaned and shot a look at Andrew. He flushed a sheepish pink and ducked away, suddenly interested in straightening a cluster of champagne glasses on the other side of the table. She was positive this press pass was probably something Howard had printed off at home. "Listen, Howard. How about I give you an exclusive some other day? When I'm not in the middle of one of the most important events of my new career?"

"That's a deal. And I'll hold you to that." Howard walked away, scribbling in his little notebook.

Jessamine turned back to Emilia and caught her failing to hide her laughter. "Do you know that guy?"

"Oh, Howard is harmless, incredibly annoying, but harmless. He's always running around trying to create a story out of nothing. No one calls him 'Click,' by the way." Emilia gave a slight shake of her head.

"I could have guessed that." Jessamine laughed.

"Ms. Rhodes! May I please speak to you? I've been trying to catch you all day."

Now what? Jessamine looked around to find who was shouting at her. The huffy voice belonged to a stout woman with bright red hair and lipstick to match. Her wrists were covered in sparkly bracelets, and her dress looked to be two sizes too small, but it was her annoyed look that held Jessamine's attention.

"Yes, of course. What can I do for you?" Jessamine had absolutely no idea who this woman was or what she could want.

Emilia politely excused herself from the conversation, but not before Jessamine caught a sympathetic look.

"I am Eugenie Price, a long-time benefactor of this art center, and I came to your opening hoping for a chance to purchase *Tranquil*. I've had my eye on that painting ever since Ms. Everhart revealed it on her website. I thought to myself that I must have it for my art collection! It is perfect for my newly painted sitting room; that turquoise and sage together is the best color combination I have ever come up with. I really outdid myself this time. Anyway, I need that painting! But I just found out that it has already been promised to Victor Carlisle. I cannot stand that man! He is always one step ahead of me when it comes to purchasing art."

When Eugenie finally paused to catch her breath, Jessamine couldn't help but stare with wide eyes at the uptight lady a moment before sorting through her long complaint. She recognized the name Price from the donor's list and knew, indeed, that Mrs. Price wasn't lying about how much she and her husband cared about art.

"Nothing has been announced yet, Mrs. Price, and the art center has nothing to do with the sale of *Tranquil*. It's just on display for the event. The artist will make all final decisions about the painting." As Jessamine tried to calm Mrs. Price down, she racked her brain on how the news could have gotten out. Only Gabriella, the Carlisles, herself, and her staff knew the painting had already been promised, and they were all in agreement not to share the news until the deal had gone through. "May I ask how you found out about the deal?"

"Victor just had to brag about it, of course. He delights in lording his art collection over mine. But if this is out of your hands, I'll have to have a word with Ms. Everhart then, won't I?" Spitting out the last two words, Mrs. Price spun on her heel and left the conversation in a humph, presumably in search of Gabriella.

Jessamine gritted her teeth at the drama unfolding and knew it was time to step in. To find Gabriella before Mrs. Price had the chance to pester the artist about *Tranquil*, Jessamine took off through the crowded classroom, sidestepping around Rose Shore residents laughing, drinking, and admiring the various displays.

"Hopefully, I can at least sideline some of this drama," she mumbled to herself.

Jessamine spotted Gabriella chatting away with Victor and Madeleine near *Tranquil's* spot next to the glass doors leading out to a large balcony. The painting, reminiscent of the calm of the ocean, with layers of small waves swirling around the entire canvas, sat on an easel beside a framed biography of Gabriella. The artist, who looked stunning in her black tunic dress with her long, dark curls hung loosely around her shoulders, laughed at something Victor had said. As Victor stood next to *Tranquil*, Jessamine realized the bow tie he wore matched the same aqua blue featured in the painting. *He sure takes his love of purchasing art to a whole new level!*

Jessamine was trying to think of an excuse to speak with Gabriella alone when she saw Mrs. Price hurrying through the crowd toward the artist. Sighing, she gave up on forming a plan and rushed to reach Gabriella first. Along the way, she was cut off by a woman with questions about an upcoming children's art class, and by the time she broke free, Gabriella, Mrs. Price, and the Carlisles were nowhere in sight.

When she finally reached the spot where she'd last seen them, she realized something else had vanished as well.

"*Tranquil*," Jessamine whispered. *Where's the painting?* Jessamine inhaled sharply and took a hurried look around the area. Maybe it fell behind a curtain? Maybe someone picked it up to take a better look? These were ridiculous solutions, she knew, but she had to ward off panic as her gaze swept around the classroom.

A moment later, the lights went out in the Rose Shore Community Art Center, leaving the building in total darkness. A startled gasp carried throughout the crowd, and guests panicked as they moved toward the front doors in the foyer. Jessamine pulled out her cell phone from her wristlet and used the flashlight feature to get a sense of what was going on.

Before she could process anything, a new sense of terror arose as the piercing shatter of breaking glass silenced the flustered crowd. Then, a bone-chilling scream echoed through the silence.

Chapter Two

"Everyone stay calm!" Jessamine said, though it was easier said than done as guests of the event had already gone into full panic mode.

She heard people running in all directions, knocking over tables and chairs in the dark. Jessamine cringed at the sound of more glass breaking and knew poor Emilia would be down a few teacups at the end of all of this.

An uncontrollable sobbing from the foyer had replaced the screaming.

"Please move. Pardon me!" Jessamine weaved through the panic toward the sobbing, her phone's small light leading the way. She noticed Molly standing near the entrance to the foyer, helping guests exit through the doorway.

"Molly, call nine-one-one!" Jessamine hurried past.

"Certainly, Ms. Rhodes." Molly, her phone already out, dialed the number.

The sight that greeted Jessamine in the middle of the foyer was horrific. On the ground, unconscious, Victor's blue shirt metamorphosed to bright red from a large pool of blood flowing from his chest. Madeleine stood in shock over Victor, and Gabriella stood beside her, sobbing loudly.

Mrs. Price stood nearby, fanning herself with what looked to be a checkbook as she muttered repeatedly, "Oh my. Oh my. Oh my!"

"What happened?" Jessamine grabbed a soft, cotton coat off the nearby coatrack and squatted down next to Victor, with the intention of pressing the balled-up fabric onto his wound with as much force as she dared. Instead, the sight of a large piece of glass protruding from his chest made her immediately reach for Victor's wrist to check for a pulse, fearing the worst.

Gabriella only blubbered, Madeleine stood silent with wide eyes, and Mrs. Price, looking like she was about to collapse, still repeated her "Oh mys."

"Ms. Rhodes, the police and an ambulance are on the way, and Andrew is working on getting the lights turned back on," a breathless Molly informed her.

"Thank you." Jessamine turned to the few remaining guests in the foyer. "Did anyone see what happened?"

From the glow of streetlamps through the windows, she only saw shaking heads. One person, however, caught her attention—a tall, heavyset man wearing a dark green raincoat. He glared at her before slipping out through the front doorway with the rest of the crowd.

Before she had a chance to react to the mysterious man, the lights suddenly snapped back on. Jessamine caught Madeleine's fearful, questioning look and responded with a solemn shake of her head.

Victor hadn't made it.

Standing, Jessamine hurried to reach Madeleine's side, and, putting her arm around the woman's shoulders, she led her away from Victor's body and back into the main classroom. They sat closely next to each other in a pair of chairs near the door.

"Why . . ." Madeleine started to ask before finally breaking down into sobs and throwing her face against Jessamine's shoulder.

"I don't . . . I don't know."

"We'll need a list of everyone who attended your opening today, Ms. Rhodes, both guests and staff. And a copy of any security tapes if you have cameras." Constable Chris Todd had been one of the first responders on the scene of the 911 call and was taking Jessamine's statement in her office in the back of the art center. From his graying hair, she guessed he'd been an officer for many years, but she wondered how often something like this happened in Rose Shore.

"Of course. I already have a member of my staff working on that."

"Good. Now, can you tell me exactly what you saw earlier?" He looked serious as he prepared to jot down her responses in his notebook.

Jessamine took her time summarizing what happened that afternoon and evening, including how upset Mrs. Price had been about the sale of *Tranquil* and how she'd been on her way to warn Gabriella when the lights went out. Andrew had reported to her earlier that someone had simply flipped the main switch on the electrical panel behind the reception desk in the foyer, and she passed on that information to Constable Todd. As she spoke, she fought to remain professional against the looming panic weighing against her chest.

"Then, something crashed in the foyer, followed by a scream. I rushed to the foyer to find Mr. Carlisle lying on the ground, bleeding from the chest. Ms. Everhart, Mrs. Price, and Mrs. Carlisle were all standing near him and were very upset." She decided to keep the part about the strange man slipping away to herself until she knew if it was of significance or not.

"Now, what can you tell me about the missing painting?" Constable Todd didn't make eye contact as he hastily scrawled down notes.

"Well, *Tranquil* is a private piece of Ms. Everhart's. She was only lending it to the art center to display for this event as part of her portfolio. The piece had already been promised to Mr. Carlisle before it was brought here, but I know that others were interested, such as Mrs. Price. Here's a photo of the painting." Jessamine handed him her phone with the picture Gabriella had sent her a few days prior up on the screen.

"Thank you. After I get the guest and staff list, that will be all for now, but I'll be in contact." He gave her a look that was almost like a warning.

Does he really think I'll just take off or something? "Of course. You can reach me either here or on my cell." She forced a smile in hopes to lighten the mood.

Constable Todd gave no response as he held open the office door for her. The pair headed back to the foyer, and Constable Todd walked over to talk with another officer near the front door. A few other police officers were questioning the remaining guests, and the paramedics had just loaded Victor's body onto a stretcher and into the ambulance parked outside.

Jessamine noticed one of the paramedics was her neighbor, Jackson Yeung. He'd helped her move into her lakeside cottage a few weeks ago when she first moved to Rose Shore, though she had a feeling he'd been reluctantly volunteered by their other neighbor, Clara Connors. She'd barely seen him since the day she moved in. The expression on his face now as he lifted the stretcher was of extreme distress, and she wondered if perhaps he'd known the art collector personally. She thought about walking over to say hi but figured it best to stay out of the way as Jackson got into the ambulance with the other paramedics and drove off.

So, instead, she walked over to Constable Todd to see if there was anything else she could do.

"Not a thing, Ms. Rhodes. Just sit tight, and we'll be out of here soon."

"Thank you for staying so calm through all of this. I'm sure it was quite the shock," the other officer said kindly and reached out to shake Jessamine's hand. "I'm Constable Lauren Marsh, Andrew's sister."

"Nice to meet you, though I wish it was under better circumstances. It's been great working with Andrew." Jessamine was surprised she hadn't noticed the resemblance right away. Andrew and Lauren had the same hazel eyes and coppery-red hair.

"I know he loves his job here."

Constable Todd cleared his throat, and Jessamine took it to mean their time for small talk was over.

"I'll just go sit tight then." She awkwardly pointed to a chair in the foyer. "Again, please let me know if there's anything you need."

After everyone had left, Jessamine went home, poured herself a cup of herbal tea, and went upstairs to her loft bedroom to settle in bed with a book. She stared at the cover of her rom-com novel, and even though it was one of her favorites, a book she'd read half a dozen times at least, she couldn't seem to muster the energy to get past the title. Margo, her beagle she'd adopted from a local rescue a few years ago and named after her favorite surrealist artist, Boris Margo, snored under the fluffy gray and white comforter beside her. Despite having her own dog bed on the floor beside Jessamine's, Margo seemed to think the elegant queen-sized sleigh bed was all hers. But Jessamine didn't mind; she hadn't realized how much she needed a furry companion in her life until Margo was a part of it.

Being too anxious about the day to concentrate on anything, she lit a candle on her bedside table and let the comforting scent of lavender soothe her nerves. Her body relaxed, which produced a yawn, but her mind focused on the events at the art center earlier that evening.

Since she had to wait around for the police to finish their search before locking up, Jessamine had learned the only clue they'd found—at least that the police had shared with her—three broken champagne glasses near Victor's body. Supposedly, the glasses, which had been left on the reception desk, were the origins of the crashing noise right before Gabriella started screaming—and also the broken glasses were the source of the large chunk of glass that ultimately killed Victor.

It had to have been murder, right? It seemed like an unlikely accident.

Maybe Constable Todd would keep her up-to-date like he promised; Jessamine wasn't sure if he would, but hopefully, she could count on Lauren.

Her thoughts drifted back to *Tranquil.* She couldn't believe her opening day had resulted in the theft of a $10, 000 painting on loan to her and a murder! Something this big could ruin her art center *and* her reputation. Jessamine decided right then she couldn't step aside and wait for the answers to come to her; she needed to do something to save face. She set her morning alarm for earlier than usual, intending to look around the art center for clues on her own. Jessamine was determined to uncover the person who had murdered Victor and stolen the painting before her new business was completely destroyed.

Chapter Three

Arriving at the Rose Shore Community Art Center early the next day with a travel mug filled with spicy Chai, Jessamine unlocked the front door. On Sundays, the art center was only scheduled to be open for a few hours in the afternoon, which gave her the entire morning to search for anything that might lead to answers. The community art center was by no means large, with the foyer and reception area flowing into a long hallway with the large classroom and two smaller ones branching off. At the end of the hallway, an employee's only section hosted her and Molly's offices and a small break room. Her favorite part of the art center was the large balcony attached to the main classroom that stretched out over Opal Lake, which ran along Rose Shore and was named for the beautiful iridescence hues of the water. She was already daydreaming about what a perfect setting it would make for hosting events during the warmer months of the year.

Setting her coat, purse, and travel mug on the small table by the front door, she started her search near the area where Victor had been stabbed. The police had done a thorough sweep of the area last night, but she hoped fresh eyes might uncover a new discovery.

Nothing really stood out as unusual to Jessamine in the lobby except for a forgotten jacket on the coat rack. Considering the autumn air, the previous night had been quite crisp, she assumed that everyone would have remembered their coat before leaving the art center. Plucking the jacket from the coat rack, Jessamine dug through each of the pockets.

Her fingers brushed a crinkled piece of paper, which she quickly pulled out of the pocket. Smoothing out the paper, she was surprised to discover a copy of the insurance policy on *Tranquil,* with Gabriella Everhart's signature and last week's date on it. *Is this Gabriella's coat?* The charcoal black jacket was a ladies' size medium, about the size Jessamine figured the artist would wear, but, before she could decide what to do with the paper, a sound at the front door grabbed her attention, and she quickly stuffed it into her own pocket.

To her surprise, Andrew and Molly stepped through the front doorway, Molly putting her keys back into her purse.

"Good morning, I wasn't expecting you two until the afternoon."

"Andrew and I both had the same idea—that you might need some extra help today after what happened. We figured you'd be in early." Molly's voice sounded sincere with concern. "We're worried you might think this incident could hurt the art center, so we want to aid in making sure it doesn't. This place is as important to Andrew and me as it is to you."

Andrew nodded in agreement and gave her a thumbs-up.

Jessamine was touched. "Thank you, both! I really appreciate it. We can start by cleaning up after last night—and then I'll try to do some damage control with Gabriella." By damage control, Jessamine meant talking with the artist about the insurance policy she found, but she wasn't ready to share that information with Andrew and Molly yet. "And please keep your eyes open for anything out of the ordinary."

"Will do." Andrew's cheerfulness turned into an animated face of disgust. "What would you like us to do about that blood stain on the carpet?"

Jessamine sighed. "Let's try to get it out, and if it doesn't, we'll throw a floor mat over it or something, for now. It's ugly carpet, anyway. We really should change it to something laminate."

After spending the morning putting away chairs, wiping down tables, cleaning the floors of the art center, and doing some unsuccessful sleuthing, Jessamine decided to treat Andrew and Molly to lunch. They locked up the front door and headed down the street to Emilia's Secret Garden Tea Shop. Even though Emilia specialized in brunches and afternoon teas, she always had something delicious available for a quick lunch as well.

They stepped into the cozy, inviting tea shop. A small fireplace glowed from a corner, and tables and chairs dotted the open eating area. The place bustled with a busy weekend crowd, and the takeout counter hosted a line of waiting customers. Behind the counter, shelves were lined with silver tins filled with every blend of loose-leaf tea imaginable. Jessamine breathed in the wonderful smells coming from the kitchen, which matched the autumn atmosphere—a mixture of cinnamon and cloves as well as pumpkin scones warm from the oven. Emilia was busy with some customers when they arrived, so Jessamine, Andrew, and Molly seated themselves and looked at the menu.

"I had no idea there were so many different types of teas before Emilia opened her shop a few years back." Andrew stared at the menu with a blank expression. "I always just enjoyed the classic English breakfast if I was even going to drink tea, though nothing beats a good cup of coffee."

"Don't let Emilia overhear that comment, or you'll never win her over!" Jessamine teased.

"The Secret Garden's English breakfast blend is rather wonderful and sounds perfect for the cool weather today," Molly said. "What are you going to have, Ms. Rhodes?"

"I think I'll try this lavender Earl Grey."

Each table had a small pair of bookends where the menus lived, and Jessamine slid hers back. The table was beautifully decorated with a lace tablecloth, a round transparent vase filled with water and floating tea light candles, and a matching set of bone china teacups and saucers placed in front of each chair. Jessamine picked hers up to admire the delicate light pink petals that blossomed into flowers painted around the cup.

Emilia walked over to their table. "Sorry about the wait. I was chatting with my neighbors, Mr. and Mrs. Liu. They just got back from visiting family in Hong Kong and brought some teas they thought I might enjoy. Now, what can I get for you?"

They all placed their orders for sandwiches and their selected teas.

After Emilia walked away, the conversation turned back to the previous night's incident.

"Do you think the missing painting and Victor's death are connected?" Andrew asked.

"It would be a huge coincidence if they weren't, considering *Tranquil* was promised to him." Molly's eyebrows knit together. "But who would do such a thing?"

"There were so many people there yesterday, but I can't imagine anyone from Rose Shore doing such a thing," Andrew said.

Andrew and Molly discussed the topic back and forth while Jessamine stayed quiet.

"You look deep in thought, Jess." Andrew leaned in closer. "Do you know something about the missing painting?"

"Possibly. I don't know if it's significant or not—"

Her thought was interrupted as Emilia brought over their food and small teapots filled with fragrant loose-leaf tea. Jessamine had ordered the Monte Cristo, Molly went for the turkey club, and Andrew had chosen the open-faced Reuben, all with small salads on the side. Emilia's tray had one extra turkey club for herself, and she sat at their table next to Andrew. Jessamine tried to hide a laugh at the look of joy on his face.

"I overheard you talking about what happened last night. Addison is taking over for my lunch, so I can join you. Are you trying to figure out who killed Victor?"

Addison Coleman was Emilia's right-hand woman, who had as much of a passion for tea as Emilia did.

Andrew nodded. "Jessamine was about to tell us she knows something."

"Tell us, Jess!" Emilia said.

"First of all, I'm so sorry so many of your teacups and saucers were broken in the mass panic yesterday." Jessamine frowned at Emilia.

Emilia waved her hand. "Don't worry about it. I literally have hundreds of them. Now, tell us what you know!"

"Okay, fine. I'll tell you, but this doesn't leave the table. Right now, all of this is just speculation." She paused as everyone nodded in agreement. "I have three thoughts as to who it might have been. The first is Eugenie Price. She was very upset yesterday after finding out *Tranquil* had been promised to Victor and was actually speaking to him and Gabriella when the lights went out."

"It has to be Mrs. Price!" Andrew jumped in, without even waiting to hear who the other suspects were. "She had motive. She had an opportunity."

Suddenly we're all detectives. "Let's not jump to a conclusion yet. I have two more suspects, and I really can't imagine Mrs. Price killing anyone. Maybe she just took the painting. Anyway, I also saw a man standing near Victor after he'd been stabbed. I have no idea who he was, but he glared at me as I was feeling for Victor's pulse. He suddenly left the art center before the lights came back on."

"What did he look like?" Andrew took a huge bite of his sandwich.

"He was tall, wearing a raincoat, and it looked like he had graying brown hair. I really didn't get a good look at him."

"Could be anyone," Emilia said. "So, who's the third suspect?"

"Gabriella Everhart."

She heard small gasps from everyone.

Molly almost dropped her teacup. "Ms. Everhart? Why would she steal her own painting?"

"Why would she murder someone who was going to pay big bucks for it?" Andrew pointed out.

"I know it doesn't make any sense, but she was standing so close to Victor when he was stabbed."

"But she was totally shaken up. No way is she *that* good of an actor." Emilia was siding with Molly and Andrew. "Oh, that reminds me. Did you ever find out why she was so late?"

"No. I never got the chance to ask her, but there *is* something else." Jessamine pulled the piece of paper she found that morning out of her pocket. "I found this insurance policy about *Tranquil* in a jacket that was left in the foyer. I think it might belong to Gabriella. It says the retail worth of *Tranquil* is ten thousand dollars, but I don't know if that was the actual amount Victor would be paying. It's possible Gabriella would receive more money from the insurance company if *Tranquil* was stolen than if it was sold to Victor."

Everyone just stared at her.

Finally, Emilia broke the silence. "Well, we can't solve this without a little dessert, can we? I'll get us some macarons, on the tea shop, of course."

As their lunch came to an end, Jessamine received a call from an unknown number. She answered it and was surprised to hear Lauren Marsh's voice.

"Hi, Constable Marsh. How can I help you?" Jessamine noticed the look of surprise on Andrew's face that his sister was calling.

"Please, call me Lauren. I was hoping you'd be able to come down to the police station this afternoon. We've come across some information that might be interesting to you."

"Yes, of course. I'll be there as soon as I can." Jessamine hung up and answered her friends' questioning looks with the little information she'd received from Lauren.

"I'm going to head over there right now. I'm very curious about what this could be about." She paused for a moment, "Do you think I should hand over the insurance policy I found right away? We still have no idea if Gabriella is involved."

"I think you should, even if it's just to prevent Constable Todd from being all grumpy once he's found out you've been keeping it from the police," Emilia said, and the others agreed.

Jessamine knew her friends were right.

She pulled up to the police station after walking back to the art center to pick up her car. The station was on the other side of Rose Shore, and she hadn't been to that area of town yet since moving. She was about to open the front door when it swung out at her and almost smacked her in the nose.

"Ms. Rhodes! I'm still waiting for that exclusive you promised."

Jessamine held out a hand as if to physically stop Howard McCoy from coming any closer to her. "Why are you at the police station?"

"You really are new to town if you don't realize a missing painting *and* a murder is the biggest thing to hit these parts in years. This is going to be great for my blog. I *must* stay on top of the story, so I was gathering some info from the cops. Why are *you* here? Are you here to confess?" Howard eagerly leaned in as if to read any guilt in her eyes.

"No, of course not." Jessamine moved to get around him.

Howard stopped her again. "I just want you to know *I'm* going to solve this case before the cops do. That'll sure up my readership! So, if you did it, know I'm on to you. I'll be by the art center later this week for my exclusive." And with that remark, Howard stepped aside and let Jessamine into the building.

Just what I need on top of everything else. This only makes me want to solve the case even more quickly before Howard "Click" McCoy finds some way to pin it on me for a better story! She walked into the station and told the officer at the front desk who she was and that she was there to see Constable Marsh.

"She'll be with you in a moment, Ms. Rhodes. Please take a seat." The officer pointed to a nearby waiting area.

Jessamine had barely sat down when Lauren came into the lobby and greeted her warmly, motioning for her to follow. They reached Lauren's desk in the back of the station and sat down across from each other.

"Lauren, before we get started, I have something to show you." Jessamine thought it best to hand the insurance policy over right away. She pulled the paper out of her purse and handed it to Lauren. "I found this in a pocket of a jacket that had been left in the art center from last night. I think it might connect Gabriella Everhart to the missing painting in more ways than we previously thought. She might have even stolen it herself to claim the insurance if Victor wasn't offering her the full ten thousand dollars." Once Jessamine got started with explaining her theory, she couldn't seem to stop talking.

Lauren raised an eyebrow. "You aren't trying to solve this yourself, are you? I don't think that's a good idea."

"I'm not, not really. Everything just happened in *my* art center. I'm nervous this is going to ruin my business before it even has a chance to get off the ground, so I want it resolved as quickly as possible." Her voice shook as she struggled to keep her emotions at bay.

Lauren gave her a sympathetic look. "I understand your concern, and I assure you we're working as fast as we can, but you really should stay out of this. It could be dangerous, and I think protecting your life is more important than protecting your business." Jessamine opened her mouth to start arguing again, but Lauren held up a hand. "I don't want to be responding to another nine-one-one call to find you injured, or worse, all right?"

Jessamine stayed quiet, purposefully not voicing any promise to stay out of it.

Lauren didn't seem to notice Jessamine's lack of an answer and set the insurance policy aside with a promise to look into it. "So, I wanted to let you know we've pulled a suspect in for questioning. Eugenie Price was brought in about two hours ago because, well, not only did you mention she was upset with Gabriella and Victor about the painting, but multiple attendants at the art center saw her arguing with both of them right before the stabbing."

Jessamine wasn't sure how she felt about the information. Since Mrs. Price was one of her own suspects, she wasn't surprised to hear the woman had been brought in, especially after her dramatic scene about *Tranquil*, but it was still upsetting to think her capable of murdering someone. "Has Mrs. Price admitted anything?"

"Nothing we don't already know. She admits she was upset about *Tranquil* and that she and Victor didn't get along, but she's insisting she didn't steal the painting nor did she stab anyone. We're currently waiting for a warrant to search her home."

"I think I believe her, at least about not stabbing Victor. I feel like this whole thing is more personal than just wanting a painting because it goes with your sitting room." Jessamine thought carefully about the situation. She wasn't ready to cross Mrs. Price off her suspect list just yet, but something wasn't sitting well with her. And it wasn't that third macaron she ate.

"Well, I'll definitely look more into Gabriella with this new clue you brought in. Thank you for giving it to me."

"No problem. Did anything show up on the security tapes?"

"We're still going through them. With so many people going in and out of the classroom during the event, it's hard to tell if anyone was in the crowd who wasn't supposed to be there."

Jessamine nodded. It would most likely take days to comb through that footage. "One more thing, was a Howard McCoy in here earlier?"

Lauren sighed. "That kid? Yeah, he was pestering everyone in earshot about getting some insider information for his blog."

"Did he get any info from you?"

"No. Of course not. Why do you ask?" Lauren tilted her head.

"I ran into him outside, and he gave me an odd threat. He seems to think I'm behind this and is determined to solve the case first in order to have a great story."

"I wouldn't worry too much about Howard. He's all talk, but I'll keep an eye on him for you, just in case."

"Thanks, Lauren. I should be getting back to the art center now." Jessamine stood.

Lauren followed and walked her back to the front lobby. "I'll try to keep you as up to date as best I can, even things I normally wouldn't be sharing with the victims. I don't want you or my brother stressing," she said in a low voice.

Jessamine let Lauren know how grateful she was for that before leaving the police station and getting into her car. She did need to get back to the art center, but she was going to make one stop on the way. Ignoring Lauren's warnings, she wanted to find out more about the insurance policy from Gabriella before the police had a chance to question her. Besides, she *did* need to return the jacket anyway. It was the perfect excuse to talk to the artist.

Chapter Four

Gabriella was staying at the Rose Shore Resort & Spa, the town's only five-star hotel, where travelers came from all over to relax along the gorgeous lakeside. The resort was close to the community art center, and Jessamine could have easily walked if she didn't already have her car. There was even a wooded path between the buildings. She hoped her business would benefit from the proximity during the heavy tourist times of the year. *Once this whole mess is cleaned up, that is.*

She had grabbed the lost coat from the art center foyer earlier when she went back to pick up her car and brought it with her inside the resort now.

Jessamine walked in through the front doorway and was greeted warmly by the hotel staff. The grand lobby was filled with a faint floral scent drifting from the beautiful bouquets scattered around the room. This was her first time in the hotel, and the beauty of the architecture took her breath away. Several paintings were hung along the walls of the lobby, and so, before setting out to find Gabriella, she walked around to take a close look at them and even found one by Ms. Everhart. Jessamine was quickly realizing art was a big part of the Rose Shore community, and she was glad to have found a small town so supportive of their local artists. After jotting down some names of various artists for future reference in the small journal she usually carried, always having preferred taking notes the old-fashioned way instead of using her phone, Jessamine walked over to the front desk.

"Hello, I'm Jessamine Rhodes, and I'm looking for Gabriella Everhart. I run the art center she was working with this weekend."

The front desk clerk gave Jessamine a look of pity. "I heard what happened there yesterday. What a shame! I hope this doesn't impact your business." The woman's words fueled Jessamine's eagerness to find Victor's killer and the missing painting; she didn't want everyone in town to immediately associate her and her business with what had happened.

"Yes, it really was. Would it be possible to talk with Ms. Everhart? It's quite urgent."

"I'm not able to give out the room number, but I can telephone Ms. Everhart and let her know you're here."

"That would be very helpful. Thank you."

The front desk clerk dialed the number and explained that Jessamine was there to see the artist.

She turned back to Jessamine. "Ms. Everhart's assistant would like to know why you're here."

"I have something I need to return to her." She only felt the need to explain part of the reason for her visit, though she was a little nervous about Gabriella's assistant being so cautious. Hopefully, they didn't think Jessamine was somehow involved in the missing painting.

The desk clerk relayed the message into the phone before hanging up, letting Jessamine know that Gabriella would be right down. She thanked the front desk clerk and went to wait near the elevators.

She hadn't met Gabriella's assistant before; she'd only been in contact with Fay Grimsey through email and wondered if Fay would be coming down with Gabriella. The assistant had been invited to the art center's painting class, but to Jessamine's knowledge, Fay hadn't attended.

Gabriella seemed to be taking her own sweet time coming downstairs, and just as Jessamine started to get annoyed at the artist's consistent lack of punctuality, she finally noticed one of the elevators descending from the top floor. *Of course, Gabriella would be staying in a penthouse suite.* The doors of the elevator opened, and out stepped Gabriella, followed by another woman who looked strikingly similar to the artist.

"Jessamine! I'm so delighted to see you again. I barely got to spend any time with you yesterday." Gabriella appeared to have fully recovered from the previous night's trauma. She was dressed professionally with model-perfect hair and makeup. She hooked her arm through Jessamine's and led her and the other woman to a pair of couches in the back corner of the hotel lobby. "And I must apologize again for having been so late to the class. The time had simply gotten away from me. Jessamine, may I introduce my assistant and sister, Fay."

Well, that explained the resemblance between the two women. "It's so nice to finally meet you in person, Fay." Jessamine smiled at her.

Despite having a similar physical look, the two women were quite different in how they dressed and presented themselves. From a distance, they looked almost identical, but up close, Fay didn't appear to have the same zest for life Gabriella did. Fay wore jeans and a beige shirt and no makeup around her dull brown eyes.

"I must have missed you at the art center yesterday." Jessamine sat across from the sisters and placed her purse on the floor.

"Oh, Fay doesn't like attending special events," Gabriella answered for her sister. "She prefers to stay at the hotel and make use of the spa and room

service. She isn't very social. She hasn't even had a boyfriend since college."
Gabriella gave a small laugh as she spoke about Fay, like her sister wasn't even
there.

Fay gave Gabriella a side-glance but didn't respond to her sister's
comments about her personal life. "My apologies for not attending your
painting class. I had too many emails to catch up on, which took far longer
than expected with this sprained wrist." She held up her right hand, which
had a tensor bandage wrapped snuggly around it, and smiled. "And yes, I did
make good use of room service."

"Oh, don't worry about it. I understand. The art world can be very busy.
I hope you can make it to a future event, though."

"I have to tell you I was *so* delighted by your invitation to attend. It's
been years since we've been to Rose Shore. Not since our family moved away
when we were just children." Gabriella looked a little lost in thought for a
moment. "Anyway, what did you need to return? I'm terribly sorry, but I do
only have a few minutes before I need to rush off to an appointment." Her
voice sounded coy as she said the word "appointment."

Not wanting to sound too suspicious, Jessamine tried to keep the
conversation light. She presented the black coat, which had been tucked under
her arm. "I was wondering if this is your coat. It was left behind in the foyer of
the art center last night, and I haven't been able to find the owner yet."

Gabriella immediately reached for it. "It is! Thank you for returning it."

"I was also hoping you could tell me some more about *Tranquil*. I'm
naturally very curious about its disappearance." She kept a close look on
Gabriella's face for a reaction, but the artist didn't offer any clue as to her
involvement with the missing painting.

"Well, let's see. I painted *Tranquil* last spring, and it was inspired by
someone very special to me. I was originally not planning on selling the piece,
but the person who it reminds me of hurt me. I don't wish to bore you with

the details, but I had to get the painting out of my life. Victor has always had a keen interest in my work, so I contacted him first. He made me an offer below what I was hoping for, but I needed to get rid of it. I quickly accepted his offer, and we arranged for the sale to take place here in Rose Shore. This all happened last week, so I don't really have much else to tell you." Gabriella's story confirmed Jessamine's hunch about Victor not intending to purchase *Tranquil* for the full $10, 000.

"Do you have any idea of who might have stolen *Tranquil*?"

"No, not at all. Despite offering it to Victor, other art collectors mentioned interest, but no one was serious about it. Well, except for that crazy Mrs. Price. I've never been yelled at like that before over an art sale! I hope to never have to deal with her again."

"I heard she was arguing with both you and Victor yesterday," Jessamine said.

"*That* was not an argument. Arguments aren't one-sided. That was Mrs. Price going on and on about her sitting room." Gabriella slouched like she was defeated by the memory of Mrs. Price's words. "The more I think about that episode with her, the more I think she's the guilty one. But, if you'll excuse me, I really must be leaving now. Thank you for stopping by." The artist stood to leave, and Jessamine could tell she was trying to keep a composed appearance.

"Thank you for chatting with me," Jessamine called after her as Gabriella rushed to the front doors of the lobby. Jessamine had hoped she would also be able to talk to Gabriella about continuing to work together, but that would have to wait until the artist wasn't in a rush. One more thing was bothering her, though.

"I do have one more question before I leave, if that's okay?" Jessamine turned to Fay, who still sat on the couch and had been quiet during the entire conversation. Jessamine got the feeling Fay was often bulldozed by her sister.

Fay bit her bottom lip. "What is it?"

"I noticed neither you nor your sister wears a wedding ring, but you have different last names. May I ask why?"

A look of annoyance crossed Fay's face briefly before she smiled pleasantly back at Jessamine. "We don't actually have different last names. Gabriella just goes by Everhart as a pseudonym because she's too high and mighty for a name like Grimsey. Gabriella Grimsey isn't an artistic-enough sounding name, according to my sister."

Jessamine hid a smirk. She knew plenty of artists who went by different names for similar reasons. "Well, I should be going as well. Thank you for your time, Fay. I'm sure I'll be seeing you again."

Fay nodded and stood with Jessamine, giving a quick goodbye before heading back to the hotel elevators.

Jessamine hurried back to the art center. Molly was scheduled to host an acrylic painting class for families with elementary school-aged children, so Jessamine needed to put the case aside for the rest of the afternoon to focus on helping with the class. That was, if parents weren't scared off by the previous day's events and still allowed their children to attend.

However, she did think about the case during the short drive. Many of the clues still pointed toward Mrs. Price, but now Gabriella confirmed she wasn't getting as much money from selling *Tranquil* as it was actually worth. Perhaps she'd stolen the painting and had been caught by Victor, some sort of scuffle occurred, and she accidentally stabbed him? That could explain her genuine shock after the stabbing; she hadn't planned on killing anyone. But then, who was that mysterious man who had slipped away afterward?

As Jessamine pulled into the small parking lot of the art center, she noticed a man leaving in a hurry out the front doorway. As he got into his car, she realized it was the man from the day before—the very man she had just been thinking about. She leaped out of her car to catch up to him, but he sped out of the parking lot before she was even close enough to get a better look at his face.

Maybe I should follow him. Pulling her sleeve up to glance at her watch, Jessamine decided to stick to her original plan and focus on the art center. Now she at least knew he drove a white, beat-up old car.

Inside, Andrew typed away on his computer at the reception desk.

"Hey, a man just left here in a hurry. Do you know who he was?"

"That must have been Frank Bates. I saw him come in earlier to take a quick look around. It must be hard on him to spend time here. I'm not sure why he even came in, considering what happened."

"Wait. Hold on a moment. I have no idea what you're talking about." Jessamine placed both her hands flat on Andrew's desk and leaned in closer.

"Oh," Andrew's voice dropped a bit lower. "Bates put an offer on the art center before you bought it. He was well-known in this town for having a keen interest in the building to turn it into a fancy art gallery and host classes similar to what you're doing. Many people were surprised when you showed up as the new owner instead of him."

She was taken aback. Jessamine had rarely felt like an outsider since moving to Rose Shore, but, at this moment, that was exactly how she felt. Small towns were known for being tight-knit and for supporting their neighbors, but it hadn't even crossed her mind there would have been locals interested in purchasing the art center. Her realtor had mentioned something about outbidding another party, but Jessamine had been too caught up in her own excitement to give it much thought. That party must have been Frank Bates.

Andrew seemed to sense her thoughts. "Now that I think about it, he did leave quite suddenly as soon as you pulled up. It's probably too hard to be around you anyway, knowing you own the business he dreamt about. Before it seemed like he was just here to admire the art we have displayed or check out the class schedule, but now it's almost like . . . creepy!" Andrew's eyes grew wide. "It's like he won't let himself get over the loss."

This had Jessamine concerned. Was Bates really that bitter? Was he stalking her if he knew she hadn't been at the art center? Should she be worried for her safety?

"Andrew, could you do me a favor? If he comes back, could you keep an eye on him? I don't want him near the offices, if possible."

"Sure thing, Jess."

"Thanks, and I'll let Molly know as well. Now, I need to get ready for this painting class."

"Molly is pretty much all set up already in the large classroom."

Jessamine chuckled. "Of course, she is."

After dropping off her purse in her office, Jessamine headed into the main classroom. Andrew was right. Molly had gotten everything ready. Each table was set up for two students, with small square blank canvases in front of each chair and half a dozen paintbrushes placed between them. On either side of the classroom were tables topped with large selections of acrylic paint bottles in dozens of colors and shades. Molly was setting down a pile of plastic paint palettes on one of the tables.

"This looks great, Molly!"

Molly's back was turned to Jessamine, and she gave a slight jump, her hands flying up, causing the paint palettes to drop with a loud clatter.

"Oops. Sorry for startling you."

Molly lowered her hands from her chest. "I'm still a little jumpy after last night, I guess. Thank you, though. I still need to fill the jars of water, and then we're all set. The families should be arriving soon."

"Perfect. Let me help you with the jars."

As they worked, picking up the paint palettes and filling the jars, Jessamine filled Molly in on her trip to the police station as well as warned her about Frank Bates. Their conversation was soon broken by laughter and chatter from the foyer, followed by multiple footsteps thundering down the hallway.

"Sounds like they're excited." This overshadowed Jessamine's worries about everything. Sharing her love of art was the perfect balm to her anxious mood.

Through the doorway flew in a handful of children, all around ages seven to ten. Three sets of parents hurried to catch up with them.

"Welcome, welcome." Jessamine directed the families to the front of the classroom and indicated that they should each take a seat. "We're still waiting for some more families to join us, and then we'll get started." She headed back over to Molly and said in a low voice, "I hope more families show up. This was booked to be a full class."

"Do you think people will be nervous to come here after what happened?"

Jessamine resisted the urge to shudder at the memory. "I hope not."

Another family of four soon arrived, followed by a girl and her mother. Jessamine gave Molly a small shrug before heading over to greet the newcomers. *Well, at least some people showed up.*

Only one more mom and her young son joined the group before Molly got started. Jessamine switched between sitting among the class to offer tips and helping the young artists create their own paint palettes. Some parents painted their own creations, and others simply helped their kids.

"Wow, you have a real eye for color," Jessamine said to the little girl sitting closest to her. "I love your mixture of orange and pink. It looks like a sunset."

The little girl ducked her head shyly and didn't respond.

"She was scared to come here," the boy next to her, Jessamine assumed her brother, said loudly.

"Oh? Why is that?"

"Because someone was murdered here! Lizzie was scared she was gonna be next."

Paintbrushes dropped, and necks craned as everyone in the classroom swung their attention to the boy's declaration.

"Zander!" His mother turned to Jessamine. "I'm so sorry. We tried to explain to Zander and Lizzie that there had been an accident here but that there was nothing to worry about. I think some of the neighborhood kids spooked them with scarier stories."

Jessamine tried to hide her wince, debating whether it was her place to explain that it most likely hadn't been an accident and that Victor *had* been murdered in the art center. Deciding on not wanting to frighten the children any more than they already were, she donned her brightest smile. "You're completely safe here. Everything is just fine."

Maybe if she could convince everyone else, she could convince herself.

Chapter Five

That evening marked the end of a very tiring day, and Jessamine's head was swimming with different theories, each thought being so quickly interrupted by the next that she couldn't concentrate or make sense of anything. She decided to bring Margo for a walk along the waterfront by their cottage in hopes it would help focus her mind. Margo's brown and tan tail wagged furiously as soon as her little paws hit the beach, and she took off running ahead into the shallow waters along the shore. Despite her weariness, Jessamine was soon distracted by Margo's playfulness at pouncing on the small waves created by the far-off boats on Opal Lake. It looked like they weren't the only ones making the most of the change in weather; it was most likely one of the last warm evenings of the year.

"Your dog seems to be enjoying her new lakeside life," a voice said from behind her.

Jessamine turned to find her neighbor, Jackson Yeung, walking a dog.

"Oh! Who is this?" She squatted down next to the small Italian Greyhound and scratched behind the dog's bouncy ears.

"His name's Poe."

The white and gray dog gave Jessamine a big lick on the face. She laughed and looked up to find Jackson smiling at them. "Aw, like Edgar Allan Poe?"

"Er, no. More like Poe Dameron from *Star Wars*."

"You didn't go with *Paw* Dameron?"

Jackson raised an eyebrow, and Jessamine gave an awkward chuckle. "Never mind. Terrible pun, I know."

This time Jackson laughed before changing the subject. "And are you enjoying your new lakeside life as well?"

Jessamine took a moment to respond. "I am, though a murder and a missing painting have me extremely stressed out."

"I can imagine. That crime scene was pretty intense. For Rose Shore, at least." Jackson gritted his teeth and shook his head.

"Have you responded to many calls like that here?"

"No, not for many years. Mostly a lot of falls and broken bones, a few car accidents. It's pretty quiet here most days."

They walked along the beach together for a few moments with the only sound being the gentle waves lapping onto the shore.

"I hope this isn't too personal," Jessamine said, breaking the silence, "but I noticed yesterday when you were getting into the ambulance, you looked really upset. Did you know Victor?"

Jackson gave her a look of surprise. "You're quite observant. I'm impressed. Yeah, I did know Victor. He helped me out of a jam a long time ago, and we stayed pretty close over the years."

Jessamine waited for him to expand on his story, but when he kept silent, she didn't push. Though, now she felt even more awful. The realization that someone had been murdered at her event hit her all over again. Someone who had friends and family and—

"Hey, hey. It's going to be all right." Jackson, as if he'd read her thoughts, put his hand on her shoulder and gently turned her to face him. "The police are going to find out who did this."

Jessamine fought back tears. "I know. I just can't believe this is happening. I've dreamt about owning my own art center for so long, and then our very first class was an absolute disaster, and I'm sure my entire business won't be far behind."

"Have you heard from the police today? Are they close to figuring out who did it?"

"I went to the station this afternoon, but there wasn't much of an update."

"Well, I'm positive this will be their number one priority, so I'm sure your painting will show up in no time, and Victor's killer will be behind bars." He gave her an encouraging smile, and Jessamine, after wiping away the last few rogue tears, found herself distracted by the thought that her neighbor was rather handsome with his dark hair and chestnut eyes.

"Anyway, I don't really want to talk about this anymore, if that's okay. Tell me about Rose Shore." She gestured a hand around the beach. "What's there to do for fun around here?"

Over the next half hour, Jackson told her all about what Rose Shore was like during the autumn months. There seemed to be quite a bit to look forward to with the different festivals and community events.

"On weekends throughout October, Halloween movies are shown outside at Centennial Park."

"Outside? Won't it be too cold?"

"That's the fun of it. Everyone gets all bundled up, and hot chocolate is served. Make sure to bring a pair of mittens and a blanket."

Jessamine couldn't tell if he was hinting at inviting her to one of the movies or not, and she wasn't sure how she would respond if he did.

As they continued to talk about what life in Rose Shore was like, with Opal Lake on one side of them and the golden leaves of the nearby Birch trees on the other, Margo and Poe made a game of racing ahead down the beach only to scurry back just as quickly. The two new friends got twice as much exercise as their owners did.

Jessamine was washing off Margo's sandy feet outside her back door when she heard Clara Connors, another neighbor, calling her.

"Did I just see you walking along the beach with Jackson? Isn't he handsome?"

Jessamine had only spoken to Clara a few times before but was quickly learning that her elderly neighbor was a bit of a gossip.

"Hi, Clara. How are you this evening?" Jessamine ignored the nosy questions as she met her neighbor near the low fence between their two cottages.

"Oh, fine as always. I heard about that dreadful business at your art center. What excitement! Are there any ideas of who would do such a thing? Has the painting been recovered? Whatever does this mean for your business?" Clara peppered her with questions without even giving Jessamine a chance to get an answer in, but just then, Margo trotted over, and Clara let out a small shriek.

"No, no, no! You stay away from me, doggie. You miscreant animal!" Clara backed as far away from Margo as possible, despite the low fence.

The beagle's only response was a questioning tilt of the head.

"Clara? Are you scared of dogs?"

"Yes! What vile creatures. They jump and bite and bark and knock people over."

"Yes, you're right. That's exactly what dogs do," Jessamine responded with dry sarcasm. "Well then, I best get Margo inside and away from you." She was sure she didn't quite succeed in keeping the smirk off her face at this newfound tactic of avoiding her busybody neighbor. "C'mon, Margo, let's get you your dinner. I'll talk to you later, Clara." And with that, Jessamine headed back to her own cottage for a quiet evening with Margo happily following behind.

Jessamine followed Lauren's advice to stay out of the investigation until about noon the next day. She'd completed most of her paperwork at the art center in the morning, but she still couldn't get Frank Bates off her mind. She wasn't sure what to think about Bates wanting the art center building for himself. Deciding a quick Google search wouldn't be of any harm, since it wasn't really investigating, she typed "Frank Bates, Rose Shore" into the search bar.

At first, nothing much showed up. It seemed like he had lived in Rose Shore his whole life, wasn't married, and, in years past, had often been praised in newspapers for his donations of large sums of money to the art center. *That's funny.* She'd looked through the donor lists from the last five years soon after purchasing the art center, but his name hadn't appeared on any of them. Something must have happened over five years ago to make him stop donating.

"Ms. Rhodes, are you busy?" Molly appeared in the doorway of Jessamine's office. "Is everything all right? You seem deep in thought."

"I'm fine. Just looking a bit into Frank Bates. It looks like he was a frequent donor to the art center up until five years ago but then suddenly stopped."

"I thought Constable Marsh told you not to investigate anymore."

"I'm not." Even to herself, Jessamine sounded unconvincing. "Not really. Just a bit of Googling. I'm too curious about this to let it go completely."

"I understand. In fact, I was looking into Frank Bates myself. I remember him working at the Rose Shore Resort and Spa when I was a child. I believe he was in some sort of manager's position. Well, it seems like he was let go about five years ago, though I have no idea why."

"That actually explains quite a bit. Thank you, Molly. That explains why the donations stopped coming in around that time and why the lobby of the resort is filled with beautiful paintings. I bet he was the one responsible for their acquisition if he has such a keen interest in art. I even saw another Gabriella Everhart painting there. But he still would have had to come into some funds lately to even put an offer on the art center."

"Hey, hey, hey! Ms. Rhodes! I'm here for my exclusive," interrupted a loud voice from outside the offices.

Jessamine turned to Molly and couldn't help but roll her eyes. "I guess I should get this over with or 'Click' will never leave me alone."

Molly gave her a sympathetic smile as Jessamine walked out of her office toward the reception area.

"Hello, Howard, what can I do for you?" Jessamine mustered up the most patient tone she could manage.

"Like I said, I'm here for my exclusive." Howard was dressed like a reporter from a black and white 1930s gangster film, complete with a fedora.

This guy is something else. "What exactly would you like to know?" Jessamine plastered on a fake smile and led him down the hallway and into one of the two smaller classrooms. She perched lightly on the edge of one of the desks, and Howard plopped himself in a chair across from her.

"Where were you when Victor was murdered?"

"I thought you wanted an exclusive of why I moved here from Vancouver."

"Oh, that's old news. No one cares about that anymore. Now it's all about the crime!" Howard showed off his jazz hands.

"If you must know, I was in the large classroom with our guests."

"So, right beside Victor when he was stabbed. You admit it!" Howard started to write something in a notebook he pulled out of his coat pocket.

"No. Victor was stabbed in the foyer," Jessamine said slowly, as if explaining to a small child how the game of Clue was played.

"Oh, right. Well, do you know who killed him?" Howard quickly moved on from his mistake.

"No."

"Any guesses?"

"No." She wasn't going to give this guy anything, but Howard couldn't seem to catch the hint.

"I have some guesses." He leaned closer.

"I thought I was your guess. You've mentioned that already, and I can assure you it wasn't me."

"Fine! But when I *do* find out who really did it, I will *not* be sharing that information with you, Ms. Rhodes." Howard stood and walked right out of the classroom and out the front doorway without another word.

Jessamine sighed and headed back to her office. Molly was still there, flipping through an art history textbook, and she gave Molly a rundown of her conversation with Howard.

"He seems convinced I did it." Jessamine sunk her face in her hands.

"Hello? Anyone around and hungry for lunch?" called another voice from the reception area before Molly could respond.

"That sounds like Emilia, a much more welcome surprise than Howard."

Jessamine smiled and rose to head back out to greet Emilia, with Molly behind her. As she reached over the desk to grab her office key, Jessamine knocked her purse onto the floor. The contents of it scattered everywhere.

"Are you all right?" Molly asked.

"Yes. Just a little klutzy today apparently." She got down on the floor to gather her things. Among the Chapstick, pens, and other loose items, she saw a crumpled piece of paper under her desk, something she didn't remember putting in her purse. She opened it to find a nasty note.

Stop snooping around, Rhodes!
This does NOT concern you!

"What is it?" Molly leaned down to help.

Jessamine showed her the note. "This must have fallen out of my purse. I don't remember anyone being close enough to stick it in there, though."

"Is it possible it was in your office already and not in your purse?"

"That would mean someone had access to my office." Jessamine had a suspicious thought it might have been Bates who was responsible. "Neither conclusion is comforting. Though I do find it amusing whoever wrote this note referred to me only by my last name. I haven't been called Rhodes since my high school track and field team."

Chapter Six

Jessamine and Molly left the office after locking up and wandered into the reception area. Emilia stood there with two large baskets that looked to be filled with scones, teacakes, sandwiches, and other goodies.

"Hey, how's it going?" Emilia held up her baskets without waiting for a reply. "I thought you detectives could use some lunch."

"That's super sweet of you, Em," Jessamine said. "You aren't needed at your shop?"

"Nope. It's my day off, but I still popped in for a little bit to help with the lunch rush and picked up some stuff to bring here."

"Well, we really appreciate it." Jessamine reached out to take a basket from Emilia and Molly nodded her agreement. "And I have lots to catch you up on. Including how I shouldn't be playing detective and the threatening note I just found in my office."

"That piques my curiosity. Before you tell me all about it, where can we set up this picnic?" Emilia asked.

Jessamine and Molly led Emilia to their small break room. It wasn't much, since they were such a small staff, but Jessamine was glad they at least had somewhere they could all sit together.

Emilia busied herself setting up the food. "Molly, could you please start boiling some water for tea? I brought my house blend of Dragon Jasmine green tea."

"That sounds wonderful." Molly immediately started filling up the electric tea kettle on the counter next to her.

Jessamine left the two of them and searched for Andrew to see if he wanted to join them for lunch. On quiet days like this, Andrew liked to tend to the gardens around the art center, and she found him near the flower beds behind the building.

"A special someone is here to see you," she teased as she approached.

"I was hoping my mother would pop in today." Andrew lifted his black-framed glasses up onto his red hair to wipe his brow.

"Very funny. Sorry to disappoint you, but Emilia brought us a delicious lunch from her tea shop."

"Perfect! I could eat her food every meal of the week, but, before we go back inside, there's something I should show you. I found a business card in the flowers when I was weeding the garden beds by the front door." He pulled the small rectangular piece of paper out of his jacket pocket and handed it to Jessamine.

"'Rose Shore Resort and Spa. Crimson Orchard Spa. Liza Monroe, Nail Technician,'" Jessamine read. "This really doesn't mean anything. Who knows how long it's been hiding in the flowers?"

"That's the thing. I spent quite a while on the flower beds, making them look perfect, right before our opening day. So, this card had to have been dropped in those flowers *during* the event or in the last two days."

"It could be something to look into then, but let's keep it to ourselves for now. Everyone's imaginations are already running pretty wild, so I don't want to share this until I'm confident if it's important or not."

Andrew agreed, and they walked back into the art center together. In the break room, Emilia had everything ready, and the small group sat down.

"Before you fill me in on the case, I was wondering if everyone was available on Friday for a small get-together?" Emilia asked.

Heads around the break room table all nodded.

"Good answer. Because it's my birthday." She gave a sly wink.

"Why didn't you say something sooner?" Jessamine asked. "We could have thrown you a big birthday bash."

"No, no. I actually wasn't even going to say anything because I didn't want to take the attention away from your opening, but now, I feel like we could all use a night of fun to forget about everything that happened. We'll just do something small, and please don't feel like you need to get me a gift or anything."

"We could have it at my place," Jessamine said.

"And please don't bake your own birthday cake. I'll oversee the food," Molly said.

"Brilliant." Emilia grinned. "I would appreciate that. Thanks, Molly."

The four friends finished sorting out the details for Emilia's birthday before Jessamine and Molly brought Andrew and Emilia up to date on what they'd learned about Bates and the note Jessamine found in her office.

"That's crazy someone would threaten you like that!" Emilia's tone became defensive.

"But it could mean you might be getting close to figuring out who's responsible," Andrew pointed out.

"I think we should bring the note to the police." Molly fidgeted with her napkin.

"I'll think about it. I promise." Jessamine gave Molly's hand a quick squeeze to reassure her.

"Do you think Bates still has some hope this building could be his?" Andrew asked. "Do you think he wrote the note?"

"I don't know. I hope not." Jessamine shrugged. "I think it's time for him to move on."

"Perhaps he'll try to purchase another art center or gallery," Molly said.

"I heard today from a customer of mine that there's actually an art gallery for sale a few towns away," Emilia said. "Maybe he should look into that one."

"But if he was outbid on this place, he might not be able to afford another." Jessamine stood to begin clearing the table.

Molly joined her and put their plates in the small kitchen sink.

"Has he not worked in five years then?" Emilia had also brought some dessert goodies for everyone but had only placed one cookie on the platter before Andrew snatched it up and shoved it into his mouth. "Really?" She scowled. "You couldn't wait until I was done?"

Andrew gave her a grin filled with cookie crumbs in response.

"I heard he did a little of this and a little of that." Molly ignored Andrew. "But nothing significant enough to keep donating to the art center, I'm assuming."

"What if he has looked into that art gallery, or any other potential buildings for sale for that matter, but didn't have enough funds? You don't think he would have stolen *Tranquil* for the money? To make sure he wouldn't get outbid a second time?" Jessamine asked. "I mean, he obviously didn't have the painting when I saw him at the end of the night."

"Stealing *Tranquil* would be beneficial to Bates in more ways than that. He'd have money to go toward purchasing a gallery, but it would also have the potential to ruin your business, which would be his competition if he did art classes as well." Andrew seemed to be on to something.

"Maybe he stashed it somewhere," Emilia said. "Have you looked around for the painting?"

"Yes, of course. So have the police." Jessamine tried not to be annoyed with her friend for assuming she hadn't done the obvious.

"Well, maybe we should all take a quick look again after lunch, just in case." Emilia seemed determined to be involved. She sat quietly for another moment before giving her friends a wide smile. "I have another idea. I'm going to call this art gallery that's for sale and pretend to be Frank Bates' assistant."

Her suggestion was met with blank stares.

"And why are you going to do that?" Andrew's eyebrows rose.

"To see if I can get some info about whether or not Bates is planning on buying it."

"Doesn't that seem too sneaky?" Molly bit her lower lip.

"I won't be trying to get anything personal out of them. I just want to know if he's interested or not." Emilia looked over to Jessamine for approval. "Come on, Jess. This could be important. This could help save your reputation."

Jessamine sighed. "All right. I'm willing to try anything at this point."

The four of them gathered in Jessamine's office, and Emilia looked up the number for the Indigo Art Gallery in Birch Cove, a town just over forty-five minutes away. "Hello, my name is Jeannie Nelson, and I'm Frank Bates' assistant." Her English accent was replaced with a fake and slightly nasally, generic North American one. She paused. "Why, yes, he *is* still interested. I was just calling to see if the current owners had a deadline for an offer." She paused again. "Yes. Thank you very much. Have a good afternoon."

"Okay. You are *way* too good at thinking up lies and an alias on the spot." Jessamine gave a small laugh, not sure if she should be impressed or wary of her friend's apparent secret talent.

"Really, you guys didn't pick up on Jeannie Nelson right away? *I Dream of Jeannie?*"

Jessamine had a vague recollection of Emilia mentioning when they first met that she had a thing for retro sitcoms.

"Anyway, yes, Bates is interested in purchasing the Indigo Art Gallery and apparently had called them yesterday saying he was planning on making an offer very soon." Emilia paused and looked each of them in the eyes. "We may have just figured out who stole your missing painting."

Chapter Seven

Jessamine took Margo for an early walk the following morning and decided to head over to Emilia's house to see if her friend was interested in joining them. It was a bit of a walk, but she was anxious to talk about the case some more and bounce theories off Emilia. Together with Andrew and Molly, they had searched high and low throughout the art center looking for *Tranquil* after lunch the previous day, but nothing, not even a small clue, turned up.

Emilia lived in an adorable single-story cottage right next to her tea shop. The outside was painted bright red, which matched Emilia's personality perfectly, and her wrap-around porch was inviting with its hanging flower baskets holding on to their last few summer blossoms and comfy-looking wicker furniture snuggled together. The steps leading up to the porch were already decked out for fall with bright mini pumpkins lining the way.

"Good morning, Jess. What brings you here?" Emilia was curled up on one of the wicker chairs sipping a cup of tea, her raven ringlets still damp from her shower.

"Good morning. Margo and I were wondering if you wanted to go for a walk with us."

"I'd love to. Just let me finish my tea first. Would you like some? It's a creamy Earl Grey."

"Sure. Thank you." Jessamine took the seat beside her friend as Margo explored the porch around them with her little nose pressed to the ground.

"I thought I'd take advantage of these last few balmy mornings before the cool weather hits for good, though I am looking forward to pulling out my scarfs and sweaters." Emilia quickly ducked inside and brought back out a matching teacup and saucer for Jessamine.

"I love your tea cozy." Jessamine admired the multi-colored cozy as she poured the Earl Grey from the ceramic teapot that had been on the side table.

"Thanks. My Gran knitted it for me years ago."

Jessamine sipped her tea quietly for a few minutes, lost in her own thoughts, which had quickly turned back to the case.

"What are you brooding about?" Emilia broke the silence after a while.

Jessamine pinched her lips together before blowing out a long breath. "I'm really starting to think Frank Bates is the guilty party and not Mrs. Price, but I'm not sure how to let the police know without it seeming like I've been investigating again."

"What does it matter if they're upset with you? If you think Bates is guilty, then you should let them know. It might keep us all safe."

Jessamine sighed. "You're always right, aren't you?"

"Of course, I am." Emilia gave her a good-natured tap on the arm. "I know it might be a little awkward, but I do think it'd be best."

Jessamine was giving it some more thought when she spotted someone she recognized across the street. "Look, there's Gabriella."

"Who's that handsome chap she's with?" Emilia tilted her head to the side.

"I have no idea, but they seem quite close."

Laughing at whatever her companion had said, Gabriella slid her arm through his and snuggled in close.

"I can't quite seem to figure her out. I thought she'd never recover after her reaction to Victor's death, but the next day, she acted like nothing happened."

"Speaking of which, are you going to see Victor's wife? She might have some answers for you."

Jessamine gave her friend a pointed look. "Well, I was planning on seeing her to offer my condolences—not necessarily to interrogate the poor woman."

Emilia held her hands up in defense. "I'm just saying. Two birds and all that."

"Maybe I'll head over there this morning since I don't have anything too pressing at the art center today. Would you like to come?"

"I better not. We have a large party coming in for a five-course afternoon tea today, complete with smoked salmon and caviar cones, sundried tomato egg salad sandwiches with truffles, and orange zest crème brûlée." Emilia dramatically ticked the items off on her fingers. "On that note, if we're going for our walk, we should probably get going."

Jessamine put her teacup down and picked up Margo's leash before following Emilia off the porch. Emilia led them down her street to a small park nestled between the two houses at the end. There, Jessamine let Margo off her leash and found a stick to toss for her happy beagle.

"So, I invited a few more people to the party on Friday. I hope that's okay."

"Of course. It's your birthday. Who'd you invite?"

"I've invited Addison, and she's bringing her fiancé. I also asked Lauren and my friend Jackson. He's your neighbor, actually. Have you met him yet?"

"I—yeah, I have," she stuttered slightly. "He actually helped me move in my furniture."

Emilia gave her a playful look but didn't say anything else. They continued their walk back around the block and soon returned to Emilia's front porch.

"Well, best of luck with your five-course afternoon tea today."

"Thanks. I'll save you leftovers if there are any."

Jessamine bid her friend goodbye before continuing on her way with Margo.

Two streets away from her own cottage, Jessamine spotted Frank Bates pulling out of a driveway in his old, white car. It almost felt eerie to see where he lived, that the man who may have stolen *Tranquil* and murdered Victor lived in a normal house in a normal neighborhood. *What were you expecting, Jess? A dark and gloomy secret lair?* He drove off in the opposite direction, and she continued toward his home.

Before she could stop herself, Jessamine ducked into his backyard, just to take a quick look. *Not a serious investigation or anything.* His backyard was basic with some neatly trimmed grass and a garden shed. Jessamine peered into a window of his house and identified a home office. His desktop computer was left on with the screen frozen on Gabriella's website. Then she noticed what appeared to be a framed painting wrapped in brown kraft paper on the ground, leaning against a wall. It was the size and shape of *Tranquil!* Frank must have smuggled it out of the art center somehow.

Jessamine couldn't believe it, but before she even had a chance to give it a second thought, a car pulled up in the driveway. *That can't be Bates back so soon!* Hurrying to the side of the house to peek around the corner at the driveway, Jessamine saw her prime suspect get out of his car a few feet away from her. Her stomach tightened, and her hands went instantly clammy. She had to get out of there!

"Margo, I have a bad feeling about this," she whispered to her dog, who had no sense of the urgency and looked at Jessamine with a goofy grin.

Bates walked up to his front door and unlocked it. Once he went inside, Jessamine planned out her escape route. There was a large bush in front of the living room bay window, which could block her from view. Jumping on her chance, she left the safety of the house's side and ducked down in front of the bush before scurrying across the lawn. Jessamine let out a sigh of relief as she approached the sidewalk; she was almost there. It would be easy enough to continue their walk without drawing any attention.

Just then, a squirrel ran up a nearby Douglas maple. Jessamine held her breath, hoping against odds Margo hadn't seen it.

No such luck.

Margo lost it! The beagle barked and barked at the exciting prospect of chasing the squirrel.

"Shhh, Margo!" Jessamine tried to quiet the dog, but it was of no use.

Margo was just too excited about the squirrel.

"Hey! What's going on? Why are you on my lawn?" Bates opened his front door and peered out at them. He held the wrapped painting. "I know you! You stole the community art center out from under my nose."

"Ooookay, that's definitely not how I saw it," Jessamine muttered to herself before turning her attention to him. "Mr. Bates, I feel like we've started off on the wrong foot. Might I introduce myself, and we can start over?"

"I know who you are. You're the bigshot from Vancouver who stole my art center. That's all I need to know about you. What are you doing on my lawn?"

"I was just taking my dog for a walk, and she got excited about the squirrel in your tree. I had no idea this was your house." Jessamine wasn't exactly proud of her little white lie, but she was too nervous about how Bates would react to the truth. He could become violent. "I'd like us to try and become friends. I believe fellow art enthusiasts should stick together."

"I don't need to become friends with the competition. Now, get away from my house!" He turned to head back inside.

"Wait! May I ask what that painting is?" Jessamine tried to keep the nervousness out of her voice. If it was *Tranquil*, she had no idea what she'd do next.

"Are you serious?" Frank barked out a venomous laugh. "It isn't your missing painting, if that's what you're accusing me of. You have some nerve!" He viciously ripped off the brown kraft paper to reveal a painting that certainly wasn't *Tranquil*. It looked like a city skyline on a bright, sunny day. And with that, Bates slammed the door and ended their conversation.

Jessamine closed her eyes for a moment and blew out a breath. "Well, baby girl, I definitely wasn't expecting to make an enemy so quickly after moving here." She led her dog back down the street, quickening the pace toward home.

After dropping Margo off back at home, Jessamine took a detour out to the Carlisles' vacation home just outside Rose Shore along the lake.

She pulled up in their circular driveway and parked behind another car near the front door. After getting out of her car, Jessamine stood in amazement, admiring the grandness of the home. The house was modern looking with sharp edges and floor-to-ceiling windows. There was a large water fountain in the front yard with a path circling around it, leading to the backyard.

The front door opened, and two women walked out onto the front step.

"Hello? Can I help you?"

"Hi, sorry. I was distracted by the gorgeous architecture. I'm here to see Madeleine Carlisle. Is she home?"

"Yes, she is. I'm Sarah, Madeleine's sister." The woman who spoke waved her closer after saying a short goodbye to the other visitor.

The visitor gave Jessamine a quick, polite smile as they passed each other on the front step before getting into her car.

"I'm Jessamine Rhodes. I work at the local art center and wanted to stop by to offer my condolences to Madeleine."

Sarah nodded. "Please, come in."

She followed Sarah through the doorway and into the house. It was even more gorgeous on the inside than on the outside. She wondered if their interior designer would do her small cottage as well. It would only take them a fraction of the time to decorate her place as it probably took to do this mansion.

"Why don't you take a seat in the library, and I'll send Madeleine in. She's just going through some photos of Victor upstairs for the funeral, and I'm sure she would love the break." Sarah led her into the nearby library.

Jessamine took a seat in one of the overstuffed armchairs and imagined how easy it would be to get lost in a good book in such a perfect space. Tall bookshelves lined three of the four walls, and the large windows were bright with the late morning sunlight streaming in. The only thing missing was a wrap-around ladder to swing from like Belle in *Beauty and the Beast*.

"Jessamine, I'm so glad you dropped by." Madeleine rushed into the library, and Jessamine stood to accept her hug. "I feel so alone without Victor."

"I'm so sorry for your loss. It was such a terrible thing to happen." Jessamine grabbed a tissue from a box off the top of a side table and handed it to Madeleine.

"Thank you." Madeleine dabbed her eyes and indicated for Jessamine to take a seat again.

"It's nice your sister could be here with you."

"Yes, Sarah is such a dear. She caught a flight from Toronto the moment I told her about Victor. I still can't believe this happened. I keep expecting him to walk through the doorway."

"If you need anything, please don't hesitate to ask."

"Thank you. You're too kind."

"Your home is beautiful, by the way."

"Victor had it designed entirely around his home art gallery. Speaking of which, do you know if that painting has been recovered?"

"No. *Tranquil* is still missing."

"I blame his obsession with art for this. I always knew it would get him into trouble."

"What do you mean?"

"Victor could get such tunnel vision when it came to his art collection. He wouldn't let anyone or anything get in his way once he had his sights set on a piece."

"I understand there was quite a bit of other interest in *Tranquil*. Do you think that could have been the reason for his death?"

"Possibly. Though, if you're referring to that dreadful Mrs. Price, I don't think she was the one to stab him."

"No?"

Madeleine shook her head. "After she came over to us and started throwing a fit over the painting, Gabriella suggested we move away from the crowd so as to not cause a scene." She gave a dark chuckle. "Oh, the sad irony of that. Anyway, Mrs. Price was with us in the foyer when the lights went off, but she was holding her checkbook and a pen right before it happened, no champagne glass. She wanted to make an offer right there and then."

So, that had been a checkbook she'd seen Mrs. Price holding. That, and based on her genuine shock, it was looking like she could cross the other art collector off the suspect list.

"Was there anything else unusual you noticed before the lights went out?" Jessamine asked.

"No." Madeleine looked thoughtful for a moment before stifling a yawn. "Oh, pardon me. I haven't gotten much sleep since Victor died."

"I should be going anyway. I'll let you get some rest. Again, please let me know if there's anything you need."

"Thank you, Jessamine." Madeleine walked her to the front door and gave her another hug goodbye.

As Jessamine drove away, she ached with sympathy for Madeleine. She was such a nice person and didn't deserve to have her husband murdered.

Chapter Eight

After finishing washing and drying her dinner dishes, Jessamine changed into a pair of pajama bottoms and her favorite sweater to settle in for a cozy evening with a blanket and cup of herbal tea on her back deck. It was the perfect weather for her fruity tea, infused with dried apples, strawberries, orange zest, and cinnamon. The sunset dipping down over the lake was one of the most gorgeous ones she'd witnessed since moving to Rose Shore, and she could just imagine how beautiful the dusty ambers and pinks would make painted on a canvas.

She still couldn't believe what a great deal she got on purchasing her cottage. The place was small, with only a living room, home office, powder room, and kitchen downstairs and her loft bedroom and en suite upstairs. It was all the space she and Margo needed, however, and she couldn't even begin to put a price on the gorgeous view that came with it.

The large back deck had obviously been an add-on some years after the cottage was originally built, and she was thankful to whoever had the idea.

Jessamine already looked forward to the backyard barbecues she was going to host next summer; though, for now, she would just enjoy the changing leaves on the surrounding clusters of trees.

Margo, who had been sleeping on the ground beside her, suddenly looked around and started to whine.

"What's up, girl? What's wrong?" She reached down to pat the beagle's head.

Margo got up and hid behind Jessamine's chair.

"Oh, Jessamine! Yoo-hoo! Are you home?" rang an approaching voice.

Clara! What does she want now? So, the dislike Clara had for Margo was mutual. *Well, at least now I have a Clara Connors warning alarm!* She smirked mischievously at the thought.

Jessamine pushed aside her blanket and rose to intercept Clara before her neighbor reached her property. Margo, the smart dog that she was, stayed behind on the deck.

"Oh, hello!" Clara seemed surprised to see Jessamine greet her at their shared low fence, despite having called out to her just a moment before.

"Hi, Clara. How are you?" Jessamine plastered on her friendliest smile.

"Oh, just fine, dear." She looked uneasily behind Jessamine. "Is that dog of yours about?"

"Margo stayed on the deck. Don't worry."

"Good! Now, tell me, how is your exciting case going, dear? Who knew you were a detective as well as an owner of an art center? Rose Shore has certainly become more interesting since you moved here." Clara's voice picked up speed with excitement.

"I'm not a detective, Clara, and who told you I was trying to solve anything?"

"Oh, I heard from Beatrice Dawson, who heard from Alan Forrester, whose daughter-in-law saw you visit Madeleine Carlisle today. She was dropping off some casseroles for the poor woman."

Jessamine had heard about how fast news could travel around a small town, but this was ridiculous. If all those people figured she was trying to solve the case, surely Lauren and Constable Todd had assumed it as well. Besides, how did they guess that was exactly what she was trying to do? She'd wanted to visit Madeleine anyway; the answers to her questions were only a bonus. Jessamine's thoughts wandered away from whatever Clara blabbered on about, but she quickly snapped back to attention when she heard something else her neighbor said about the murdered man. "Sorry, did you just say something about being friends with Victor?"

Clara looked a little put off that Jessamine hadn't been completely paying attention to her. "Yes, dear. I was talking about how Victor and I were both part of the Literary Classics Book Club that meets at the local library. Well, Victor only came when he was in town, which was usually only during the summer months. But he brought the most delicious lemon squares their personal chef makes. Oh, she must use the freshest lemons! She also uses them in her famous strawberry lemonade."

"Could you please tell me more about the book club?" Jessamine struggled to put some extra sweetness in her voice as she tried to get a word in.

"Of course, dear. That's what I'm doing. This week we're tackling Mary Shelley's *Frankenstein*. Did you know she was only eighteen when she started writing the story—"

"I meant could you tell me more about Victor's involvement with the book club."

Clara gave her the evil eye for interrupting. "Well, Victor was a very active member of our little club when he was in town, quite popular with everyone. Except that grumpy old Barb Waters, but she doesn't like anyone. Anyway, the book club and the art center were really the only two places in town Victor was involved with."

"Are drop-ins welcome at your book club? I love literary classics." Jessamine made sure Clara was done speaking this time to avoid another disproving glare from those icy blue eyes.

"Yes, of course, dear. We would love to have you join us sometime. We meet every Thursday evening at seven in the back room of the library. Please bring a little something to snack on, perhaps a little something from Emilia's tea shop." Clara absently patted her stomach.

Jessamine had a suspicion that her neighbor went to these book club discussions more for the food and gossip than for the literature. "I'll make sure to pick something up." She turned to head back to her cottage.

"Oh, and did you hear Gabriella Everhart might have gotten back together with her fiancé?"

"I didn't know she had a fiancé to get back together with." Jessamine shook her head slightly, feeling a little lost in this new topic of conversation.

"She was engaged to some fancy fashion designer named Carlos Leoz from San Francisco. He gave her the biggest diamond you ever laid eyes upon. I'm surprised you didn't see a picture of the ring. It was featured in all sorts of magazines and all over Facebook. My daughter got me set up on that thing. Now I can see photos of all her travels. Did I tell you she's currently in Vienna? I believe Berlin is next on her list. Have you been to Europe?" Clara paused to catch her breath. "Anyway, they split up for whatever reason a few weeks ago. Gabriella and Carlos, I mean. Rumor has it she was inspired by their relationship to paint *Tranquil*, which is why she was so eager to sell it after she broke off their engagement."

Surprisingly, Clara's story was actually aligning with what Gabriella herself had told Jessamine the other day. "How do you know they've gotten back together?"

"Oh, that's just a rumor, dear. Don't believe everything you hear."

She's one to talk. "Okay." Jessamine took a deep breath. "Then do you know how the rumor started?"

"Leonard Franklyn from the grocery store said his wife's cousin was meeting an old friend for brunch at Emilia's. I personally prefer the afternoon teas to the brunches. There are more chocolate items with the tea menus. I went there with Beatrice a few weeks ago, and it was simply divine and we—"

"Clara, please, what does any of this have to do with Gabriella and Carlos?" Jessamine couldn't help herself this time; she needed the information from Clara and not all the fluff that was coming with it.

Clara closed her eyes for a moment and took in a deep breath. Jessamine braced herself for the lecture she feared was coming, but then her neighbor simply said, "Gabriella and Carlos walked by the tea shop, arm in arm."

Realization dawned on her. That was who she saw that very morning while drinking tea with Emilia. Gabriella and Carlos must have been coming back from wherever they had walked to when Leonard Franklyn's wife's . . . whoever . . . saw them at brunch.

"That's interesting. Do you think it's true?"

"Who am I to say? But I do think Gabriella was silly to let him go in the first place. Carlos Leoz is quite the handsome man."

Clara spent a few more minutes talking about the local gossip, but Jessamine was eager to share this new information with Emilia. Her friend had been just as curious about who Gabriella was with as she had been. She was finally able to excuse herself when Clara grew distracted by a weed in one of her flower beds. Jessamine hurried back to her deck, picked up her forgotten cup of tea, and headed inside the cottage, with Margo quick at her heels.

Pouring the last bit of the now-cold tea down the kitchen sink drain, she looked around for her phone. Margo started whining again, and Jessamine figured her dog must smell Clara's scent still. But Margo barked, and another sound came from her home office in the front of the cottage. It sounded like something had crashed to the floor. Margo's barking became more frantic.

"Hello? Is anyone here? Emilia? Is that you?" Jessamine called out and tried to keep the worry out of her voice. It had to be Emilia. She was the only other person with a key. Or maybe something fell that hadn't been put away properly. Another noise followed—one that sounded like running footsteps.

Someone was in her house!

Chapter Nine

The footsteps headed straight to the front door, which opened and slammed before Jessamine even left her kitchen. She followed, opened her front door, and stepped out onto the porch. A woman, who unquestionably was not Emilia, ran down the sidewalk, away from her house. Jessamine ran back inside to grab a pair of shoes. Slipping on her runners and lacing them up as quickly as she could, she took off after the woman. But the other woman was fast, and by the time Jessamine got back out onto her porch, the woman had already headed into a nearby forested park. It seemed hopeless to try and catch up, but Jessamine took off running anyway.

The chase was on. The woman zigzagged through the trees, and Jessamine pushed herself to keep up, her ragged breath a reality check of how out of shape she was. Soon, the intruder was out of sight. Jessamine slowed down, knowing she had lost whoever it was, and instead, searched the area for any clue, anything the woman could have possibly dropped.

Was that Gabriella? Whoever it was had the same long, dark hair.

Jessamine was lost in her thoughts as she searched the jogging path and around the trees when the sound of someone approaching grabbed her attention. Thinking it must be her intruder, she slipped behind a large rock and grabbed a stick off the ground to use as a weapon.

The running footsteps slowed to a stop just on the other side of the rock. Jessamine's already-racing heart sped up even more. Her grip on the stick was shaky—she could be found at any moment! Determined to use the element of surprise to her full advantage, she leaped out from behind the rock and took a swing with the stick.

"Jessamine! Stop! What are you doing?"

She realized just in time it was Jackson she was about to attack like a birthday party piñata.

"Jackson, you scared me! Why are you sneaking around the forest?"

"Why are *you* hiding behind large rocks and jumping out at people with sticks? And why were you booking it down the street in your pajamas?" He was dressed in shorts and an old T-shirt, clearly having been out for a jog.

Jessamine looked down; she had completely forgotten her legs were covered in purple plaid fleece. "I'd just been enjoying my lazy evening. But then someone broke . . . ." she wasn't sure how much she should tell Jackson. "I was just out for a run."

He clearly didn't believe her sad attempt at a lie. "What's going on?"

Jessamine sighed. "Okay, fine. I may have been doing a little investigating on the side after stumbling upon a few clues here and there. I know the police don't want me to get involved, but I can't sit back and do nothing. And then tonight, someone was in my house, and I—"

"What do you mean someone was in your house?" Jackson's voice was filled with concern.

"It's fine. Nothing happened. When I came inside from the back deck, she ran. I chased her to the forest before losing her in the trees."

"You're sure it was a woman?"

"Yes. I think it might have actually been Gabriella Everhart," she whispered as if the trees were listening in.

"The artist whose painting was stolen?"

"Yes." Jessamine read earnest curiosity in his eyes and knew she could trust him. "I think Gabriella might have been the one to steal her own painting, actually. For the insurance money."

Jackson let out a low whistle and his eyes grew wide. "Okay. I'm in."

"What do you mean 'in'?"

"I'm in—in with the investigation. I want to help you figure this out."

"Why?" Jessamine put a hand on her hip.

"Like I said the other night, I had a personal connection with Victor. I want to find whoever killed him. And besides, you seem like you could use someone looking out for you if your house is getting broken into."

She scoffed at the last part. "It's just been the one time. I can take care of myself."

Jackson gave her a gentle smile. "I didn't mean it like that. I'm sure you can. But I still want to help."

"All right, but don't tattle on me to Constable Todd. That man scares me."

Together, they searched around the forest for a few minutes but found no trace of the mysterious woman. After giving up their search, Jackson suggested they head back to her cottage to look around inside and try to figure out what the intruder might have been looking for.

"I didn't even think to check if anything was stolen first," Jessamine admitted as they walked down the street. It was completely dark by now, and the street lights had come on. "I just took off on instinct."

Once they arrived at her cottage, Jessamine led Jackson to her home office. She kept her office simple and tidy, with a white L-shaped desk in one corner and tall bookshelves lining the other walls. The bright window and beautiful French door made the small room feel much larger than it actually was. There were still a few decorations to unpack to brighten up the space, but overall, she was quite happy with it. At first glance, nothing seemed out of place except for a stack of notebooks on the floor. The books had been neatly stacked between decorative bookends on her desk next to her laptop.

"I first heard a crash when I realized someone was here. This must have been what fell."

"Are any of them missing?"

She took a closer look at them. The notebooks contained lists of potential future guest teachers for the art center and ideas for classes. Not always finding the time during the workday to fill out her ideas, she kept copies at home. Jessamine flipped through the books, but no pages seemed to be missing, and she doubted the intruder would have had the time to copy down any information written in them, not that there was anything too private. She put the books back down exactly as they had been on the ground, looked up, and noticed the closet door was slightly ajar. She always left it closed so Margo wouldn't get into trouble.

"Nothing is missing from the notebooks, but Gabriella, or whoever she was, was in that closet." She walked over and opened the door. Nothing seemed amiss inside there either. "This is so strange. Nothing is missing. What was she after?"

"She must have been looking for something specific since your laptop is still here."

"Good point. That would've been easy to steal."

"Do you know how she broke in?" Jackson asked.

"No. The front door was locked, and I would have noticed if she came in through the back. Maybe she climbed in through a window." They walked through the ground floor of the cottage and, sure enough, the window in the living room next to her upright piano had its screen popped out.

"Well, that's what I get for trying to get some fresh air in the house." Jessamine's effort at humor fell flat. "I should probably keep all the windows and doors locked until this case is wrapped up."

He nodded in agreement. "We should also probably report this to the police."

Jessamine groaned. "I know. You're right." She picked up her cell phone off the coffee table and called Lauren directly. After explaining what happened and repeatedly insisting she wasn't hurt, Jessamine hung up and turned back to Jackson. "The police are on their way. Constable Marsh asked if you wouldn't mind staying as well and giving your story, even though I know you didn't actually witness anything."

"It's all right. I understand. I want to stay a little while longer anyway, in case the intruder comes back."

"Do you want any of the leftover dessert from the art center catering while we wait?"

Jackson beamed. "Sounds good."

She wasn't quite sure what to make of Jackson's comment about wanting to stay. She understood he was being cautious, but she could take care of herself. Still, it would be nice to have some company; it was a little unsettling knowing someone had broken in only an hour ago. Jessamine boiled some water and made a pot of rooibos tea to go with the goodies she plated.

When she got back to the living room, Jackson was looking through a photo album that had been in a basket underneath the coffee table. The album was filled with pictures of paintings.

"Are these all paintings you featured at your art gallery in Vancouver?"

"Actually, they're ones I painted myself."

"Wow, these are amazing." His voice was an odd mix of admiration and intrigue.

Jessamine shrugged, not knowing how to decipher his interest in her art. "Most of those are ones I sold at small art shows or gave away as gifts."

He looked like he was about to say something else when a car door slammed in her driveway, and they both looked out the window. Lauren and Constable Todd were walking up to the front door.

"Jess! Are you all right?" Lauren asked as soon as Jessamine opened the door.

"Yes, yes, I'm fine. And I don't think anything was actually taken." She stepped aside, inviting the two officers inside.

Lauren and Constable Todd took their time looking around her small cottage and taking pictures of the knocked-over notebooks and broken-in screen window. Jessamine had to keep biting her lip to keep her sassy remarks at bay every time Constable Todd asked if she had "disturbed" anything. *Yes, I completely rearranged my entire house right before you got here,* she thought sarcastically after he asked her for the fourth time in under twenty minutes.

Finally, after the officers seemed satisfied with their search, including their dusting for fingerprints, they went over the events of the evening with Jessamine and Jackson. They sat in the living room, with Jessamine and Jackson together on the couch and Lauren and Constable Todd sitting across from them in the two armchairs. Jessamine started with what she'd heard and seen at the time of the break-in. Jackson didn't have too much to add, since he hadn't actually witnessed anything, but she was glad he was there for support. She was also glad he kept to their unspoken agreement not to mention anything about them wanting to investigate, and they breezed over the part about searching around the forest for clues.

"Well, we'll be in contact once we find out who broke in." Constable Todd closed his notebook. He stood, and Lauren followed.

"Have a good evening Ms. Rhodes, Mr. Yeung." He nodded at them and headed out the front doorway.

"I'll let you know about the fingerprints," Lauren said quietly to Jessamine before following her partner outside.

Jessamine smiled her thanks.

"Well, that went well," Jackson said flatly as he closed the door behind Lauren. "Officer Uptight almost seems to think *you* had something to do with this."

"You caught that as well? I'm so glad I have Lauren on my side, even though I know she's doing it more for her brother's sake. She still doesn't like me investigating, but she at least promised to keep me up to date on the case."

"Are you going to talk to Gabriella yourself?"

"Yeah. I'm going to head there sometime tomorrow morning. I'm sure the police will go tonight, but I don't want it to seem too suspicious if I show up this late. Do you want to come?"

He shook his head. "I can't. I have an early shift at the station tomorrow."

Jessamine wasn't sure what to do with the hint of disappointment that swelled inside of her.

"But here, I'll give you my number so you can keep me updated." Jackson reached out a hand, and Jessamine handed him her phone so he could type in his number.

"Thanks. I'll talk to you tomorrow."

The next morning, Jessamine headed back to the Rose Shore Resort & Spa. She again purposely hadn't called ahead of time, in hopes that Gabriella wouldn't be prepared with a lie or cover story.

"Is Ms. Gabriella Everhart around? I need to speak to her," she asked the front desk clerk, a different employee from the last time she was there.

The front desk clerk immediately called up to Gabriella's room without asking any questions. After hanging up, the desk clerk assured Jessamine that someone would be with her shortly and, inviting her to take a seat in the lobby, gestured toward the same couches Jessamine, Gabriella, and Fay had sat on last time.

The elevator doors opened, and Fay walked out. Something about her was different from when Jessamine saw her last, and she realized it was the way Fay was dressed. Now, her outfit was more similar to something Gabriella would wear, with a sleek pair of dress pants and a sky-blue chiffon top.

As soon as Jessamine saw her, she realized Gabriella's sister could have very well been the one in her cottage. They had the exact same long, dark curls, but the idea of Fay breaking in had never even crossed her mind.

Fay greeted Jessamine with a quick handshake. "You wanted to speak with my sister again?"

"I have a few questions for her. Is she on her way down?"

"Gabriella isn't feeling well and is still sleeping in our suite. You're stuck with me, I'm afraid. What can I do for you?"

Jessamine wasn't too annoyed as it gave her the opportunity to figure out if it had been Fay who'd broken in. "Do you know where your sister was last night? And were you with her?"

Fay didn't say anything for a moment. "I assume Gabriella was in bed all last night. She said she wasn't feeling well after our early dinner together here at the resort's restaurant and headed up to our suite right afterward."

"You assume? So, you don't know for certain?"

"I had my own plans for the evening."

Jessamine gave Fay a look she hoped would be interpreted as an invitation to continue.

It worked. "I met a friend for drinks, and I didn't get back until almost midnight. I went straight to bed and didn't check on Gabriella until this morning. She was still fast asleep right before I came down here."

"So, it's possible Gabriella could have left sometime between last night's dinner with you and this morning?"

"It's possible, but I doubt it. Gabriella doesn't know anyone in town anymore nor does she really enjoy the small-town scene. Unless there was another extravagant party somewhere, she would have stayed here. What's this all about anyway?"

"Fay, someone broke into my home last night, and the person seen fleeing the scene matches your sister's description."

Fay sat quietly for a moment, and it was hard to tell if her lack of surprise was because it had been her who broke in or because the police had already questioned her. "Was anything taken?"

"No, which adds to the mystery. Do you have any idea why your sister might break into my home?"

"No, none. Were you the witness? Are you sure it was her?"

Again, it was hard to tell if Fay was trying to defend Gabriella or get a sense of whether she was a suspect as well. Possibly both.

"No, I'm not sure. I only saw the person from behind. All I know is the intruder had long, dark hair."

Fay instantly brought a hand up to her own hair, showing off perfectly manicured nails as she did, and stood. "I really must go check in on how Gabriella is doing. I'm sorry I couldn't be more help."

"Before you go, do you mind giving me the name of the place you went for drinks so I can confirm your story?"

"So, you *do* suspect me." She glared at Jessamine. "Well, I met my friend at the Waterfront Kitchen out in Birch Cove. That's why I got back so late, but I'm sure they'll be happy to confirm my *story*—as you put it. I believe our server's name was James."

And before Jessamine could respond, Fay left the hotel lobby.

Jessamine stopped in at Emilia's Secret Garden Tea Shop for lunch after leaving the resort. She took her place at the back of the line for the takeout counter and stood on her tiptoes to try and read the chalkboard menu. She still couldn't quite see what was listed under the Daily Specials and had to squint.

"Do you need to get your eyes checked or something?" said a teasing voice behind her.

She turned around to find Jackson had just stepped in through the entrance, apparently with the same craving for Emilia's food as she had.

Jessamine scowled at him. "No, the letters are too tiny. That's hardly my fault."

Jackson laughed. "So, how did talking with Gabriella go?"

"I didn't see her, actually. I talked to her sister, Fay, who said Gabriella was sleeping in because she wasn't feeling well."

He raised his eyebrows. "Sleeping in because she wasn't feeling well or sleeping in after some tiring B and E escapades?"

"Shhh, not so loud." Jessamine stifled a laugh. "We're trying to keep this on the down-low, remember?"

"Right, right." Jackson's voice dropped into an exaggerated whisper. "So, what else did Fay have to say?"

She laughed again at his attempt to be covert. "Well, it's not so much what she said as to who she looks like. Fay has the same hairstyle and color as her sister. So, she could have been the one who broke in."

"Sneaky."

"But she said she was out in Birch Cove last night, so I'm going to call the restaurant she said she was at after lunch and find out."

"Maybe she and Gabriella are in on it together. Whatever 'it' is."

"What is 'it'? What are you two talking about? The case?" They had reached the front of the line, and Emilia's way of greeting them was to pepper them with curiosity.

Now it was Jackson's turn to scowl. "You're not also trying to solve this, are you? We can't all investigate, or we'll draw attention to ourselves."

Emilia gave him her best innocent look, a sad attempt that didn't so much say "Who me?" as it did "Of course I am!" "I'm just curious. How about a trade? Some info for a free lunch? Come on, buddy; I need to know what's going on!"

Jackson shook his head in defeat. "How about this? You give me my free lunch, and then I head back to work. Whatever Jessamine then decides to tell you is up to her."

"Deal!" Emilia agreed and eagerly packed up a turkey club sandwich for him without even waiting to hear what he wanted to order. "Here you go! Now, see you later."

Jackson took the bag and walked out the doorway, laughing and shaking his head.

"Now tell me!" Emilia leaned against the counter and blinked her wide, pleading eyes.

Jessamine checked behind her, and since no one else had gotten in line, she gave a quick rundown of the break-in and conversation with Fay that followed.

"So, who do you think was there last night? Gabriella or Fay?"

"I have no idea. They could be twins they look so similar, especially from behind, and we can't make much more progress until I call this restaurant."

"We?" Emilia repeated. "Are you two working together now or something?"

"I guess so. Jackson apparently has his reasons for wanting to solve this case as well, though I don't know what they are."

"If you're worried about trusting him, don't."

"Don't trust him?" Jessamine raised an eyebrow.

"No. I mean don't worry. Jackson is a stand-up guy."

The line behind Jessamine started to form again, so she quickly ordered her lunch and stepped aside as Emilia took the next few orders. Once Emilia was free, Jessamine thanked her for the lunch and grabbed the takeout bag to bring back to the art center.

Chapter Ten

Jessamine was too jittery to concentrate on her work when she arrived at the community art center. Calling the restaurant had to be a priority before she would be able to get anything else done. She found the number for the Waterfront Kitchen easily and was able to speak with James the server.

Yes, he remembered that someone with Fay's description had dined there the night before with a friend. Yes, she only had dessert and drinks. And yes, they stayed until closing time and left the restaurant just after eleven P.M.

"Is there anything else I can help you with?" James asked politely.

"No. Thank you, though. You've been very helpful." Jessamine hung up. *Well, that was a bust. I guess I can cross Fay off the list.* Fay hadn't been at the art center opening, nor had she been the one to break into her cottage— double strike against Fay being a suspect.

Jessamine forced herself to turn back to her work and set the case aside for the rest of the afternoon. There was payroll to sort through and potential art teachers to contact, and she needed to finally get around to contacting a flooring company about changing over the carpet in the foyer. That blood stain wasn't coming out. She got a solid three hours of work done at her desk before her cell phone rang. Looking at the caller I.D., she was surprised to see it was Emilia, considering it was the height of afternoon tea time and the tea shop had already been picking up when she left earlier.

"Hey, Em. What's up?"

"You said Fay and Gabriella look similar, right? So similar they could almost pass off as twins?"

Jessamine was getting used to the way her friend tended to leap into a conversation without a formal greeting first. "Yes, they do. Why? What's going on?"

"Because Carlos and someone who looks a lot like Gabriella but isn't Gabriella are sharing an intimate afternoon tea right now."

"Define intimate."

"Laughing, giggling, can't keep their hands off each other. Oh. And she just pecked his cheek." Emilia sounded very unimpressed with the PDA of her customers.

"But we saw him with Gabriella just yesterday, and it looked like they'd gotten back together. Clara even said they did." Jessamine paused. "Not that I believe everything Clara says."

"Listen, neither of them knows who I am or that I know who they are. I'm casually going to play the nosy server and see what kind of information I can get from them."

"Be careful. If Carlos was involved with the murder, he could be dangerous."

"Nothing bad ever happened in a cozy tea shop. I'll be fine." Emilia ended the call, and Jessamine stared blankly at her phone.

Should I go over there? Or would that blow Emilia's cover because Fay knows who I am?

Jessamine decided to stay at the art center and not fret about it. She trusted Emilia. Despite the curiosity coursing through her, she turned back to her work, though it wasn't long before her phone rang again.

"That was quick. Tell me everything!"

"Okay. You would have been very impressed with my acting skills, Jess! I was so casual. They didn't suspect a thing." Emilia clearly enjoyed playing detective. "So, I walked over to their table with a refill of tea and made comments about how cute they were as a couple. Then I asked how long they'd been together. Fay immediately rambled on and on about how they had just started dating a few weeks ago and how before that, she had a crush on Carlos for forever and was so happy they'd finally gotten together. And the look on Carlos' face! Clearly, he didn't agree. He kept trying to interrupt her, and it seemed like he was trying to downplay their relationship, but Fay wouldn't let him get a word in."

"That's so strange. The first time I met Fay, she barely said one word. I can't imagine her gushing like that."

"She's clearly head over heels for the guy, but he doesn't seem to feel the same."

"Did you find anything else out?"

"Just that Fay mentioned they're going for an evening stroll along Willows Beach later today."

"Where is that? I haven't heard of Willows Beach." Jessamine pulled up Google maps on her computer.

"It's a gorgeous path along the lake, close to all of those lakeside condo rentals along Kingfisher Way. Willows Beach is very popular with young couples."

"Well, I'm impressed with your detective work. Thanks for the info."

"No problem. Anytime, but I really must get back to work. Everyone and their gran are here for afternoon tea today."

"Thanks again, Em. I'll talk to you later." Jessamine ended the call and pushed her work aside. She wasn't quite sure how Carlos Leoz fit into the mystery yet, but she had a feeling he did. Jessamine gathered her things and headed out of her office.

"Hey, Andrew, I'm leaving early for the day. Emilia called with a great tip for the case."

"Sounds good, Jess. Just be careful."

She got in her car intending to drive to Willows Beach when she remembered she now had another partner in crime—or partner in solving crime, that was. She pulled her phone back out of her purse and called Jackson.

"Hello?" Jackson picked up on the first ring.

"Hey, Jackson. It's Jessamine."

"Oh, hey. Long time, no talk. Is everything all right?"

"Yeah, everything's fine. Is this an okay time to talk?"

"It's perfect. I'm on a break. What's up?"

"Two things. So, I called the restaurant in Birch Cove, and also, Emilia called me about something interesting."

She told him everything the server from the Waterfront Kitchen had said and what Emilia said about Carlos and Fay having afternoon tea at the Secret Garden Tea Shop. "So, I was wondering if you wanted to head over to Willows Beach this evening and look into this ourselves?"

There was a pause before amusement soaked his words. "You know that place has a reputation for being something of a lovers' lane, right?"

"I'm not asking you out!"

Jackson laughed. "I'm just teasing. Sure. Sounds like a good idea. And you can go over exactly who this Carlos is because I'm still a little confused about how he plays into this."

Me too. "Sure. What time do you get off work?"

"At six. Do you want to meet in the parking lot at the beach around seven?"

"Sure."

"Now, I know this isn't a date," his voice became playful, "but we can grab a late dinner there at one of the food trucks, if you're interested."

It was Jessamine's turn to laugh. "Sounds good. See you then."

After ending the call, she wasn't sure what to do with herself while she waited for Jackson, so Jessamine headed to Willows Beach anyway, thinking a walk in the fresh air would do her some good. She'd pulled into the parking lot when her phone rang again.

"Who is it now?" she muttered to herself and reached for her phone. The caller I.D. this time read "Lauren Marsh." "Hey, Lauren. What's up?"

"Hi, Jess. I'm calling with some updates about the case."

"That's great. What have you learned?"

"Mrs. Price is no longer a suspect. Our interviews with both Madeleine and Gabriella about the incident revealed that Mrs. Price wasn't anywhere near a champagne glass before the stabbing occurred."

A twinge of guilt hit Jessamine at having already known that information from her own conversation with Madeleine but having kept it from the police. She offered no indication that she already knew that Mrs. Price's hands had been full with her checkbook and pen, so she waited for Lauren to continue.

"Also, Mrs. Price is no longer a suspect because we did a thorough search of her home, and there was no trace of *Tranquil*."

"Did you see that sitting room of hers she keeps bragging about?" Jessamine asked flatly.

"Yes, and I must say that, even though I don't know a thing about color schemes, Mrs. Price sure is right about that turquoise and sage." Lauren let out a laugh, and Jessamine joined in.

"Well, I have to say I'm not really surprised Mrs. Price is no longer a suspect. She seems a little nutty, but not nutty enough to actually steal a painting or stab someone."

"I agree. I've also finished analyzing the fingerprints found in your house but didn't find any that weren't yours or Jackson's. Oh, hold on a minute."

Jessamine could hear Lauren covering the phone with her hand, so she listened with curiosity to the muffled voices on the other end. Something about Gabriella and the painting.

"Hey, Jess?" Lauren came back on the line. "A witness just called with a new tip about the case. Someone at the event saw Gabriella pick *Tranquil* up off the easel a few minutes before the lights went out. Sounds like I'll have to speak to her again. The witness admitted at the time she didn't think there was anything unusual about an artist handling her own painting, but, after reading the article in the newspaper this morning asking for anyone to come forward with any info, she thought it might be useful. She said she didn't realize the investigation was so far from being solved." Lauren sounded a little annoyed at the last part.

"Did the witness leave a name?"

"Yes, a Dina Layton."

"Hmm. I don't recognize the name, but I didn't know most of the people at the event. Molly or Andrew should know her, though, if you want to get in contact with them."

"I'll do that. Thanks."

"And thank you for the info, Lauren. I appreciate it."

"No problem. Take care."

"Bye."

"So, Gabriella and Carlos were engaged, and then they broke up, and then Carlos dates Gabriella's sister who is also her assistant?" Jackson was trying to sort everything out. "Do you really think this all has something to do with the missing painting and Victor's murder? It sounds like messy family drama to me."

"I agree it's all very dramatic, but it's still too much of a coincidence."

Jackson had just arrived in the parking lot and seemed eager to proceed. She'd been surprised at how busy Willows Beach had gotten before remembering how unusually warm it was for a fall evening. She was sensing Rose Shore residents tended to take every advantage they could to spend time outdoors.

"But, can we eat first before we dive into this some more? I'm starving," Jackson said.

"Yeah, me too. That sandwich from Emilia's was delicious but didn't quite fill me up."

They headed toward the four parked food trucks, and the delicious smells made Jessamine's mouth water. There was a gourmet grilled cheese truck, a taco truck, a butter chicken truck, and one called The Sweetest Sweets You Ever Did Eat, which seemed to offer every deep-fried dessert imaginable.

"I think I'm going with the butter chicken." Jessamine looked at the nearby colorful menu board.

"Okay. I'm going to grab a few tacos. Let's order and then meet by those picnic tables over there."

Jessamine nodded and went to get her food. She didn't want to admit it, but she hadn't eaten outside in a park since she was a child, and she certainly had never ordered from a food truck before. She was secretly gleeful at this new experience. It all seemed so small town to her.

Finding a table was easy enough, despite the growing crowd. Jessamine happened to be next to a table as another couple was leaving, and she quickly slid onto a seat while waving Jackson over at the same time.

"These food trucks have become very popular over the last few years." Jackson looked around at the packed picnic tables. "There are almost always some here or over at the Centennial Park pitch and putt."

"There seems to be a lot to do around Rose Shore, for being such a small town."

"It may be small, but it's a fast-growing town. Many people, like you, are looking to escape big-city life. But you're right, community recreation here is a big thing. Do you miss living in Vancouver?" Jackson took a big bite out of a taco.

"No, not really. I'm finding I'm much more suited to small-town life anyway. So is Margo."

"How long have you had her? I know she was a rescue, but tell me her story."

Jessamine smiled to herself and thought back to the day she walked into the rescue shelter and saw that small, malnourished beagle for the first time. Those big puppy-dog eyes looked at her, pleading for Jessamine to love her. "Well, I grew up with dogs actually but didn't think I'd have time for one of my own once I started working at the gallery in Vancouver. But I was missing having a furry companion and looked into adopting an older dog, one that hopefully wouldn't need quite so much training. I popped in at a local rescue one day and immediately fell in love with Margo. She was about three at the time and just needed someone to love her after having been found on the street almost starving. I took her home with me right then and there."

"Poe has a similar story, though I adopted him when he was only a few months old."

"Oh, I didn't know he was a rescue as well."

"Yeah, my sister actually found out about him for me. She insisted I needed him in my life. Turns out, as always, she was right. And it's been just Poe and me for quite a few years now."

"No special someone in your life?" Jessamine glanced down at her food.

"Yes, I just told you about him. His name is Poe," Jackson teased. "But no special humans, if that's what you're asking. What about yourself?"

"Not for several years now."

After an awkward pause, Jessamine quickly moved on to a new topic. She steered the conversation back to the case and told Jackson what she'd learned from Lauren earlier that day.

Jackson was shaking his head and stifling a grin when she got to the part about Mrs. Price.

"What's so funny?"

"Oh, that Mrs. Price. I've responded to a few not-quite-emergency calls from her over the years. Very dramatic, that one is."

"She *is* quite the character. I think she and Clara Connors would get along."

Jackson laughed even harder. "You would think that, but they don't! Just the opposite, actually. There's some mysterious feud between the two of them, and no one knows what it's about."

"That sounds like one mystery I don't want to get involved in."

Jackson's laughter died down. "So, what do you think of the lack of fingerprints in your house? That's kinda eerie."

"Not really. I've given it some thought. If it was Gabriella, or anyone in the art world, for that matter, they would most likely have a pair of white cotton gloves handy for handling delicate paintings. Therefore, no fingerprints." Jessamine wiggled her fingers for emphasis.

Jackson nodded and pointed his taco at her. "Smart thinking."

Jessamine was thoughtful for a moment. "Perhaps we're looking at this case the wrong way."

"What do you mean?"

"Perhaps the culprit isn't at all connected to the art world. It's possible that instead of *Tranquil* being the target and Victor getting in the way, it was the other way around."

"You mean someone *meant* to kill Victor and stealing a ten-thousand-dollar painting was just a bonus?"

"Yes. I think it's definitely something to look into." Jessamine pulled her journal out of her purse to jot this new idea down. She looked back up and saw someone she thought she recognized walking through the parking lot toward the food trucks and picnic area. "Is that Howard McCoy?"

"It is. I wonder what he's up to." Jackson sounded as suspicious as she felt.

Howard walked up to each of the food trucks and talked to whoever was working in them. Each person gave a shake of the head in response to whatever Howard asked until the butter chicken food truck. After a quick conversation, Howard handed the young guy working there some money, and then Butter Chicken Guy immediately pointed in the direction of Jessamine and Jackson. Howard gave them a wide-eyed stare and hurried back across the parking lot. Butter Chicken Guy started laughing and pocketed the money.

"What was that all about?" Jessamine asked.

"I'm not sure, but I'm going to find out." Jackson walked over to the butter food truck.

Jessamine couldn't hear the conversation, but Butter Chicken Guy seemed very nervous and held his hands up in a position of defense.

After a few minutes, Jackson walked back over. "Apparently, Howard has been attempting to trail you, though he doesn't seem to be doing a very good job. The guy working at the food truck said Howard was in the parking lot and saw us walk over here. He wanted to know where you took off after that and gave the guy ten bucks to tell him."

"And he just pointed over here," Jessamine finished.

Jackson nodded. "Howard didn't realize we hadn't left the area."

"So, now he's given himself away, gained no information, and is out ten dollars?"

"Exactly."

"Why was the guy so nervous when you were talking with him?"

"I was maybe a little aggressive. He thought Howard was a wanted criminal or something. He must have been scared I thought they were working together, but he relaxed when I explained that Howard was some rogue blogger and that I just wanted to know what their conversation had been about."

"I hope this makes Howard give up on his trailing attempt. That guy is starting to give me the creeps."

Jackson rubbed the back of his neck but didn't say anything else.

They finished up their butter chicken and street tacos, and Jessamine suggested checking out the dessert food truck. The smell of deep-fried mixed with cinnamon sugar was too good to pass up. "I don't think I can finish a whole churro funnel cake by myself. Want to share one?"

Jackson took in a deep inhale of the sugary-sweet aroma. "Absolutely!"

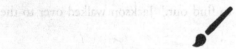

An hour into their time at Willows Beach, Jessamine realized she'd almost completely forgotten why they came in the first place. She also realized, and had no idea how she felt about it, that she really enjoyed spending time with Jackson. But since she didn't know *why* he was so eager to work on the case with her, she was still a little cautious around him.

After finishing their delicious dessert, they walked along the trail that hugged the shoreline of Opal Lake. Here, the beach was quite sandy, and Jessamine was tempted to slip off her shoes and squish her toes in the damp sand. Ahead of her, a couple had done just that. They were laughing and teasing each other, and it suddenly seemed like a very romantic thing to do. Jessamine's face warmed, and she hurried ahead a few steps, keeping to the trail instead of the sand.

Before Jackson could comment on her change of pace, Jessamine held out her arm in an indication to stop walking. There, walking toward them, were Fay and Carlos. Fay, with her arm looped through Carlos' elbow, had her head thrown back in laughter, whereas Carlos' expression showed slight annoyance.

Jessamine nudged Jackson in the side. "There they are. We probably should have thought up more of a game plan for starting a conversation with them."

"Just be casual. Act like you're excited to see her." Jackson deliberately took a step to the side so he was right in front of Fay and Carlos, pulling Jessamine gently by the arm with him.

She followed his lead. "Hello, Fay! Nice to see you again. Enjoying an evening walk?"

The laughter from Fay's eyes disappeared for a moment, and her expression became almost cold and uninviting. "Yes, we were just finishing up our evening and heading back to the parking lot. Why are you here?"

Jessamine thought quickly before blurting out, "We're on a date."

Jackson covered his surprised laugh with a cough and a side look at her. "Yep, our first date."

Fay's eyebrows disappeared up into her bangs. She clearly didn't believe them, but Jessamine ignored her and reached out to shake hands with Carlos, realizing Clara was right about one thing: he *was* very handsome. "Hi, I'm Jessamine Rhodes, and this is Jackson Yeung."

"Carlos Leoz. How do you know Fay?" Carlos had a slight Spanish accent and didn't seem nearly as eager as Fay did to get away, slipping his arm out of hers.

"I own the Rose Shore Community Art Center here in town."

"Oh, have you spoken to Gabriella recently then?" Carlos' amber eyes lit up when he said Gabriella's name. "How is she? I know this awful business has her all shook up. That painting was very special to us."

"I *have* spoken with her. She seems to be doing all right, despite everything. How do you know Gabriella?" Jessamine feigned curiosity.

"We were in love, deeply in love. Gabriella painted *Tranquil* the night we got engaged." A sad smile danced upon Carlos' lips.

"I didn't know Gabriella was engaged." Jessamine continued with her small lies.

"Yes," Carlos sounded like he was lost in a dream. "We got engaged last spring and were so in love. We met at a mutual friend's beach house down in California the previous summer, and so, when we got engaged and Gabriella painted *Tranquil* to celebrate, she chose colors to represent the ocean. But we are both passionate about our artistic work and let that passion come between us. After a couple of massive fights about priorities, she broke things off for good a few weeks ago."

"You wouldn't happen to know anything about where *Tranquil* is now, would you?" Jackson asked.

"No, of course not." Carlos crossed his arms. "I haven't seen *Tranquil* since it was housed in Gabriella's personal studio, the day before we broke up."

"Which doesn't matter anymore since we're now happily together. And we really must get going." Fay grabbed Carlos' hand. "Thank you for saying hello. Have a good rest of your evening." Fay gave Jessamine a quick smile and led Carlos toward the parking lot.

"That was odd," Jessamine said. "They don't seem to be on the same page about their relationship. That's what Emilia commented on as well. And clearly, Carlos still has feelings for Gabriella."

"Yeah, I picked up on that. Something doesn't add up here."

"Well, shall we head back as well?"

"Not just yet. We don't want Fay and Carlos to get suspicious and think we're following them. Let's at least finish walking the path." Jackson started walking down the trail again and turned back with an inviting smile.

Chapter Eleven

Despite having eaten so much dessert the previous night, Jessamine was starving when she woke up the next morning. *I must have walked off all that churro funnel cake.* She toasted herself a bagel and sliced an orange while she waited for her tea kettle to boil. Her tea corner was filled with a few different types of loose-leaf from all over the world, though much more meager than Emilia's collection, and she picked her usual Chai from Mumbai to start off her day. She steeped the tea strong and added a splash of milk to get that perfect creamy caramel color. Jessamine sat down with her breakfast and turned her cell phone on to see the time.

The screen lit up to reveal a missed text message from Lauren sent a few minutes prior:

L: Just wanted to let you know Gabriella has been brought in for questioning. Will keep you updated.

Jessamine replied immediately.

J: Thanks, should be interesting

"Surprise!"

Jessamine cringed at the overly cheerful voice that had snuck up behind her. She whirled around from her place at the front of one of the small classrooms to find Clara grinning at her. From the doorway, Andrew flashed an apologetic look before darting back into the hall.

"I decided to join one of your classes. See what your art center is all about, considering I wasn't invited to the opening." Her neighbor gave a small huff.

"Are you here for the beginner drawing class? That doesn't start for another thirty minutes."

"Yes, yes. That cutie receptionist of yours tried to make me wait in the foyer, but I assured him you wouldn't mind if I came early."

"Um, no, I guess not. But there really isn't anything interesting happening in here yet. I'm just getting set up for the class. Wouldn't you rather look through some of the art books we have out by the reception desk?"

"No, no. You just do your thing, and you won't even know I'm here."

Clara took a seat at one of the tables in the front row, and Jessamine turned back to her portfolio she'd been flipping through. She tried to select some of her drawing examples to display for the class, but it was hard to concentrate over Clara's loud sighing.

"Is something the matter?" Jessamine forced some cheerfulness into her voice.

"Oh, just ignore me, dear. It's all right. You keep working."

"Okay." She grabbed a handful of sketching paper and began to divvy it out among the tables.

After another long sigh, Clara said, "Well, if you must know, Beatrice and I aren't speaking to each other."

"Oh? Why is that?" *I'm majorly going to regret asking that.*

"Well, she's convinced it was Gabriella who murdered Victor when obviously it was that Eugenie Price who killed the poor man. I informed Beatrice she was wrong, and she said some awful things to me. And don't ask me to repeat them. I'm too much of a lady." The look Clara gave Jessamine practically begged her to ask.

Jessamine didn't take the bait. "I'm surprised you two are fighting over something like that."

"Fighting? Oh, that sounds so juvenile. We aren't fighting. Simply having a disagreement in which she is wrong."

Right. Clara would never act juvenile. "Well, I don't think either of you should be worrying about it." *Or spreading gossip about it.*

Clara gave another huff. "In my opinion—"

"Oh! I think I hear the others arriving. I'm going to go help Andrew out front. Why don't you make yourself comfortable here?" Jessamine darted out of the classroom before Clara could share her latest opinion.

Once she'd helped Andrew sign everyone in and gotten them settled in the classroom, she finished handing out the art supplies and got started with the drawing class.

"Welcome to our beginner drawing class. Many people often think drawing is a talent they either have or they don't, but drawing is definitely something that can be learned. If you think you can't draw and want to change that, you're in the right place."

Quite a few heads nodded around the classroom.

"All it takes is a little practice and patience."

Jessamine got started with the basics of contour line drawing and was pleased with how enthusiastic her students were. It gave her hope the art center would be successful.

"Jessamine, I'm done!" Clara said in a loud singsong voice three minutes into the first exercise. She waved her paper excitedly in the air like it was a winning lottery ticket.

"That's great. Just sit tight until everyone else is done with the exercise, and then we'll move on to shading."

"Oooh, shading! I can do that without a lesson." Clara bent her head back down over her paper and got started.

"I . . . oh, never mind," Jessamine said under her breath.

A few of the ladies near her had seemed to hear and gave sympathetic smiles.

"She means well," one of them whispered, and her friends nodded their encouragement.

"Thanks," Jessamine whispered back.

The rest of the class went by with more interruptions from Clara, but the other students didn't seem to mind. At the end, Jessamine was pleased that some participants even sighed up for the next level class.

After the drawing class, Jessamine headed back to her office to get some paperwork done, but first, she had a little bit of Googling to do.

"Victor Carlisle," she muttered to herself as she typed his name in the search bar. She sat back and tied her long, wavy hair into a braid as she waited for the results to pop up on the screen. She saw numerous pages of information and articles about Victor, but most of it was stuff she already knew. He'd been a lawyer from Toronto who'd been beginning to wind down many of his cases, with hopes of retiring sometime in the next year. He'd spent his summers at the vacation home he owned near Rose Shore with his wife and had two impressive art collections: one in Rose Shore and one back in Toronto. Victor had been known for being a bit of a bully when it came to art. He would never take no for an answer when he came across a piece he desired.

Oh wait, here's something interesting. Jessamine came across an older article written seven years ago. "'Trial Wraps Up on Victor Carlisle Case Against Art Thief'" she read the headline out loud. The article explained how someone by the name of Pierce Naismith had broken into Victor's Toronto home and stolen over $30,000 worth of artwork from Victor's private collection to pay off some gambling debts. The thief didn't get very far before he was caught, but Victor was still angry about it. *You don't cross Victor Carlisle when it comes to art!* Jessamine shook her head at the thief's mistake. The article continued, reporting that though Victor didn't handle the case himself, through his money and connections as a lawyer, he hired the best of the best to represent him. Pierce Naismith was sentenced to ten years in prison after a short trial.

Jessamine let out a long breath and continued with her search. She came across another article published just last week. "Art Thief Dies from Heart Attack in Prison Three Years Before Release."

She had read about half of the article, trying to figure out what to make of this new information, when Molly poked her head in the doorway.

"May I please have a moment of your time?"

"Of course. What is it, Molly?" Jessamine's gaze quickly skimmed the last few sentences of the article.

"The next couple artists we had lined up to teach classes have all canceled on us, and Andrew and I were brainstorming on what we could do instead. Would you like to see our notes?"

Jessamine sighed. "Yes, I would. Did anyone explain why they canceled?"

Molly's answer was what Jessamine had feared. "They all said the same thing. They don't want to be associated with an art center that lost such a famous painting."

Jessamine shook her head in frustration and caught a glance at the clock on the wall. She hadn't realized it was almost one already, and suddenly she was starving again. "Well, I don't want to stress about this on an empty stomach. Leave your notes on my desk for now, and I'll look at them after lunch. Do you have any plans? You can join me if you'd like."

"Are you going to Emilia's again?" Molly asked.

"Hmm, I really should try out some of the other local restaurants, shouldn't I? What do you recommend?"

"I've always liked Heidi's Bavarian Restaurant, though it can be quite the hearty meal. I'll see what Andrew is thinking of doing for lunch." Molly gave a nod and left Jessamine's office.

Jessamine took a few minutes to gather up her things and lock her office door before heading out into the hallway to find Molly.

"Andrew and Lauren are going out for lunch and have invited us to join them. Are you interested?"

"Yes. That would be fun. Where are they going?"

Andrew walked over. "Wherever you ladies would like to go. We hadn't settled on anything."

Jessamine looked at Molly. "I think Heidi's Bavarian Restaurant sounds great."

"Mmm! That does sound good." Andrew rubbed his stomach appreciatively. "Schnitzel and apple strudel would hit the spot today. I'll let Lauren know."

Jessamine laughed. "That settles it then."

Jessamine, Molly, and Andrew walked into Heidi's and were instantly greeted with both the smells and sounds from Bavaria. Jessamine's nose tingled at the sweet aroma of the freshly baked apples as a server carried a tray of apple strudel near the front door. From the kitchen came the smell of schnitzel cooking, a special house recipe, no doubt, which made her mouth water. Traditional yodeling accompanied by an accordion filled the air as the music floated from cleverly disguised speakers, which were hidden into the half-timber look of the restaurant.

Lauren had beaten them there and was already seated in a corner booth near the back of the restaurant. She waved them over, and the host brought them some more menus.

"Well, this place is darling!" Jessamine said.

"I thought you'd like it," Molly said. "How are you doing, Lauren?"

"Hungry! What a great suggestion. I haven't been here in years."

They took a few minutes to look at the menu and order.

"I'll have to come back another time when I'm not still on duty and order one of their famous German beers." Lauren grinned and flipped to the back page to where the beers were listed.

"Yeah, I don't know how the boss would feel if I had a drink during the workday." Andrew winked at Jessamine.

Jessamine shook her head. "I'm just excited they have rosehip fruit tea here. That was one of my favorites when I visited Germany a few years ago."

The four of them made small talk while they waited for their food to arrive, mostly about the different countries they had visited. It turned out that Jessamine, Molly, and Lauren had visited some of the same European countries.

"I think Austria was my favorite place to visit when I was in Europe, though it's so hard to choose just one country," Jessamine said.

"That was one of the only places I didn't get to," Lauren said. "I did, however, spend two months in Spain alone and loved it. What about you, Molly?"

Molly's gray eyes looked thoughtful. "The museums throughout France were all very interesting. If I had to go back anywhere, that would probably be it, though I hate flying."

"Aw, I feel left out. I need to travel more." Andrew playfully rolled his eyes.

Once their pork roast, schnitzel, roasted potatoes, and other various Bavarian dishes arrived, Lauren shared information from her interview with Gabriella.

"Gabriella's story mostly matched the rumors about her and Carlos' broken engagement, except for one major point."

"What is it?" Jessamine tilted her head.

"According to Gabriella, she and Carlos are back together. They're engaged again."

Jessamine, Molly, and Andrew all stared at Lauren, waiting for her to finish the story.

"Gabriella said she *did* break things off with Carlos a few weeks ago, but after that day at the art center, she went to Carlos for comfort, and they mended their relationship."

"Do you know why Carlos is in Rose Shore?" Jessamine asked.

"He came to support her at the opening of the art center, I guess—hoping Gabriella would change her mind and invite him as her guest."

"She didn't, though, right? I offered her a plus one, but she didn't bring anyone. Fay didn't even come." Jessamine had double-checked the crossed-off guest list, and neither Carlos nor Fay had been added beside Gabriella's name. She looked at Andrew to confirm.

"That's right. She arrived by herself."

"But now Gabriella and Carlos are back together?" Molly asked.

Lauren nodded. "She said they don't want to announce anything until the case is solved."

"Is that why she isn't wearing her engagement ring?" Jessamine tapped her ring finger on her left hand.

"Gabriella said Carlos has been renting a vacation home down by the lake. That's where he was when she went to see him. Her engagement ring is back in San Francisco. He apparently put it away in a ring box and locked it up with the hopes they would get back together."

"But none of this makes sense." Jessamine took a minute to tell them about Carlos and Fay having afternoon tea together and then heading to Willows Beach. She casually left out the part of her and Jackson also going to Willows Beach to follow them. "Carlos has been seen out with Fay at least twice in the last two days." She turned to Lauren. "And what did Gabriella say when you asked her about picking up *Tranquil* that day? Did you mention a witness had come forward?"

"She again said I was mistaken or the witness was, at least. Gabriella said she was around *Tranquil* and *did* touch the painting to straighten it on the easel, but she never picked it up or moved it. And I called this Dina Layton back, but she had no other info for me."

"Well, someone isn't telling the truth, either Gabriella or the witness about the painting. And this supposed love triangle between Gabriella, Fay, and Carlos seems full of holes as well."

"I can't believe all this is happening in Rose Shore!" Andrew made a motion like his head was exploding from all the drama.

Lauren shushed her younger brother. "Jessamine, we've also looked into Gabriella's finances, and there doesn't seem to be any evidence Gabriella would have stolen *Tranquil* for the insurance money. She's quite financially stable and gives large donations to various causes every year."

"It sounds like your investigation has been one step forward and two steps back," Molly said sympathetically.

Lauren nodded.

"Did you ask her about breaking into my home?"

"She denies it was her."

"I don't know who it could have been then. But I do have some new information about Victor, though I'm not sure how helpful it is." Jessamine gave a rundown of what she had learned about Victor during her Google search that morning.

"Jess!" Lauren scolded. "You're supposed to be staying out of this."

"I know, I know. Some Googling never hurt anyone though, right?"

Lauren just shook her head. "I do remember hearing about that case. I have a friend on the police force in Toronto. I'll see if he can dig up some old files for me."

"Do you think it's important?" Jessamine asked. "Since Pierce Naismith passed away before the art center opening, he obviously wasn't there to stab Victor. It seems like it might be another dead end."

"There might be another angle. Maybe some evidence in the police files were kept out of the press," Lauren said.

"Mr. Carlisle had been a lawyer for many years. Perhaps looking into some of the other criminals he helped put away might lead to something as well." Molly took a sip of her water.

"That's a good idea. Can you see if any of them have been released from prison in the last few months?" Jessamine asked Lauren.

"I'll look into it, as long as you concentrate on your art center and not on the case."

Jessamine gave a tight smile and fought against the guilt in her chest. She could voice no such promise. She was too involved to let it go now.

Chapter Twelve

She hadn't been lying to Clara when she'd mentioned she enjoyed classic literature, but that was only part of the reason why Jessamine headed over to the library on Thursday night. If, as Clara had alluded to, Victor had only interacted with a handful of people in Rose Shore, the book club could be a good place to gain some more information about him.

She pulled into the small parking lot of the library and reached for the plastic container of freshly baked chocolate chip cookies on the back seat of her car. Emilia had generously donated the cookies for the book club, and even though Jessamine had offered to pay, Emilia argued it was her way of keeping up with the investigation as it had been difficult to get away from the tea shop the past few days.

Before getting out of her car, Jessamine snatched up a cookie and took a huge bite, letting the gooey goodness melt in her mouth. The delicious and tempting smell had been teasing her senses the entire drive there, and Jessamine had to give in to her sweet tooth.

One cookie quickly led to another, and as she brushed the crumbs from her mouth, a rap on her car window startled her. With her cheeks still puffed with cookies, Jessamine froze in surprise and slight embarrassment at being caught eating the snacks meant for the book club.

"Do you generally make a habit of sitting in library parking lots, eating entire containers of chocolate chip cookies?" Jackson grinned as she rolled down her window.

"I'm just bringing something for my first book club meeting," Jessamine said dryly. "Wait, are you part of the club?"

"Would that affect *your* attendance?" Jackson raised one eyebrow.

"No, of course not. Just want to plan out where to sit," Jessamine mumbled the last part teasingly and knew from Jackson's amused smile he had heard.

"Don't worry. I'm just here to drop off a book." Jackson indicated to a hardcover novel tucked under his arm. "Though now that I know you're going, I might reconsider."

Jessamine scowled to hide her warm face as she got out of the car. "Well, just to let you know, Victor was a part of this club so someone here might have some insider information on him."

Jackson looked at his watch. "In that case, I think I *will* join you. I didn't have any other plans for this evening."

"Okay, but remember, if anyone asks . . . we're just here to brush up on our classic literature." She led him across the parking lot to the library entrance.

Jackson laughed and followed her. "Got it. Hey, do you even know what book they're discussing tonight?"

"*Frankenstein.* Don't worry. I'll share my copy with you."

It looked like most of the book club members were already there when Jessamine and Jackson walked into the back room of the library. Right away, they spotted Clara in the center of the room, talking to three other ladies. It was obvious Clara was also the center of the conversation. Their neighbor gave them an animated wave and excused herself from her friends.

"Well, I'm just tickled you decided to join us, dear. It's always so nice to have a new face join our little club. And you brought the handsome Jackson Yeung." Clara practically waggled her eyebrows at him.

"Hi, Mrs. C. How are you this evening?" Jackson asked.

"Oh, just dandy! And I have to say, you two make quite the lovely couple."

"Oh! We're not—" Jessamine started at the same time Jackson awkwardly started coughing.

Clara wiggled her eyebrows again at them. "Hmm, isn't that interesting." She thankfully didn't make another comment on the matter as she reached out to grab the container of cookies from Jessamine. "Well, thank you so much for bringing such delicious-looking cookies! I'll put them right over here with the other snacks."

Jessamine and Jackson awkwardly turned to each other after Clara left with the cookies.

"I should get some water." Jackson's voice indeed sounded dry, and he followed Clara over to the snack table.

Jessamine took a moment to look around the room. Most of the people mingling about were unfamiliar, but one familiar face stood out.

"Molly, I didn't know you were a part of this book club." Jessamine walked over to her employee.

Molly was already seated in one of the chairs in the circle, flipping through her copy of *Frankenstein*.

Molly blinked up at her in surprise. "Ms. Rhodes—I mean Jessamine! What are you doing here?"

"Just wanted to check out Rose Shore's book club and meet some new people." Jessamine plopped into a chair next to Molly.

Molly looked at her for a moment before lowering her voice. "Do you suspect someone here killed Mr. Carlisle and took *Tranquil?*"

"I honestly have no idea. I just know Victor was a part of this club."

Molly nodded. "He was, but he hadn't shown up in weeks. I didn't even think to mention it to you."

"Don't worry about it." Jessamine waved her hand dismissingly.

"He only participated during the summer when he was in Rose Shore on his extended vacations."

"That's what Clara was saying as well, but, just in case, can you tell me anything about the members here?"

Jackson joined them then and took a seat on Jessamine's other side. He leaned in to hear what Molly had to say.

Molly greeted him quickly before looking around. "The ladies talking to Clara are Beatrice Dawson, Carol Forrester, and Kay Franklyn. The official town busybodies as they seem to have appointed themselves."

Jessamine smiled inwardly at Molly's small joke. All three of those names sounded familiar, and she soon remembered they had all played a role in Clara's grapevines of information about Victor and Gabriella.

Molly indicated her head toward a group of people who looked to be college-aged. "That's Sofia, Leigh, and Ben. Ben has been coming for a few years now, but Sofia and Leigh just started this fall, so I'm not sure if they even met Mr. Carlisle."

Jessamine nodded along, appreciating all the information. "What about the woman standing by the bookshelf over there with the scowl?"

"Oh, that's Barb Waters. I'm not sure why she attends since she never seems to enjoy herself."

"Clara mentioned her as well. She said she was the only person here who didn't like Victor."

"Well, Mrs. Waters doesn't like anyone, it seems, so I wouldn't worry too much about her being involved. This is also her first week back after visiting some family in Ontario, so she wasn't around during the art center opening." Molly then pointed toward the last two people in the room. "And that's Ms. Silva, an English teacher from the high school, and Mr. Park. He teaches at the high school as well. Biology, I believe. But I think he only comes to spend time with Ms. Silva, though."

Jessamine watched as Mr. Park chattered on and on, despite Ms. Silva occasionally glancing at her notebook as if she wanted to go over something she'd written down about *Frankenstein* before the meeting began. A few moments later, Jessamine realized why it seemed important to Ms. Silva to prepare, as the English teacher was the one to begin leading the discussion.

"All right everyone, we are going to get started in a few moments," Ms. Silva's clear voice rang out among the group.

Jessamine muffled a laugh as she saw, out of the corner of her eye, Clara loading up her plate with a large mound of goodies before taking a seat.

"Thanks for the info, Molly," Jessamine whispered to her friend as she rummaged through her bag to find her copy of *Frankenstein*. Her collection of literary classics was decent, her bookshelf satisfyingly full and organized. It had been a tradition of her father's, a book publisher, to gift one to her each Christmas.

By now, everyone had settled into their seats, and Jessamine took another look around at the group, assuming everyone who was coming was there by then. No one looked like someone who would go around murdering art collectors or stealing paintings.

Ms. Silva turned to her and Jackson and asked them to introduce themselves. Jessamine was caught off guard and stumbled over her words. It was even worse when she physically cringed at the murmur that went through the group when she mentioned where she worked. But Jessamine quickly realized her advantage and used that opportunity to take note of everyone's expressions. There was nothing but pity from most of the group and unchanging bitterness from Barb Waters. Nothing to indicate someone was guilty of any knowledge about the incident.

Jackson reached over and gave her hand a comforting squeeze before introducing himself. When the attention had turned away from them, she looked over and gave him a smile in appreciation. She then opened her book and leaned closer to Jackson so they could share the story together.

The hour and a half-long discussion flew by. Jessamine had actually enjoyed herself and even considered joining the group. *That is once Tranquil is found, and I have time for these types of things.*

"I'm going to try and talk to a few people before everyone disperses for the evening," Jessamine said quietly to Molly and Jackson as soon as the discussion wrapped up.

"I'll do the same," Jackson said.

"I have to run home. Sorry I cannot introduce you to everyone." Molly gathered her belongings.

"That's all right. I'll be fine. See you tomorrow."

Jessamine said goodbye to her friend before heading over to Ms. Silva.

"That was a really interesting discussion. It's been several years since I read *Frankenstein*," Jessamine said to the book club leader.

"I am glad you enjoyed it. Will you be joining us again next week?" Ms. Silva stuck out her hand to shake Jessamine's.

"I hope to. Maybe I shouldn't admit this, but I've never actually read *Wuthering Heights*." Jessamine chuckled.

Ms. Silva smiled. "Well, you are welcome any time. I'm sure you need a distraction from what happened at your art center, if you don't mind me saying so. How is Victor's wife doing? I forget her name. Have you heard anything?"

"Madeleine is doing all right, as best as expected. I just saw her the other day. Were you good friends with Victor?"

"Oh, I just knew him from the book club. He always had fairly intense opinions about the books we read." Ms. Silva smiled. "But he never talked much about his personal life. Aside from his personal art collections, that is, which he managed to bring up in a surprisingly large number of conversations."

Jessamine had to laugh at that. "That sounds exactly like Victor."

"He was quite the character, but we did enjoy having him around."

"Do you know if he ever got together with anyone outside of the club?"

"Perhaps Ben." Ms. Silva nodded over at the blond college guy. "The two of them were always friendly, and I often saw them chatting together before or after the discussions. But if you'll excuse me, I must be getting home. I still have a few papers to grade before school tomorrow."

"Yes, of course. Thank you again for having me."

Ms. Silva smiled at Jessamine before heading out into the main part of the library, with Mr. Park quick at her heels.

Jessamine took the opportunity to wander over to Ben, who was just saying goodbye to Sofia and Leigh before he started tidying up the snack table.

"Hi. You're Ben, right?" She guessed him to be about ten years younger than her.

He responded with a warm smile. "That's right! How did you like tonight's discussion?" He reached out to shake her hand.

"Oh, I really enjoyed it. Hopefully, I can keep coming back."

"Well, let me know if you have any suggestions for reading material. I help Ms. Silva pick the books each week. I can even get you a list of ones we've already read."

"That would be great. How long have you been part of the club?" Jessamine tried to figure out a way to steer the conversation toward Victor. It had been so easy with Ms. Silva bringing up the subject herself.

"Since I started university three years ago. It's my little escape to enjoy some reading that isn't out of a textbook." Ben gave a slight eye roll at this, making Jessamine laugh. "Though, I actually listen to most of the books on audiobook during my commute to the university."

"How long of a drive is it?"

"Just under two hours each way."

Jessamine's eyes widened. She lived in dorm rooms her entire time in university and couldn't imagine anything other than just waking up a few minutes before classes started. "I bet you get through a lot of books!"

Ben heartedly agreed and handed Jessamine her empty container. "Thanks for bringing the cookies. They were a hit."

"I can't take any credit. They were made at Emilia's Secret Garden Tea Shop." Before Ben could get back to his task, Jessamine asked, "Do many people drop in for only a discussion or two?"

"Yeah, it isn't uncommon, though everyone you saw tonight are regulars."

"I heard Victor Carlisle sometimes came."

A soft look of sorrow flashed across Ben's face. "Yeah, he does . . . well he did, I mean."

"Did you know Victor well?"

"Yeah," Ben breathed out the word. "Victor was my mentor, actually. I'm hoping to get into law school after I get my Bachelor's, and Victor was helping me work on my networking. We'd gotten pretty close over the last few years after meeting here at the book club."

Jessamine nodded with understanding. "Do you know of anyone in Rose Shore who might have wanted to kill him?"

Ben's blue eyes widened. "No, none. I thought it was an accident. That some glass shattered into his heart during the chaos of the power outage or something like that. That's what I've heard at least. But you think someone stabbed him on purpose?"

Jessamine wasn't sure what to say. She thought with the missing painting it was obvious that none of this was an accident, but she realized that various versions of the story must be floating around Rose Shore by now. Not wanting to worry Ben any more than he already was, she simply gave a small shrug and offered a smile of sympathy. "I'm really not sure exactly what happened, but I know the police are putting all their resources into it."

Ben relaxed a bit. "Thank you for letting me know. Do you know how his wife is doing?"

"She's doing okay. Her sister came to be with her."

"That's good. I should visit her sometime."

Jessamine smiled again. "I'm sure she would like that. Well, I should be getting home. Enjoy the rest of your evening."

"You too. Hopefully, we'll see you next week." Ben gave a wave as Jessamine turned to find Jackson.

"Did you learn anything?" she asked as they headed out of the library.

"No, nothing important. It seemed like everyone knew *of* Victor but didn't really know him."

"Yeah, I got the same impression from Ms. Silva, though Ben knew him quite well." Jessamine gave Jackson a quick rundown of what she had learned from Victor's mentee.

"Do you think he was involved?"

"No, he's quite upset about Victor's death and has absolutely no motive anyway."

They reached Jessamine's car, and Jackson held open the driver's side door for her. "Well, I'll see you tomorrow for Emilia's birthday party."

"Yeah, see you then." She gave a little wave before driving off.

Chapter Thirteen

"Come on, Margo. Let's go for a quick walk before everyone gets here." Jessamine had taken the afternoon off on Friday to tidy up her cottage for Emilia's birthday party and had just finished up with thirty minutes to spare.

The beagle happily trotted toward Jessamine, wagging her tail in excitement. After putting on her warm, rust-colored overcoat, Jessamine attached Margo's leash to her harness and headed to the front door. Right as she reached out to turn the doorknob, a knock came from the other side. *That's probably Molly here early with the food.*

"Jackson!" Jessamine was surprised to find her neighbor standing on the front porch. He was bundled up in a gray crewneck sweater, and Jessamine noticed he had a hint of shyness in his warm brown eyes.

"Poe and I were wondering if you wanted to go for an evening walk together before the party."

Poe gave a happy bark, and Margo playfully growled in return, her tail wagging.

"Okay, sure. We were just stepping out for a walk ourselves." Jessamine shut the door behind her.

They headed down the street toward the forested area, where Jessamine had jumped out at Jackson a few days earlier.

"Excited about this evening?" Jackson broke the comfortable silence between them.

"Yeah, I am. I'm looking forward to setting the case aside and having a good time with everyone."

"I'm sure it will get solved soon. Between the police working hard at it, and us sneakily working at it, odds are it has to be."

Jessamine liked his confidence. "Hey, can I ask why this is so important for you as well? I respect that you might not want to say, and I understand, but I *am* curious."

Jackson looked over and gave her a weary smile. "I suppose you should know, especially since we're working closely together." He took in a deep breath. "Well, I got into a little bit of trouble with the law when I was a teenager. Nothing too crazy, just needed to break into a neighbor's home one day. I got caught, and Victor represented my case—completely pro bono. He got me off completely clean, no juvie record or anything."

"What do you mean 'needed to'?"

Jackson looked queasy, and this part of the story seemed harder to tell than his run-in with the law. "It was just my mom raising my siblings and me, and we didn't have a lot of money. One month it was particularly bad, and I desperately wanted to help my mom out. But being the prideful teenager I was, instead of asking someone for help or going to a food bank, I broke into our neighbor's house when they were on vacation and wiped their cupboards clean."

"Oh, Jackson, I had no idea," she said softly.

He gave a small shrug. "Anyway, that's all in the past. My mom got a financially stable job a few years after that and has been working hard at it ever since. She's doing great, I'm doing great, my brother and sister are doing great. It's all good."

"Great even?" Jessamine smiled to break the tension.

Jackson laughed. "Yeah, great. Anyway, so I've kept in contact with Victor over the years, and now, I feel like I owe it to him to find whoever killed him. I can finally repay him."

They turned around and arrived back at Jessamine's cottage to find Molly unloading her car in the driveway. Her arms were filled with baskets and cloth bags overflowing with food.

"That's quite the spread! You know there is only a handful of us tonight, right?" Jessamine chuckled.

"Oh, Ms. Rhodes, I know. But once I started baking, I couldn't stop." Molly looked like even she couldn't believe how much food there was. "And then I thought I needed some salty and healthy snacks to offset all the sweets I made."

"And suddenly you have enough food for the whole town!" Jessamine laughed.

Jackson and Jessamine helped Molly bring the food inside. They set everything out on a small table Jessamine had set up against a wall in her living room, and she now tilted her head as she looked at the wide variety of snacks and thought it seemed a little random.

Molly must have noticed her reaction. "I know the choices seem odd, but I made everyone's favorite snacks, which might not necessarily all go together, apparently."

Jessamine took a closer look at everything. She noticed her favorite pineapple salsa and pita bread next to a large plate of sugar cookies and snickerdoodles, obviously Andrew's favorite. "This is really creative, actually. And I'm super impressed you've taken note of everyone's favorite. I don't think I've ever mentioned how much I like pineapple salsa before."

Molly only gave a small nod and continued placing everything on the table. Jessamine took note of not only how thoughtful and observant Molly was but also how modest. Instead of commenting some more on how much work Molly put into the food, which she figured would only embarrass her, Jessamine put on her favorite jazz playlist as they waited for the other guests to arrive. The bold and playful notes of George Gershwin's "Rhapsody in Blue" soon filled the air.

Next, Jessamine went about setting up her kitchen counter as a sort of tea station. She boiled water in her kettle and picked out three different types of loose-leaf tea. She chose a delicate white tea flavored with jasmine pearls, a black currant tea, and an oolong tea that came from Taiwan. She steeped each selection in their own small teapot and set out her favorite teacups along the counter. *Emilia will be impressed with this setup!*

"Did you learn anything at the book club after I left yesterday?" a voice asked quietly behind her.

Jessamine jumped; she hadn't realized Molly had followed her into the kitchen.

"No, nothing really. Ben seemed to have been the only one to really know Victor personally, but I also didn't get the chance to talk to everyone. Though, as you said, Sofia and Leigh probably never even met him, and I doubt the Clara clique had anything to do with it."

Molly nodded. "I'm sorry nothing came out of it for you, but I'm glad to know no one in my book club is a murderer and art thief."

"Well, it wasn't a complete waste of time. I did enjoy the discussion, and I think I might join. It'll be nice to feel more like I belong in Rose Shore anyway."

The doorbell rang loudly just then, and Andrew, Emilia, Addison, and

Addison's fiancé, Dave Blake, who had all shown up at the same time, walked through the front doorway. Jessamine's small cottage was instantly filled with the sounds of laughter as each of the friends joked and teased each other. They were all determined to set the case and other worries aside for the evening and have some fun. Poe and Margo joined in the party and were having a great time with so many people around to play with.

Lauren arrived a few minutes later, and Jessamine greeted her at the door. "I do want to keep the case to the side tonight, but I was wondering if you've had a chance to look into any of Victor's past cases?"

"I did, but I couldn't find anything of significance. No one he worked against has been released from prison in the last four years, but I'll keep looking into it. And I also heard back from my friend in Toronto, but he wasn't able to offer anything helpful either."

Jessamine realized the disappointment she felt must have been written all over her face because Lauren quickly assured her not to worry. Just because there wasn't a huge break in the case yet didn't mean there wasn't going to be one soon.

"Besides," she added. "Like you said, tonight should be about fun anyway and not the case."

"You're right, you're right. Let's go beat Andrew at some games." Jessamine looped her arm through Lauren's and led her to the living room, where the others had gotten started on some sort of trivia game.

Jessamine had unpacked her box of board games earlier that day and set them up on her coffee table. It had been one of her last boxes to unpack, so she was beginning to feel like an official resident of Rose Shore now. However, it quickly became evident that no one was going to beat Andrew. He was dominating the games.

"For one hundred points, 'What type of weapon is a falchion?'" Molly glanced around the room for a response.

"A sword!" Andrew blurted out before anyone even had a chance.

"Correct," Molly said as everyone else groaned.

Andrew arrogantly moved his pawn up the board and looked at Jessamine with a smirk.

"Now, for two hundred points, is everyone ready?" It was Addison's turn to read out the question.

Everyone nodded, and Jessamine shot Andrew a glare. "You're going down, Marsh."

Andrew grinned at her and took a smug bite out of a snickerdoodle.

"In which film did Humphrey Bogart say, 'We'll always have Paris?'" Addison asked.

"*Casablanca*!" Andrew spat cookie crumbs everywhere as he yelled his answer.

"Andrew!" Lauren covered her eyes with her hand and shook her head.

"That's disgusting!" Emilia said at the same time.

"Okay, okay." Jackson laughed and held up his hands in a failed attempt to calm everyone down. "One more question, and then I think we might need a break."

"Agreed." Jessamine felt a little too competitive, but she couldn't catch up to Andrew now.

"Ready?" Jackson asked, and again everyone nodded. "'How many U.S. states border the Gulf of Mexico?'"

"Five." This time the answer came from Molly, and everyone turned to look at her. Molly fidgeted nervously with her glasses.

"Nicely done, Molly." Jessamine reached over to high-five her and received an awkward one in return.

"Thank you."

"Okay, I say the final answer declares the winner, so congratulations, Molly!" Emilia said.

"Hey! No fair." Andrew crossed his arms with a smirk.

"I'm the birthday girl. I can make up rules if I want to." Emilia grinned. "How did you get so crazy good at random trivia anyway?"

Andrew shrugged. "There's more to me than my good looks. How about Molly wins if she can name all five of those states?"

Molly gave him a no-nonsense look. "Florida, Alabama, Mississippi, Louisiana, and Texas."

Everyone laughed at the surprised look on Andrew's face.

"Brilliant. So, as I said before, Molly's the trivia champion." Emilia pumped her arms in the air.

After they finished packing up the game, Jessamine took Emilia aside into the kitchen. "I know you said no gifts, but I had to get you a little something." Jessamine handed Emilia a card.

"Oh, thank you so much, Jess. You didn't have to." Emilia opened it to find a gift card for the Crimson Orchard Spa at the Rose Shore Resort. "Wow! I've never been here but have heard great things about it. Thank you."

"You're welcome. I'm sure you can find some excuse to treat yourself for a day."

"I definitely will. My nails could use a bit of love one of these days," Emilia paused awkwardly for a moment. "So, are you and Jackson like *friendly* now? I noticed the looks you were giving each other in there."

Jessamine dipped her chin down. "We've been getting along, yeah. And it's been interesting trying to solve the case together and getting to know him. We did have a lot of fun at Willows Beach the other night and then again at the book club yesterday and—"

She was cut off by Emilia's laughter. "You are *rambling*! I think you *do* like him."

"What is this? High School?" Jessamine scowled but knew her friend was right. She was starting to have feelings for Jackson.

Thankfully, before she felt the need to explain herself further, Andrew called to them from the living room. "Hey, Emilia! Jess! Come back."

Emilia smiled. "Let's see what kind of trouble Andrew is stirring up now."

They headed back into the living room just in time for the cork of the champagne bottle Andrew had opened to whiz by Jessamine's face after a loud *POP*.

"Hey! Careful," she scolded Andrew.

The rest of the small group laughed, and Jessamine was sure her surprised face had been memorable. Andrew poured the champagne into tall glasses for everyone for a toast to Emilia.

"To Emilia! May she have the best year yet." Andrew raised his glass, and everyone followed suit, clinking their glasses together.

Chapter Fourteen

"**I** think that painting would look better next to the large Marc Davids' piece over there." Jessamine pointed to the large, beautiful painting of colorful tulips and daffodils.

"Okay, but this is the last time I'm moving it. Why did you stick it in such a heavy frame?" Andrew blew out a breath as he picked up the painting.

The two of them had been rearranging the art displays throughout the entire art center all morning, but Jessamine still felt like it wasn't perfect. Business had been down since the incident at the opening, and she'd hoped a fresh look to the art center might help. It was the very least she could do at this point.

"Don't worry. That's the last piece to move. Next, we're going to reorganize the classroom supplies."

Andrew groaned as he carried the painting across the main classroom. "We just opened last week. What's there to reorganize?"

Jessamine sighed. "You're right. I know. I'm just stumped on this case, and it's making me a little antsy. Sorting paintbrushes sounds pretty calming right about now."

"So, no new leads?"

"No, nothing."

"This drama between Gabriella and Fay is pretty wild, like something out of a low-budget rom-com."

"I know." Jessamine groaned and gave a shake of her head. "So much for the drama-free, small-town life I'd been hoping for."

"Speaking of, Emilia tells me you and Jackson have big googly eyes for each other."

"She did not! And we do not."

"Yes, she did, but that isn't the topic here. So, are you going to ask him on a date?"

Jessamine laughed at Andrew's straightforwardness. "What do you think? I have a business to run, a missing painting to find, and, oh yeah, a murder to solve."

Soon after Jessamine settled in her office, she heard the front door of the art center open and close, followed by a loud, "Well, look who it is. The gentleman of the hour," from Andrew now back at the reception desk.

Jessamine groaned and had a feeling she knew who was on the receiving end of Andrew's teasing in the foyer. She hurried down the hallway to save him, and, sure enough, Jackson was holding a few brown paper bags with the Secret Garden Tea Shop logo on them. She started to give him a wide, sunbeam of a smile, but then noticed Andrew's I-told-you-so grin and plastered on her best professional expression instead.

"Hello, Mr. Yeung. How are you today?"

Jackson raised an eyebrow at her sudden formality but didn't comment on it. "I thought I'd stop by with some lunch for everyone."

"Oh, that's very sweet of you. Thank you."

"Well, don't thank me too much. It's compliments of Emilia. Something about leftover scones and tea sandwiches from a reservation no-show."

"Those no-shows really make Emilia mad. I should call her to see how she is." Andrew ducked his head and picked up the reception phone.

Jessamine had a feeling he was using the phone call as both an excuse to talk to Emilia and to leave Jessamine alone with Jackson.

"I'll grab Molly and meet you in the break room." Jessamine pointed Jackson in the right direction before heading off to find Molly.

Once everyone was settled in the break room and had divvied up the leftover goodies and sandwiches, the topic quickly turned to the case.

"So, have you two figured out how Carlos fits into everything yet?" Andrew asked Jackson and Jessamine.

They looked at each other.

Jackson shook his head. "No, not really. All I can say is Carlos seems in way over his head with Gabriella and Fay."

"I have a theory about it all," Jessamine said. "I think Carlos might have been spending time with Fay to stay close to Gabriella, which is sort of what Lauren was saying the other day about Carlos being in town with the hopes Gabriella would invite him to the opening. But maybe this has all backfired on him, and Fay has taken the time he spent with her to heart and truly believes they're now a couple."

Jackson seemed to be picking up on what she was getting at. "And Carlos doesn't know how to get out of it without hurting Fay, so he's just going along with it. That could explain a lot about his attitude toward her."

"What a mess," Andrew said. "In my opinion, the dude is acting like a coward."

"I wonder if he knows anything about *Tranquil?*" Molly asked.

"We asked him that the other night," Jackson said. "He said he doesn't know anything about where it could be."

"Though he could be lying. Carlos doesn't seem like the most trustworthy guy. Maybe he stole it back because he's so in love with Gabriella and wanted to hold onto their relationship in some way," Jessamine said.

"That's a good theory. Maybe Victor tried to stop him, and Carlos panicked and stabbed the man." Andrew demonstrated with an intense stabbing motion of his fork.

"And Carlos shut the lights off so Gabriella wouldn't recognize him," Molly finished.

"These are some interesting ideas, except Gabriella or Madeleine would have heard them fighting since Victor was right beside them, and neither of them mentioned anything."

Jackson hummed thoughtfully. "I don't know about Gabriella, but Madeleine isn't the sort of person to keep something like that to herself, though I still don't think we should cross Carlos off the suspect list just yet."

After lunch, Jessamine walked Jackson out to his car. "Thank you so much for stopping by with lunch."

"It was no problem." Jackson paused and fiddled with his car keys, looking suddenly nervous. "So—um, listen, after going to Willows Beach and doing a little investigating, and then going to the book club and doing a little investigating, I was wondering if you wanted to go out tonight and not investigate. Like a date—like a date-date. Not to stalk suspects or anything."

Jessamine was completely caught off guard. "Really? A date?"

Jackson winced at her astonished tone. "Well, I understand if you're busy. Or if it would be too weird with the investigation going on—"

She held up her hand to stop him. "I would actually like that. I was surprised, that's all."

"Oh, okay. Great! How does the Aria sound at the Rose Shore Resort?"

"Sure. I've never been there. It sounds fancy."

"They specialize in Italian and have the best Linguine alle Vongole in all of B.C."

Jessamine had to laugh at his attempt at an Italian accent.

"I'll pick you up from home around six?"

"All right. I'll be ready. See you then."

Jessamine waved at Jackson as he got into his car and drove off, before walking back inside the art center, humming happily to herself—though it wasn't long before the anxiety set in. She hurried to her office and shut the door.

A date? Now? I just told Andrew I should be focused on the art center and finding Tranquil! Plus, I haven't been on a proper date in years. She felt like she was in college again, trying to balance the struggle of being "grown-up" but also feeling giddy that her crush was turning into something more. Before she could make another decision, Jessamine picked up her phone to call Emilia to rant or gush or freak out or whatever it was she needed to do.

"Hey, it's Jessamine. Are you crazy busy right now?"

Emilia hadn't answered until about the fifth ring, so Jessamine figured she already knew the answer to that question.

"We just got a mad rush in. Apparently, all of Rose Shore needs a macaron and a cup of tea before heading back to work for the afternoon. Is something the matter? Is there a break in the case?" Emilia's English accent was coming in strong with her rush to explain.

"No, it's not that." Jessamine debated whether to bother Emilia right then. "Actually, it can wait. Call me when the rush is over?"

"Of course." As Emilia hung up, Jessamine could hear just how crazy the tea shop was on the other end of the line.

She tried to focus on her office work to not stress over the upcoming date. She checked and replied to emails, tidied up her desk drawers, wrote up artist biographies, and tidied up her desk drawers again. Finally, her phone rang.

"Emilia?"

"What is *up,* Jessamine? You seemed frazzled out about something."

"Jackson asked me out on a date. Tonight."

Emilia let out a sound that was half a squeal and half a cry of triumph. "This is so exciting! I knew he was into you. Where are you going?"

"To the Aria. Is that super fancy? What should I wear?"

"Ah, more semiformal, I would say. That dress you wore to the art center opening would be perfect. I dined there once when my parents were visiting from London, and it's a lovely place. The restaurant opens out to a beautiful rose garden behind the resort, so make sure to bring a nice cardigan or shawl for a post-dinner walk. Oh! And order the bruschetta for an appetizer."

"This is great advice. Thanks."

The two friends talked for a while longer about the date, and Jessamine decided on her coral-colored one-shouldered dress. Emilia offered to bring over a cream-colored shawl she promised would match perfectly.

Chapter Fifteen

Jessamine arrived home much later than she had planned after work. Molly had needed some help with a project she was working on to draw more involvement in the art center from the community, and Jessamine had to agree it was best not to leave it for the weekend. Her idea was to host classes at various venues around Rose Shore away from the art center building itself. Molly thought perhaps if people were away from where the incident occurred, they might not be so wary about participating in another class.

But now she was pressed for time and hurried to put some water on to boil for tea while she took Margo out for a walk. Outside, Jessamine headed in the opposite direction of Jackson's home, since her nerves couldn't handle accidentally bumping into him before their date.

She quickly realized her mistake. Clara was tending her flower beds only a few feet away.

"Hello, dear. How are you this evening?" Clara called out as Jessamine was subtly trying to tiptoe backward, attempting to make an escape. Thankfully, Clara noticed Margo and kept her distance.

"Oh, just fine, Clara, though I'm in a bit of a hurry."

"Did you hear both Gabriella and her sister, oh what's her name? It doesn't matter. Anyway, both sisters got pulled in for questioning at the police station. Can you imagine Gabriella stabbing Victor? Why do you think she did it?"

"Just because she was pulled in for questioning doesn't mean she did it."

"Well, it had to have been either her or Eugenie Price. I heard both of them were standing right next to Victor when he was stabbed."

"I'm not sure who it was, but I really must be getting home." She made another attempt to leave.

"Oh, listen, I just remembered. I cannot believe I didn't think of this sooner, but I know a single girl like you must be lonely. If you and Jackson aren't going steady, as you say, my son would be perfect for you. He lives in Calgary, but you two can do long-distance. My dear husband, bless his soul, and I did long-distance for many years before we were married. Anyway, both my children will be visiting me in December, and you can meet him in person then. Give me a moment, and I'll write down his phone number for you."

Oh, this is incredibly awkward. "Maybe some other time. Thank you, though."

"Are you sure? He really is quite the catch. And let me tell you what he does for a living." Clara rambled on and on about her son's IT job at some software company. Jessamine was about to decide that stooping down to rudeness might be her only chance of escape when Emilia pulled up in her driveway next door. It took some resistance not to sigh out loud in relief.

"Oh, there's Emilia. I've really got to get going now. Goodbye, Clara."

"Okay, dear. I'll leave my son's phone number in your mailbox."

Jessamine wasn't even sure how to respond to that promise as she hurried back to her home.

"You just saved me from being practically betrothed to Clara's son. Thank you."

"You're . . . welcome?" Emilia gave her a questioning look.

"I'll explain later. I already arrived home late, and now, I have even less time to get ready. I was going to make some peppermint tea to calm my nerves, but I don't think I have time now."

"You go get changed. I'll make the tea." Emilia held opened the front door for her.

Jessamine raced upstairs and opened the door to her walk-in closet. She flipped through her neatly pressed business outfits and hangers filled with comfy sweaters for her days off to pull out the coral dress. After taking a quick shower so her hair would be easier to work with, she curled it back into a loose side bun. A glance at her clock told her she had about ten minutes to do her makeup and dig out a pair of heels from a box of shoes still left to be unpacked in the back of her closet.

Emilia came upstairs with a steaming cup of peppermint tea. She placed it on Jessamine's dresser and then pulled out the cream-colored shawl from her shoulder bag with a dramatic wave of her wrist. "Ta-da! It goes with your dress even better than I imagined. You're going to look *fab-u-lous!*"

"Thanks, Em. I owe you one."

"Well, if you aren't going to take up Clara's offer to date her son, then maybe I will."

"You're welcome to, though he lives in Calgary, apparently."

"Hmm, maybe I'll just borrow this dress instead." Emilia reached into Jessamine's closet and pulled out a red dress with a short skirt. "I love the color."

"I don't know if it will fit you. You're quite a bit taller than me."

Emilia sighed mournfully and put the dress back. "You're right. Goodbye, cute red dress. We could've made a great pair."

Jessamine laughed at her friend's dramatics and finished getting ready.

Margo started to bark, and both friends looked out the window just as Jackson was walking up her driveway. He reached her front porch, and Jessamine's pulse picked up as she bit back a wide grin.

"Wow! He looks so good in that dark suit." Emilia squealed, as if she could read Jessamine's thoughts. "He's even wearing a bow tie. What a keeper."

Without responding, Jessamine gulped down the last bit of peppermint tea to soothe the somersaults happening in her stomach and headed downstairs.

As soon as Jessamine opened the front door and was greeted by Jackson's warm, friendly smile, her nerves instantly settled. An evening of hanging out and getting to know Jackson better would be fun. They were starting to become good friends, despite the unusual circumstances that brought them together.

"Wow, you look great." Jackson handed her a single rose.

"It's very pretty. Thank you." The peachy-pink rose matched her dress perfectly, and Jessamine wondered if Emilia had given Jackson a tip.

"Can I be the cheesy parent who takes a million pictures?" Emilia asked from the top of the stairs.

"No thanks." Jessamine gave a small laugh and hurried Jackson out the doorway before she found out if her friend was serious or not, leaving Emilia to let herself out.

Jessamine got into Jackson's car next door, and they headed off toward the Rose Shore Resort & Spa.

"No ambulance tonight?" she teased.

"Nah, that doesn't usually go over well on a first date."

"I feel like there's a story there."

Jackson laughed. "No, there really isn't. Though, I often threaten to pick people up from the airport in one. My brother-in-law thinks it would be awesome, but my sister says she'd be pretty embarrassed."

"I don't blame her."

At the resort, Jackson parked the car, and they headed toward the main lobby doors. Jackson bumped slightly against her side before he reached down and grabbed her hand.

The Aria was just off the lobby in the hotel. Despite this being the third time Jessamine had been in the lobby in the past few days, she was still impressed with its elegance. As they walked by the paintings along the walls, she told Jackson a bit about each of the artists.

"Has art always been your passion?"

"For as long as I can remember. It started with finger painting in preschool. I loved how I could create something so colorful out of a blank piece of paper."

"You were probably the kid who always colored perfectly in the lines, weren't you?"

Jessamine laughed. "If I felt the picture called for it, then yes, but sometimes I did get a little creative."

They reached the restaurant, and Jackson gave his name to the hostess. She sat them quickly at a table by the back window, and Jessamine was in awe at the view they had over the beautiful and expansive rose garden. The sun was starting to set, but she could still make out the various types of colorful roses that lined the walking paths. Fairylike white lights were strung above the garden, and they twinkled on as if by magic as she gazed out the large window. Beyond the garden was the resort's man-made white sand beach along glassy Opal Lake.

"We have to go for a walk down there after dinner," Jessamine said.

"I thought you'd like it. Did you see the gazebo?" Jackson pointed to her left.

"It looks like something out of a fairy tale."

"I was reading on their website that the roses planted here are all remontant, meaning they bloom more than once a year. Usually in the spring and then again now in late September."

Their server arrived with sparkling water and took their drink orders. Jessamine turned to the menu and considered her dinner options. Everything sounded so good. She narrowed it down to three choices and panic-picked one right as the server returned. After they had handed back their menus and the server left again, Jessamine asked Jackson if he had always wanted to be a paramedic.

"Not really. I actually went to university to study chemistry. But, in the summer after my first year, my brother got into a bad car accident and would literally not be alive today if the paramedics hadn't saved his life. So, I was inspired to look into it and took a basic first aid course, fell in love with the practice, and continued on with training from there."

Jessamine was touched by his story and reached over to give his hand a squeeze. "Do you enjoy your job, though?"

"I do. I feel like I was always meant to be a paramedic. I just didn't know it until I tried."

"What did you want to do with a chemistry degree?"

"I wanted to be a high school science teacher, actually. I still volunteer as a tutor during exam time at Rose Shore High."

"Did you grow up in Rose Shore?"

"No, I grew up in Toronto but did my training in Vancouver before being stationed out here after my courses. I think I'm more suited for the small-town life as well." He echoed her words from the other night.

They continued talking about their career choices while sharing a plate of bruschetta for an appetizer, and Jessamine thought it was probably the best she'd ever had. When their main dishes came, Jackson had ordered the Linguine alle Vongole, of course, and Jessamine dived into her Mushroom Risotto.

"This is absolutely delicious. Great choice for a date."

Jackson beamed at her.

"Did you want any dessert?" Jackson asked after their dinner plates had been cleared away.

"Let's walk around the garden first. Then maybe I'll have some room for dessert."

Jackson paid their bill and then followed Jessamine to the French doors that led out to the garden area. The doors opened onto a large terrace, which featured a wide staircase leading down to the main garden. Hanging baskets overflowing with flowers hung from the numerous pillars surrounding the area. The resort obviously took great pride in their gardening, keeping flowers in full bloom even this late in the year. The sun had completely set, and darkness stretched out around them, with only the twinkling garden lights to see by.

"The stars are just appearing." Jessamine looked up at the small bright dots poking out of the black sky. "It was definitely van Gogh's *Starry Night* that inspired me to make art my life's work."

They walked arm in arm along the roses and came to a gated outdoor pool reserved for hotel guests. The heated pool was closed for the evening, and the steamy mist coming off the surface was only lit by dim, shimmery lights.

"Want to dip our feet in the pool?" Jessamine asked only half-teasingly.

Jackson laughed. "In the restricted pool that's closed?"

"I won't tell anyone if you don't. You have to admit it does look inviting." Jessamine gazed over the low fence at the reflecting lights dancing on the surface of the pool. Then, something large and dark floating in the water caught her eye. She wasn't sure what it was but had a strong feeling it didn't belong there. She clenched Jackson's arm tighter. "What's that in the pool?"

The urgency in her voice must have made him hurry over to look. "Jess, it looks like a body." Without another word, Jackson hopped over the low fence, and Jessamine followed, ripping the skirt of her dress as she did.

Jackson was kneeling next to the edge of the water and had pulled the body out onto the deck when she caught up. It was a man wearing a dark suit, and Jessamine gasped when she recognized his face in the shadowy light.

The blank, unseeing eyes staring up at them belonged to Carlos Leoz.

Chapter Sixteen

The Rose Shore Resort & Spa's outdoor pool deck buzzed with police, paramedics, and hotel security. Bright yellow police tape had been quickly strung up haphazardly around the outer fence of the pool, and a crowd of curious hotel guests and restaurant patrons had gathered to see what was going on. After pulling Carlos out of the pool, Jackson had immediately gone into first-responder mode and assessed the body while speaking to 911 on his phone, leaving Jessamine to hurry back to the hotel to find security. The gardens had been vacant at the time, aside from the two of them, and so far, no witnesses to Carlos' death had come forward.

Nothing else seemed to be amiss around the pool deck; there were no signs of a struggle. Carlos had been fully dressed in a designer suit and tie when he was found, with a large wound on the back of his head. It remained unclear if the gash had happened before he drowned or if it was from falling into the water. *He could have knocked his head against the side of the pool or on the stair rail.* Jessamine looked around unsuccessfully for any signs of blood.

She gave her statement to a police officer and then waited by the pool gate for Jackson while he gave his. She wondered if Carlos had the same thought she did while walking through the gardens, that the shimmering water looked too tempting on a starry evening like this. But he still had his socks and shoes on, so he obviously hadn't been dipping his feet in the water. *Maybe he just wanted to sit by the pool.*

She leaned over to a nearby pair of lounge chairs. They weren't cheap plastic deck chairs but quality wicker ones covered with thick, comfy-looking cushions hiding underneath large sun umbrellas. Jessamine lifted each cushion to look underneath, trying to appear casual.

Finding nothing under the cushions or the seats, she turned to do the same to another set of lounge chairs on her other side.

What's this? Under the seat of one of the lounge chairs, she discovered a small, rectangular jewelry box. She couldn't help the small gasp that escaped her lips as she opened the lid. Inside was a diamond bracelet laced with small blue sapphires. "Wow," she said breathlessly. *It's beautiful.*

"What did you find?" Jackson approached her, and she wordlessly handed him the box. "'Jewels of the Rose,'" Jackson read the bottom of the box before looking inside.

"Do you think this bracelet is linked to Carlos and his death?"

"It's hard to say. Why don't we visit Jewels of the Rose tomorrow and find out? We'll have to hand this in to evidence, but I'll take a few photos first." Jackson pulled out his phone and took some photos of both the box and the bracelet.

"Do you know where Jewels of the Rose is?"

"It's a locally owned jewelry store over on Second Avenue. I know the couple who own it, and I'm sure they'll be happy to answer a few questions."

"Do you think they might have had something to do with this?"

"Oh no. They're a very nice couple, but they might know something important about who bought the jewelry. Anyway, I should go turn this in."

As the police were wrapping up the crime scene, Gabriella came flying through the gardens toward the pool area.

"Carlos," she sobbed with hysterical tears. "Oh, this is all my fault."

Jackson had wandered back to Jessamine's side, and they glanced at each other, eyebrows raised.

"I wonder what she means by that," Jessamine whispered. She met Gabriella on the other side of the pool gate and put a comforting arm around the artist. "Gabriella? Do you want me to call someone to be with you?"

"It's true then. It's Carlos?"

Jessamine nodded. "I'm so sorry."

"This is all my fault. If we hadn't gotten back together, Carlos would never have been here. Who would do something like this?"

"I have no idea, but I don't think this is your fault. Was Carlos on his way to see you?"

Gabriella nodded as she continued to sob.

"How about I go find your sister for you?"

"It's all right, Ms. Rhodes. We'll take care of it." A police officer had come over to talk to Gabriella, and Jessamine took it as her cue to leave.

Jackson offered to take her home, and the pair headed back toward the main building of the resort.

"I guess we can't actually go on a date without doing some sort of investigative work." Jessamine made a small attempt at a joke.

"Then we should concentrate on solving this case quickly."

"Do you think the missing painting, Victor's murder, and now Carlos' death are all connected?"

"I think so, with the most obvious linking factor being Gabriella."

The next morning, Jessamine met Jackson in a parking lot near Jewels of the Rose. They had forgone dessert the previous night, and Jackson had dropped her off at her home after they left the resort. Finding a dead body really put a damper on a first date.

"I picked up a London Fog from Emilia's for you." Jackson handed her the steaming hot cup. "She said it's one of your favorites."

"Thank you. This is perfect on such a chilly morning. It feels like we're officially into autumn now." Jessamine was glad she'd grabbed her favorite gray-and-white-striped scarf on her way out the door that morning.

Like many of the local businesses in Rose Shore, Jewels of the Rose was only open for a few hours on Sundays, and the small shop was just opening when Jessamine and Jackson walked in.

"Mrs. Liu, how are you doing today?" Jackson enthusiastically greeted the woman behind the counter.

"Jackson, so nice to see you. Is this your new girlfriend? Are you here to pick out a ring?" Mrs. Liu rushed over to greet Jackson. "Special discount for a special customer."

"No, no. I just have a few questions for you. Mrs. Liu, this is Jessamine Rhodes. She's the new owner of the Rose Shore Community Art Center. Jess, this is Mrs. Liu. She and her husband were my landlords when I first moved to Rose Shore."

The two women shook hands.

"Jackson was such a great tenant. He did all the yard work without complaint. We considered giving him a bad reference when he bought his home, just to keep him around." Mrs. Liu gave Jessamine a wink.

Jessamine was immediately fond of the woman and tried to think of where she'd seen Mrs. Liu before. A door in the back of the small store opened, and a man walked in. Jackson introduced him as Mr. Liu, and when Jessamine saw the couple together, she remembered they had been at Emilia's tea shop the day after *Tranquil* went missing. They had brought Emilia tea from Hong Kong, or something like that.

"The reason we're here is an unfortunate one, I hate to say. A body was found last night in the outdoor pool of the Rose Shore Resort and Spa."

Both Mr. and Mrs. Liu gasped.

"Who was it?" Mr. Liu asked.

"A fashion designer by the name of Carlos Leoz. He was engaged to the artist Gabriella Everhart."

"He was in here yesterday late afternoon. Oh no, you couldn't possibly think we had anything to do with his death!" Mrs. Liu looked like she was about to faint.

"No, of course not. But we did find a bracelet from here underneath a cushion on the pool deck." Jackson pulled out his phone and showed the couple the photos he took the previous night. "Does this look familiar?"

"Mr. Leoz bought that bracelet yesterday," Mrs. Liu confirmed.

"Did he say who he was buying it for?" Jessamine eyed a very sparkly diamond pendant necklace in a display case next to her. Oh, to be able to treat herself to something here one day.

"Just that it was for someone very special to him. He mentioned it matched a ring he had bought her last year," Mr. Liu said.

"That sounds like he bought it for Gabriella to match her engagement ring," Jessamine said. "Perhaps since he didn't have her ring with him, he wanted to make up for it when they got back together."

"Was there anything unusual or worth mentioning about the transaction?" Jackson asked.

"He did seem rather anxious, like he was in a hurry. I offered to wrap the box up nicely for him, but he grabbed it and ran out after he paid for the bracelet," Mrs. Liu said.

"Anything else?"

"No. I think that's it. I'm so sorry to hear he's gone. He seemed quite in love with the girl he was buying the bracelet for."

"All right. Thank you for your time, Mr. and Mrs. Liu. If you think of anything else, please contact me."

"Are you looking into the death?" Mr. Liu furrowed his brow.

Jackson hesitated, but Jessamine could tell he trusted the couple. "Let's just say I have an interest in it, but I don't necessarily want that to get around."

Both Mr. and Mrs. Liu nodded in understanding and promised to contact him if they remembered anything else of importance.

Chapter Seventeen

Opal Lake was hidden underneath a blanket of fog as Jessamine drove by on her way to the art center after saying goodbye to Jackson. When Jessamine arrived at work, she found both Andrew and Molly anxiously waiting for her in the foyer.

"Oh, Ms. Rhodes—Jessamine. We heard on the radio this morning a body was found at the Rose Shore Resort last night. That was where you and Jackson were having dinner, correct?" Molly asked.

"Yes. We are actually the ones who found the body."

"Jessamine! Trouble seems to be following you around Rose Shore." Andrew's voice was filled with both worry and curiosity. "Who was it?"

"Carlos Leoz."

"No! Was he murdered?"

"I don't think the police have been able to say yet. They're probably still waiting for the coroner's report."

"You should take it easy today. Do you want to go home? We'll be all right here," Molly said.

Jessamine started to protest and say she was completely fine when Andrew interrupted. "But first, tell us everything and don't leave anything out."

He led them all to a pair of armchairs in a corner of the foyer and rolled over his office chair for himself. Jessamine spent the next half hour going over every little detail with Andrew and Molly, excluding how romantic the beginning of the evening had been. That was something she still wanted to keep to herself. As she was finishing up, her phone rang.

"It's your sister," she said to Andrew after reading the caller I.D. and answered the call.

"Jessamine, how are you holding up with everything? I heard you were the one to find the body last night. I'm so sorry I wasn't on shift so I couldn't be there."

"Lauren, that's hardly your fault. I was fine. Have you heard anything about what might have happened?"

"Yes. I just read the coroner's report that came back."

"That was quick."

"Well, there aren't too many dead bodies showing up around Rose Shore, so Carlos was a priority."

"So, what did the coroner find? Was he murdered?"

"It seems that way. According to the report, Carlos had zero alcohol in his blood, so that nixed the theory that he'd been drunk and accidentally fallen in. The coroner also reported that he received a blow to his head before going into the water. It seems Carlos was unconscious in the water before he drowned."

"Who would have done such a thing?"

"I have no idea, but I need to get going. The police officer who visited Carlos' sister just got back, and I need to talk to him."

"He has a sister in town?"

"Not in Rose Shore, but nearby. I don't remember the name of the town Maya lives in, but it's close to here. Anyway, try not to worry about this too much. See you." Lauren hung up, and Jessamine thought trying not to worry was easier said than done.

She turned back to Andrew and Molly and filled them in on what Lauren had said about the coroner's report.

"I didn't know Carlos had family nearby," Andrew said.

"Me neither." An idea started to form in Jessamine's head, one she didn't want to share with Andrew so he wouldn't have to keep anything more about her investigating from his sister. "I think with all the excitement I *will* actually take the afternoon off. Will you be able to handle things here? We only have that small painting class from the senior's home at three-thirty. Other than that, it should be a quiet afternoon."

"We will be fine." Molly gave a firm nod .

"Just don't find any more dead bodies," Andrew called after her, and Jessamine couldn't tell if he was joking or not.

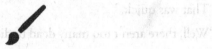

"Maya Leoz lives in Birch Cove?" Jessamine asked with surprise as she and Jackson reached the edge of the small town.

Jackson nodded from the driver's seat. "Is that significant?"

"There's an art gallery here I might want to check out later if we have some time, the Indigo Art Gallery."

After Jessamine had left the art center, she called Jackson to explain what she'd learned from Lauren and to ask if he wanted to take a trip out to visit Carlos' sister to ask a few questions. He had the afternoon off and eagerly agreed to come, saying he would find Maya's address and pick Jessamine up.

"To check out for fun or to check out for the case?"

"Um—let's go with both." Jessamine explained what little she knew of Frank Bates and his interest in the Indigo Art Gallery.

"So, this guy was at your art center opening?"

"Yes, and he was standing close to Victor after he was stabbed."

"If he did kill Victor, though, don't you think he would have run right away?"

Jessamine shrugged. "That's kinda been the whole issue with looking into Bates. Everything's a half-baked theory, so I've been concentrating on other clues and suspects first."

Jessamine was quiet for the rest of the drive as the case turned over and over in her thoughts. Maybe they should investigate Frank more. Out of their four original suspects—Mrs. Price had been cleared by the police, Fay hadn't been at the art center opening, and Gabriella seemed unlikely to have murdered Carlos, which left Frank.

They pulled up to the address Jackson had found for Carlos' sister, and Jessamine wasn't surprised to find a beautiful lakeside mansion. It looked like Maya's lifestyle of luxury matched her brother's. The mansion was surrounded by beautifully landscaped gardens, and large windows spanned every outer wall with views of both the lake below and the mountains in the distance. The property was enclosed by a tall, wrought-iron fence and gate with a security panel. Jackson rang the buzzer, and a female voice answered.

"Hello?"

"Is this Maya Leoz?"

"No, I'm her housekeeper. Who is this?"

"My name is Jackson Yeung, and I knew Ms. Leoz's brother. May I please come in? I'd like to speak to her."

After a pause, they heard the lady mumble something to someone else in the house. Finally, the gates buzzed open.

"Thank you," Jackson said, but there was no reply.

He parked close to the large double front doors stationed between tall pillars, and they got out of the car.

"I feel like Mr. Carson from *Downton Abbey* should be opening the door for us," Jessamine joked as she rang the doorbell.

"I'd feel extremely underdressed if that were to happen. Should have dressed for white tie." Jackson's eyes sparkled with some humor despite the grim reason for their visit.

They had to wait several moments on the front step before the door was finally opened by a tired-looking woman wearing black pants and a black sweater. Jessamine assumed it was the same housekeeper who had buzzed them in, and she led them into a large sitting room, all while barely speaking three words to them. She left just as briskly as soon as Jessamine and Jackson sat down.

"She seemed quite upset," Jessamine said.

"You're sure she isn't just rude?"

"Her makeup was slightly smeared, and her nose was red, as if she'd been crying."

"The news of my brother's death has certainly been a shock to us all." The sharp voice came from a dark-haired woman who appeared in the doorway of the sitting room. "I'm Maya Leoz. You said you knew my brother?"

They stood quickly to shake Maya's hand.

"Yes. I'm Jackson Yeung, and this is Jessamine Rhodes. We're so sorry for your loss and to bother you on such a tragic day, but we have a few questions."

"Are you the police?" She frowned.

"Oh no," Jessamine jumped in. "I own the art center in Rose Shore and work with Gabriella Everhart. She's quite distraught about Carlos' death, and I thought if I could find out any information about it for her, it could be a comfort."

Maya raised an eyebrow at her, and Jessamine thought she was going to be caught in her white lie, but Maya sat in an armchair across from them. "All right, but please keep it brief. There's much to do to get ready for the memorial service." She smoothed out the skirt of her elegant black dress and adjusted the small old-fashioned mourning veil she had over her eyes.

"Of course. We understand." Jackson smiled gently. "Were you and your brother close?"

"Not really. We shared an interest in exotic travel but rarely went anywhere together. We always kept each other updated on our trips, but, other than that, we spent most of our time apart."

"How well do you know Gabriella?"

"That selfish dimwit? I have no idea what Carlos ever saw in her. She broke his heart repeatedly, and he always went back to her. I was glad when she ended things for good and handed back that gorgeous diamond."

"Did you know they'd mended their engagement a few days ago?" Jessamine asked.

"No, but that doesn't surprise me." Despite her words, Maya looked just the opposite.

"Ms. Leoz, there's a strong possibility your brother was murdered. Do you know of anyone who would have wanted to harm him?" Jackson asked.

Maya gave out a small laugh in disbelief. "Murdered? Are you certain?"

"No," Jackson admitted, "but we know the police are looking into it."

"The police didn't say anything about that this morning when they came to break the news." Tears started forming in Maya's eyes.

Jackson and Jessamine looked at each other. *Oops.*

But Maya quickly regained her composure. "Aside from the trail of broken hearts he left behind every time he went on a trip, no. I can't think of anyone who wanted to harm him."

"Is there anything else you're able to tell us about your brother that might be linked to his death?" Jessamine asked.

"No, there really is nothing. He was always so caught up in his work, and I can't think of anyone who'd want to kill a fashion designer."

"Well, we won't take up any more of your time, Ms. Leoz. Thank you for seeing us. Here's my number in case you think of anything else you think we should know." Jessamine handed Maya her card, and she and Jackson stood to leave.

"I'll get Paula to show you out."

As if on cue, the housekeeper walked back into the sitting room and led them to the front door. She opened it for them, and Jackson and Jessamine stepped outside into the gloomy afternoon chill.

Paula started to close the door behind them but suddenly swung it back open. "Are you sure Carlos got back together with Gabriella?"

"Yes," Jessamine slowly answered with a questioning look.

Paula let out a frustrated sigh. "I knew I shouldn't have trusted him." And with that, she slammed the door and left Jackson and Jessamine staring at each other in surprise.

Chapter Eighteen

"First Gabriella, then Fay, and now Paula the housekeeper? Apparently, Carlos was a bit of a player," Jessamine said as they pulled out of Maya's driveway. "Even Maya mentioned the trail of broken hearts he left behind."

"Did you get the feeling Maya was hiding something?"

"Possibly, though I have no idea what. Maybe it was just her way of grieving."

"Maybe." Jackson seemed thoughtful. "She did seem genuinely surprised at the possibility of Carlos being murdered."

"She also seemed surprised Carlos and Gabriella had gotten back together. And she certainly has no love for Gabriella."

Jackson nodded in agreement. "Hey, did you still want to check out that art gallery?"

"I'd love to. Even if we don't find anything related to the case, I'd never say no to exploring a new art gallery."

The Indigo Art Gallery was the smallest art gallery Jessamine had ever visited and was in a single-story heritage house. The large front gable was painted dark blue and the rest of the siding an off-white. It reminded her of an old house her grandparents used to live in when she was a child; the two rocking chairs on the front porch even brought back memories of long summer days enjoying her grandma's homemade iced tea. There were only a few parking spots out front, all of which were empty, except for one white, beat-up car. A large "For Sale" sign was posted on the front lawn.

"It looks like business is quite slow here." Jessamine's observation worried her and once again fueled her determination to salvage her own business after that disastrous opening.

Jackson held open the front door for her, and she stepped inside, only to immediately turn around again.

"Oof," Jackson winced as Jessamine ran right into his chest. "What's going on?"

"Frank Bates is right inside," Jessamine whispered. "I knew that car looked familiar, but I couldn't place it."

"Wait . . . how do you know what his car looks like?"

Jessamine realized she never told Jackson about the time she was almost caught snooping around Frank's backyard. "Never mind. Let's just get out of here. That man hates me." She tugged at his sleeve to follow her.

Jessamine slouched down and raced back to the car, slamming her seatbelt into place the moment she was seated. Jackson was a few steps behind and was laughing by the time he reached the car.

"What's so funny? Come on, we have to go."

"You! You're acting like this is some top-secret covert ops mission." Jackson started the car and pulled out of the parking lot.

Jessamine realized how ridiculous she must have looked sneaking away from the art gallery and started to laugh as well. "He really does hate me."

"I find that hard to believe."

"He does! He thinks I stole the art center out from under his nose or something."

Jackson shook his head. "Well, if he does think that, then he's wrong. You had every right to purchase the center."

"I know." Jessamine's laughter faded away. "I don't like thinking someone hates me, though."

"That's Bates' problem, not yours. Anyway, what do you want to do now?"

"I still think we should go inside Indigo and talk to someone who works there, especially now that Frank was there. If he stole *Tranquil*, he could be using the money toward purchasing the gallery. We'll just have to wait until he leaves."

Sure enough, by the time they made it back around the block to the art gallery, Frank's car was gone.

"Okay, let's try this again." Jackson held open the front door for Jessamine a second time.

Inside, they were greeted by a friendly-looking woman with frizzy light-brown hair sitting behind a small desk.

"Hello. Welcome to the Indigo Art Gallery. Feel free to look around, and I'm available to answer any questions you have about our displays." Her small name tag read "Susan." "And I encourage you to check out our gift shop afterward." Susan pointed to a plastic folding table covered with a small selection of books, prints, and a few postcards.

They must really be getting desperate to make any sort of sale. "Actually, we were wondering if we could ask you some questions regarding the sale of this place."

The woman's smile faltered. "If you're interested in purchasing, you should act fast. Someone else has already put in a strong offer. It should go through in the next few days unless we receive a larger bid by then."

"No, it's not that. I own the Rose Shore Community Art Center. Have you heard of it?"

"Yes, the one where a Gabriella Everhart original went missing." Susan's dry reply bordered on mockery.

Jessamine cringed. Again, apparently, that was all her art center was becoming known for. She quickly introduced herself and Jackson.

"We'd like to ask a few questions about that actually," Jackson said.

"What's wrong?" Susan crossed her arms.

"Well, I think the missing painting might have a connection with the sale of this art gallery," Jessamine said.

"Ms. Rhodes, if you're suggesting we stole that painting for funds to save Indigo, you're mistaken." The friendliness in Susan's voice was completely gone by now.

That thought hadn't even crossed Jessamine's mind. She thought Frank might have done something similar, but not the current owners. It was something to look into. "I was actually going to ask about Frank Bates. I understand he was interested in purchasing the community art center but was outbid."

"I heard that as well, but I still don't understand what that has to do with the missing painting."

"I also heard he was putting an offer in for this place with the possibility of hosting art classes. Therefore, he could be in direct competition with me, and stealing *Tranquil* would be to his benefit." Jessamine started to become heated and struggled to keep her tone calm.

"Frank is a good man. He would never do something like that, and it's none of your business that he put an offer on Indigo. When he's the new owner, he'll do great things with this place. Now, I have to kindly ask you to leave if you're going to continue to make such absurd accusations."

Jackson gave Jessamine a sort of warning look, and she knew it was time to back down. "I'm sorry to upset you, but I'd honestly like to look around the gallery."

The woman rudely waved a hand in the direction of the artwork and then buried her head back behind the desk.

"I had no idea I could make so many enemies so quickly in the small-town art world," Jessamine whispered.

"I had no idea the small-town art world was so dramatic."

After the awkwardness with Susan, Jessamine only wanted to spend a few minutes looking at the paintings before ducking out the front door. The woman at the desk completely ignored them as they left.

"Well, we didn't get as much information from there as I was hoping," Jessamine said as they got into the car. "Except that she confirmed that Frank will be the new owner if the sale goes through. I think we should look into the current owners of the art gallery. Susan gave me the idea that perhaps they stole *Tranquil* for the money."

"Do you have any idea who they are?"

"No, unfortunately, I don't."

"Okay, I'll do some digging later today. I'm sure someone in Rose Shore knows the owner."

After stopping at a fast-food joint near the Indigo Art Gallery for a quick dinner, Jessamine and Jackson headed back to Rose Shore. Shortly into their drive, Jessamine's phone rang. She answered it and, after hearing Maya's voice, stuck it on speakerphone so Jackson could hear.

"Hello, Ms. Rhodes? This is Maya Leoz."

"Hi, what can I do for you?"

"I thought of something else after you left that you may want to know."

"Oh? What is it?"

"My brother was very upset a short while ago with an art collector who apparently had claims to a piece by Gabriella that was also very important to Carlos. This art collector wouldn't sell it to Carlos for any price."

"Did Carlos feel threatened by this collector?"

"No. I'm worried it might have been the other way around. Carlos could have such a temper sometimes, and he talked about making threats to this man, but I don't believe he would've ever carried anything out. He never mentioned if the issue got resolved or not."

"Do you know this art collector's name?"

"Yes, it's Victor Carlisle."

Chapter Nineteen

Jessamine slowly turned toward Jackson, who was staring right back at her; she knew her own face reflected the same wide-eyed stare. The two victims had been arguing with each other shortly before all this?

"Are you sure about that?"

"Of course, I'm sure. Whoever this Victor Carlisle is, he had my brother all up in arms."

"Was this before or after Carlos and Gabriella broke up?"

"It was after, I believe. What does it matter?" Maya seemed to be becoming impatient. "But I have to go now. I need to make sure Carlos' San Francisco friends are informed of his death." She ended the call.

"Do you think Carlos stabbed Victor at the opening? He wasn't on the guest list, but maybe he found a way to sneak in. On that note, I should probably look into tightening up some security for the next major event I hold. The cameras aren't much help with the larger crowds."

"It's a possibility. Maybe his wife knows something about Carlos. Do you want to drop by Madeleine's house and ask her?"

Jessamine nodded. "That's a good idea."

"We're getting so close to figuring it out now. I can feel it."

"I hope so. I don't want to do any more investigating after this is solved. If my business and reputation weren't at stake, I'd be staying far away."

"You've been pretty good at it though, I have to say."

Jessamine waved her hand in dismissal. "I haven't done much, just talked to a few people, like at the book club." She stopped to think for a moment. "And even if Carlos did kill Victor, that still doesn't explain who killed Carlos."

"Maybe someone close to Victor did it to avenge him."

"You don't think Madeleine did it, do you?" Jessamine's throat went dry with horror.

Jackson was quiet for a moment. "I've only met her a few times, but she always seemed very kind."

"But who knows what grief will do to a person."

"I have a hard time believing she would kill someone, though."

"We should ask her who else was close to Victor. That might give us a clue as to who may have wanted to seek revenge for him."

"See! Thinking like a detective."

The radio was playing in the car, and the local news came on.

"Brother of dead art thief declared war on art collector who pressed heavy charges. This and more are coming up next on our six o'clock news on RSWN," the news reporter said.

"Are they talking about Victor?" Jessamine asked in disbelief.

Jackson gave a slight shrug and turned the radio volume up.

"Seven years ago in Toronto, Pierce Naismith was sentenced to ten years in prison for stealing over thirty thousand dollars' worth of artwork from esteemed art collector Victor Carlisle. Mr. Naismith died of a heart attack in prison last week, and now, his brother, Watson Naismith, places the blame on Carlisle. He says Pierce Naismith had a known heart condition with a history of heart attacks running in their family. Watson Naismith believes Carlisle knew this and knew he was sentencing his brother to live the last years of his life in prison. Naismith argues that since the artwork was all recovered and returned to Mr. Carlisle only a few hours after the theft, it was morally wrong for Carlisle to press such heavy charges on his brother. Shortly after Naismith posted a public threat against Carlisle on his Facebook page, the art collector was viciously stabbed at the Rose Shore Community Art Center and died from blood loss. The mystery? Watson Naismith's airtight alibi had him on the other side of the country at the time of the murder."

Jessamine realized they'd been so caught up with looking into Carlos' death, that she'd forgotten to tell Jackson about the old article she'd come across about the art theft. As the radio announcer moved on to report other news, she filled him in on what little she knew about the old trial. "We have to find out more about this Watson Naismith. I don't believe for a moment he had nothing to do with Victor's death."

Jackson gripped the steering wheel tightly. "I don't believe it either."

They neared Rose Shore, and Jessamine pulled out her phone to send a text to Emilia asking if she'd be able to take Margo out for a quick walk and feed the dog dinner.

> **E: Sure. Out on another hot date?**
> **J: No! Just doing some more investigating.**
> **E: K. I expect a full report later. Don't worry about Margo. I'll take care of her.**
> **J: Thanks!**

They went straight to the Carlisle home, and Jessamine was a little shaky on her feet as she walked to the front door. Madeleine couldn't be a murderer, could she?

She rang the doorbell as Jackson reached her side, and Sarah answered. "Hi, Jessamine. Nice to see you again."

Jessamine introduced Jackson. "We were hoping to speak with Madeleine. Is she home?"

Sarah took a quick glance at her watch. "She is, but she's currently in a meeting, and then she's taking me to the airport in about an hour. I'm flying back home this evening."

"It'll only take a minute. Can we wait till after her meeting and quickly talk to her before you leave?"

"Sure, that should be fine. Come in." Sarah led them into the house.

They walked by the library, where Jessamine had met Madeleine the last time she was there, and she heard voices drifting out through the partly closed door. Sarah brought them into the kitchen.

"Why don't you wait here until after Madeleine is done? Can I get you anything to eat or drink?" She motioned to the bar stools tucked under the kitchen island.

Jessamine and Jackson both politely refused before Sarah excused herself to finish packing.

Jessamine immediately left the kitchen and started to creep back down the hallway toward the library.

"Where are you going?"

"Shh! I want to hear who Madeleine is meeting with."

"Detective Rhodes on the case," Jackson teased.

"Hey, zip it already."

They reached the ajar library door, and Jessamine heard Madeleine's voice speaking with another she didn't recognize. She put a hand on Jackson's arm and indicated to listen.

"Were you successful?" Madeleine asked roughly.

"Yes, it was rather gruesome, but I got it done. I hate dealing with messes like that," the unknown voice said.

"I appreciate it. Something needed to be done and quick."

"Next time you should get John to do the job for you. He has a much tougher stomach when it comes to these things. Anyway, I should be going. I want to leave this town as quickly as possible, but I'll be back in a few days."

Jessamine shuddered, her imagination running wild with all sorts of horrific thoughts as to what they could be talking about. But she knew she couldn't miss the chance to talk to the person in Madeleine's library, and she needed to act now. She gave a quick knock on the door and then strolled in like an old friend, with Jackson right behind.

"Madeleine! So good to see you. I hope you don't mind that we stopped by. Sarah let us in. Oh, you have company. My apologies." Jessamine turned to get a good look at the man Madeleine had been speaking with. His dark hair was speckled with some gray, and he was wearing a sharp-looking suit.

Madeleine sat across from the man in one of the armchairs. Her red-rimmed eyes looked surprised to see them, and she shifted uncomfortably in her seat. "Jessamine, Jackson. I didn't know you two knew each other."

"It's nice to see you again, Madeleine. Jessamine and I are neighbors."

"Jackson, you've met Brian, haven't you? Jessamine, this is Victor's step-brother, Brian. Brian, Ms. Rhodes owns the Rose Shore Community Art Center."

Jessamine resisted the urge to look at Jackson to see if he was thinking the same thing she was. Did Victor's step-brother kill Carlos?

"Nice to meet you, Ms. Rhodes, but please excuse me. I was just leaving." Brian stepped out of the library without another word.

"Please, have a seat. What can I do for you?"

"We wanted to check in. See how you were feeling." *See if you've killed anyone lately.* Jessamine inwardly winced and scolded herself. *I don't know if she did anything.*

"I'm all right. It'll be tough having Sarah leave, but she needs to return to her job."

"How much longer will you stay in Rose Shore?" Jackson asked.

"Another week or so. It'll probably be a long time before I come back here. Too many memories, you know, so I want to get everything sorted out before going back to Toronto."

"Madeleine, I wanted to let you know we've been sort of looking into who might have killed Victor and stolen the painting." Jessamine focused on Madeleine's expression, looking for any clue in her reaction. "Mind if we ask you a few questions?"

Madeleine seemed surprised by the announcement, but she had no look of guilt on her face. "Oh, you don't need to do that. Leave it up to the police. This is dangerous."

"You know I can't just stand aside and do nothing after what happened to Victor," Jackson said.

Madeleine sighed. "Jackson, I know you cared a great deal for my husband, but I couldn't bear it if something happened to you, too."

"I'll be careful. Besides, I've got Jess looking out for me. She's pretty tough." He winked at Jessamine.

"There's no stopping you once you've put your mind to something, is there?"

Jackson gave Madeleine a goofy grin. "Nope."

"Oh, all right. What do you want to know?"

"Do you know of a Carlos Leoz?" Jackson asked.

"The name sounds familiar. Is he a painter?"

"No. Carlos was the fiancé of Gabriella, the fiancé who inspired her to paint *Tranquil*," Jessamine said.

"Oh, yes. I believe their breakup finally convinced Gabriella to sell the painting to Victor."

"Did you ever meet Carlos? Or do you know if Victor did?" Jessamine asked.

"No, I've never met him in person, and I only remember Victor talking about him once. I believe Carlos called Victor to ask if he could purchase *Tranquil* after finding out Gabriella was selling it to him. Do you think he was the one who stole the painting?"

"Madeleine, Carlos was found dead last night," Jackson said quietly.

"Oh, I don't know what to say. How is Gabriella?" Madeleine sounded genuinely surprised.

Jessamine frowned. "Heartbroken, actually, they'd just reconnected right before he died."

"Oh, that poor girl."

"I hate to ask, but did you have anything to do with his death?" Jackson asked as gently as possible.

"Of course not! Why would you think that of me? I've barely even left this house since my husband's death."

"But did someone maybe want to kill Carlos on your behalf?"

"Madeleine, we overheard what Brian was saying about the gruesome mess he had to deal with." Jessamine shifted in her seat.

"Oh, that. Brian was talking about dealing with the lawyers. He hates doing stuff like that, but I'm certainly in no shape to argue insurance and liability and all that."

"Of course. That makes sense," Jackson said. "I'm sorry to have accused you."

"Oh, don't worry about it. I'm glad to know you're still looking out for Victor." Madeleine reached over and squeezed Jackson's arm.

After a small knock on the door, Sarah poked her head in. "Hi. Sorry to disturb you, but we should be heading to the airport soon."

Madeleine gave her sister a sad smile. "I wish you weren't leaving."

Sarah walked over and gave her a hug. "I know, but you'll be back in Toronto soon."

Madeleine opened her mouth to respond but yawned instead. "Oh, pardon me."

"Why don't you let me drive Sarah to the airport?" Jackson offered.

"Oh, it's fine. I'll be all right."

"It's really no problem. I have just enough time before my night shift starts anyway."

"Are you sure? I'd really appreciate it," Sarah said. "I know Madeleine could use the rest."

Jackson nodded. "We can leave whenever you're ready."

"Thank you so much, Jackson," Madeleine said.

"Are you ready to go, Jess?" Jackson asked.

"I—uh, actually, if it's not too much trouble, I was wondering if I could take a look at Victor's art collection?"

Madeleine chuckled. "Of course, you can. But do you have enough time? It's a large collection, and there's a lot to see. Though, you're welcome to stay if you have another way to get home."

"Hmm, good point. You're sure you don't mind if I stay for a bit? I won't bother you if you want to go to bed, and I really want to see the collection. I can call Emilia or someone to come pick me up in a bit."

"Sure. I'll go help Sarah gather her things, and then I'll show you where it is."

The two sisters headed up the large stairway, leaving Jackson and Jessamine in the foyer. Once they were out of earshot, Jackson turned to her.

"Well, we didn't really learn anything, but I'm glad to know Madeleine didn't have anything to do with Carlos' death."

"If she's telling the truth."

"You still suspect Madeleine?" Jackson's voice rose slightly.

"Shh, I don't want her to hear. All I'm saying is Brian was talking about some pretty nasty stuff just to be talking about insurance."

"Maybe he's had a bad experience with an insurance broker."

"I don't know . . ."

Jackson crossed his arms. "I can't believe you. If Madeleine says she didn't have anything to do with it, I trust her."

"Look, I know you were close with Victor, but we can't just cross her off completely. We need to think about this objectively."

Jackson opened his mouth like he was about to keep arguing, but the doorbell interrupted them.

"Could you please get that?" Madeleine called from upstairs.

He gave Jessamine a we'll-finish-this-later look as she walked past him to open the front door.

And the second she opened the door, she wished she hadn't.

"Well, if it isn't Ms. Detective Rhodes! Looks like you had the same idea I had."

Jessamine cringed at the obnoxious voice. *This guy keeps popping up!* "What do you want, Howard?"

"Oh, don't flatter yourself. I'm obviously not here to see you. *You* are no longer on my suspect list. I'm here to see Madeleine Carlisle."

"I'm glad I'm no longer your suspect, but why are you here to see Madeleine?"

"Obviously because she offed Carlos Leoz. I plan on getting the full confession."

Jessamine gave Jackson a look as if to say "See! Other people suspect it as well." Perhaps Howard McCoy was smarter than she gave him credit for.

"What makes you think that?" Jackson asked.

"I was interviewing Gabriella about Carlos' death, and man! That lady couldn't stop crying. I could barely understand a word she said."

"Well, her fiancé did just die." *I can't believe how insensitive Howard can be.*

"*Any*way! I asked her if the painting were to ever be recovered, if she'd want it back, and she said no because it would remind her too much of Carlos and that Victor's wife could keep it. So, naturally, Madeleine must have killed Carlos so she could keep the painting." He said this like Madeleine was some all-powerful crime boss.

Or perhaps Howard is just as clueless as I originally thought. "Howard, that doesn't make any sense. First off, Madeleine doesn't even care about collecting art; second, she didn't know Gabriella was engaged, and third—" She cut off her rant abruptly when Jackson's hand pressed against her back. He was right—she was saying too much.

"Madeleine has gone to bed already, and we were just leaving. I suggest you do the same."

"I'll just be a minute. I only have a few questions for her."

Howard tried to step around them and into the house, but Jackson held up a hand. "No, Howard. You should go home."

"Who's at the door?" Madeleine started walking down the stairs.

Howard's eyes brightened at his opportunity. "Mrs. Carlisle! I'm Click McCoy, and I have a few questions for you. Did you kill Carlos Leoz?"

"Howard!" Jessamine said at the same time Jackson yelled. "Out now! Before I call the police."

Finally, Howard seemed to back down. "All right, all right. I'll go. But I'll be back, and I *will* get my story." He walked slowly backward down the front steps, glaring at Jackson, before getting into his car and driving away.

"Jackson? Who was that?" Madeleine's voice was shaky as she came up behind them.

"No one. Just some self-made reporter who's always trying to create a story about nothing. Don't worry about it. I'll deal with him."

"He doesn't really think I killed this Carlos person, does he? I didn't even know him."

Jessamine was about to tell her the truth about what Howard had said, but the look Jackson shot her quickly changed her mind. "Let Jackson worry about Howard. You just focus on saying goodbye to Sarah and then getting some rest."

Madeleine nodded. "All right. I have to say now I'm really thankful you're staying for a bit, Jessamine. It'll make me more comfortable knowing someone else is in the house."

"I can stay for as long as you'd like me to."

"Is everything all right?" Sarah came down the stairs just then, struggling with her large suitcase.

Jackson ran up the stairs to help her. "Everything is fine. Just some pesky reporter, but we've sent him on his way."

The two sisters said their goodbyes, shed a few tears, and gave each other a ferocious hug, as Jackson stood quietly beside Jessamine. She couldn't tell if he was still upset over her suspicions about Madeleine, but, after seeing the woman's reaction to Howard's intrusion, she was starting to believe Jackson was right. Now wasn't the time or place to finish their discussion, though. It would have to wait until tomorrow morning after Jackson's shift.

After Sarah and Jackson got in the car and drove off, Madeleine led Jessamine back into the house. "Come, dear. Let me show you Victor's art gallery. It was his pride and joy, you know."

Chapter Twenty

Jessamine followed Madeleine down the hallway Sarah had led them down earlier that evening, but instead of going into the kitchen, they walked into a formal dining room. A table with twelve chairs filled the space. The dining table was staged—ready to serve an elegant dinner at a moment's notice, with crystal wine glasses placed next to the fine china plates and cloth napkins folded neatly alongside each one. A beautiful chandelier sparkled from the ceiling.

"Were you hosting a dinner party?" Jessamine asked.

"Oh, no. Victor loved having our china always out on display, and I don't see a reason to change that now."

"It's a beautiful set."

The dining room led into another sitting room, similar to the front library but without the dozens of bookshelves. From there, Madeleine opened a set of double doors and quickly ushered Jessamine inside.

"Wow," was all Jessamine could say, her words lost over the most exquisite home art gallery she'd ever seen.

"Though not my personal interest, even I have to admit it's rather impressive."

"It must have taken Victor years to collect so many pieces."

"Decades more like it. He started long before we met. Now, if you'll excuse me, I'm going to make myself a cup of tea and then head to bed. Please stay as long as you'd like and help yourself to anything in the kitchen."

Jessamine smiled at her hostess. "Thank you so much, Madeleine. I really appreciate this."

"Well, I'm glad someone can enjoy the collection now that my husband is gone."

After Madeleine left, partly closing the doors behind her, Jessamine took her time wandering around the room. One wall was completely covered in blackout blinds to keep out the natural light, and Jessamine noticed how each piece of artwork had its own spotlight, just like in a museum or professional art gallery. The other three sides of the long and narrow room were covered in paintings, each with an engraved plaque underneath stating the title of the painting, along with the name of the artist. The center of the floor was covered in a cushy area rug with four armchairs and two side tables. The whole setup was very professional. She recognized most of the artists and made some quick notes in her journal to look up the others.

She was completely lost in her own little art world when the gallery doors closed with a click.

"Madeleine? Are you there?"

Jessamine walked over to the doors and pulled at the handles. They wouldn't turn. She was locked inside.

She knocked on the door. "Hello? I'm locked in here."

She couldn't hear anything on the other side of the doors and, even though her gut told her something was wrong, she tried to remain calm and think of a logical reason for the locked doors.

Her panic didn't subside for long as another sense flared alive, and her heart started pounding. She knew what was happening even before the high-pitched alarm went off.

She could smell it.

Smoke.

Jessamine started banging on the doors even louder. "Help! I'm trapped in here!"

No answer. She took out her phone and dialed 911 and told the operator what was happening before she searched for another way out. The blackout blinds were all electronic, and once she found the switch to pull them up, they seemed to take forever to rise. Her impatience with the *whirring* sound grew worse as it was becoming more and more difficult to breathe. Jessamine held up her arm in front of her mouth to block out the smoke that started to seep into the gallery through the cracks in the double doors.

When the blinds were finally up, she let out a strangled sob when she realized that none of the windows could actually open. Hurrying to the other side of the room, she searched for another way out, but there was only a large bookshelf at that end. Her only option now was to break one of the windows. She looked around on the bookshelf for something heavy enough to do the job and read the spine of the thickest book she could find. *The Complete Collection of Jules Verne: Volume One* sat perched in the middle of the highest shelf.

Jessamine said a quick apology to the beautifully bound book as she stood on her tiptoes to reach it.

It took a moment for her to realize what was happening next. A few seconds after Jessamine picked up the book, she stumbled forward into a black hole. Her senses were completely off balance as she stood and tried to make sense of what had happened. The bookshelf had shifted sideways, and she was now in another room.

"Of course, Victor would be eccentric enough to have a secret passage in his house. What a cliché," Jessamine said out loud to the empty space. She fumbled around for a light switch and blinked as brightness filled the room. It looked to be a home office with the double-sided bookshelf serving as the door. *No wait, there's another door.* Jessamine tried the door on the other side of the room. Also locked and her loud knocking again went unanswered.

She went back into the art gallery to make another desperate attempt at finding a way out. Dark smoke swirled around the ceiling of the gallery, heading toward the bookshelf passageway she had just stepped back through.

Suddenly, a loud crash came from the office behind her.

"Hello? Anyone in here?"

"Here! I'm in here!" Jessamine hurried back toward the office and, without thinking, she grabbed the closest painting off the wall beside her and hugged it close. She tripped over the threshold of the passageway and fell smack into the chest of a firefighter.

"Hurry, we have to get out of here." The firefighter didn't wait for a response and scooped her up. The house was all a complete maze to Jessamine, but the firefighter seemed to know the way from Victor's office to the front entrance. They made it to the front lawn, where a team of paramedics surrounded them.

The moment the firefighter set her down, she was instantly immersed in a tight hug.

"Jess! Are you all right? What were you still doing in there?"

"I was trapped." Her voice was a muffle against Jackson's uniform. "The doors to the art gallery were locked from the outside."

She glanced at him and saw Jackson exchange a look with the firefighter who rescued her. The doors had been locked, right? Though now that she wasn't in a frenzied panic anymore, she thought it did seem strange they'd been locked from the outside.

Before she could question it, Jackson seemed to take note of the small painting she still clutched to her chest. "Don't tell me you went back for a painting. That's like the number one rule of fire safety."

"I didn't. I grabbed it on my way out. I had to save at least one. There are so many in there that are probably now destroyed and Madeleine—wait. Madeleine? Did you find her? She was—" Before she had a chance to warn them Madeleine might still be upstairs, an oxygen mask was placed over her face, and she was being led to the ambulance.

"We already got her, Jess. She was in the kitchen and will be just fine." Jackson held onto her hand tightly.

She sat on the back ledge of the ambulance while the paramedics assessed her and watched the firefighters work together in their chaotic routine to douse the growing fire. The flames cast a yellow glow into the night, and a crowd of curious neighbors had gathered on the front lawn. Jessamine felt completely helpless as she watched the shooting flames engulf the house. The firefighters were doing their best, but she thought the worst with every bright flare—another painting was gone.

"Ms. Rhodes! What were you doing in there?" an angry voice approached her and she looked up to see Constable Todd.

Jackson stepped in to stop the police officer. "You can talk to her later. We need to take her to the hospital. She might have smoke inhalation."

Constable Todd looked like he wanted to argue but sharply nodded his head instead. "Fine, but I'm sending an officer along to question her there." He looked behind him to bark his order at the closet-standing officer.

"Miss? We're going to head to the hospital now."

Jessamine simply nodded at the young EMT talking to her and closed her eyes, thankful she didn't have to deal with Constable Todd just then.

Jackson crawled into the back of the ambulance with her and grabbed her hand. "You're going to be okay, Jess. I've got you."

He held her hand the entire ride to the hospital.

Chapter Twenty-One

Where am I?

After struggling to open her eyes, which felt like they'd been glued shut, Jessamine realized she was flat on her back in a hospital bed. She tried to clear her foggy brain to remember what happened. Her gaze scanned the room, looking for any clue as to why she was there. She found Emilia snoozing in the chair next to her. A stinging cough escaped from deep in her lungs and triggered her memory. She'd been in the Carlisle house the night before, and there'd been a fire.

She winced at the thought of all those ruined paintings.

Jessamine tried to sit up in bed and groaned at her pounding head.

"Jess? Are you awake?" Emilia opened her eyes and reached out a hand. She grabbed Jessamine's arm and helped her sit up as she adjusted the hospital bed to a sitting position.

"What time is it?" Jessamine coughed again.

Emilia pulled up her sleeve to look at her watch. "Just after six in the morning."

"What are you doing here?"

"Jackson called me once you got to the hospital. He wanted someone to stay with you since he needed to leave and finish his shift."

"Have you been here all night?"

Emilia nodded and pressed the call button near Jessamine. "I'm supposed to let the nurse know when you're awake."

This worried Jessamine. "Am I okay? I wasn't in the smoke for too long."

"From what little they told me, you'll be fine. They wanted to keep you overnight as a precaution. You'll have a bad cough for a few days and will need to take it easy, but you'll be just fine."

Jessamine sighed and rested her head back, only to wince again at the pain.

"Oh, and bad headaches are also apparently a common symptom of smoke inhalation. You were completely bonkers to try and save those paintings; you know that, right?"

"I just saved one!"

"Really? That's not the story going around. Last I heard you came out with a whole armload of paintings."

Jessamine groaned. Rose Shore's rumor mill was like a living creature, thriving and growing with each crazy event that happened to her.

The nurse came in and examined Jessamine. She explained basically the same thing Emilia had said and told her the doctor wanted to see her before she could go home. "She should be by in the next hour or so. Just sit tight. I'll send up some breakfast for you." The kind nurse left the room.

"What happened when I got here? I only remember the ambulance ride."

"The doctor did some tests and examined you. I don't know exactly what, but I'm sure she'll tell you when she gets here. Then your adrenaline must have worn off because you pretty much passed right out after that."

"Do they know who did this?"

Emilia was quiet for a moment. "A security camera outside Madeleine's home caught the guy. They still need to analyze the footage, but, from first glance, it looks like Watson Naismith."

"I don't understand. Watson Naismith? Here in Rose Shore?"

Emilia nodded solemnly.

"How do you know this?"

"Jackson called a few hours ago with an update because he knew you'd want to know as soon as you were awake. Sounds like he heard it from Lauren. Oh, that reminds me. He also wanted me to let him know when you woke up." Emilia pulled out her phone and sent a quick text. "He was completely worried about you last night. He wanted to get out of his shift to be here, but I assured him I'd keep him updated. He still demanded I call or text him every hour." Emilia rolled her eyes.

"Have they found Naismith?"

"No, not that I'm aware of. Jackson said the police have been searching all night but haven't found him. This case is all-hands-on-deck now."

"Hey, thanks for looking out for Margo yesterday. I really appreciate it."

"No problem. I took her for a quick walk before I came to the hospital last night as well. I'm sure she misses you."

Jessamine gave a weak smile. " Hopefully, I can go home soon."

Jessamine was finishing up her simple breakfast of a bowl of fruit, some yogurt, and a glass of water when Jackson gave a soft knock on the door.

"Hey." He slipped into the room. "I'm so glad you're awake and okay."

"I think I'll go give Addison a call to let her know what's going on." Emilia stood and gathered her purse and phone.

Jessamine saw right through her friend's excuse to leave her and Jackson alone together, but she appreciated it all the same.

After Emilia shut the door, Jackson took the chair closest to Jessamine. "I was so worried about you. You can't imagine how I felt when we were driving to the Carlisle house, knowing you were still there." He grabbed her hand and held it tightly. "I'd just clocked in when we got the call."

"Is Madeleine all right?"

"Yes, she's fine. She was pulled out in time."

"Listen, Jackson. I'm sorry for being suspicious of her. Even before the fire, I was starting to think she had nothing to do with Carlos' death, but I didn't get the chance to tell you."

"It's all right. I'm sorry for arguing over something like that. You're right. We do need to work objectively together if we're going to solve this."

Despite Jackson's encouraging words, she still had a flicker of doubt telling her they'd never solve this. "Do you know if Watson has been found?"

"No, not yet. From what I've heard, so many police officers have been up all night looking for him. I think this might be Rose Shore's first manhunt. It seems he arrived in Rose Shore a few days ago and has been staying at an old motel over on West Street. Officers are being sent over there this morning to investigate.

"Listen, Jess, there's something I need to tell you. I don't know about the gallery doors, but the firefighter who pulled you out yesterday told me the door to Victor's office wasn't locked. A heavy chair had been jammed under the doorknob so it wouldn't open."

Her voice trembled. "So, Naismith knew I was in there and purposely tried to kill me."

"He knew *someone* was in there. That doesn't mean he knew it was you or that he's after you. Maybe Naismith thought Madeleine was in there. A couple of other doors were also jammed, almost as if he was gambling on which rooms you or Madeleine were in."

"I guess he had no way of knowing the art gallery and office were connected then. Just my bad luck he trapped both doors."

"We're going to get this guy. I promise."

"Are you done with your shift?"

"Yeah, and now I want to get out there and look for him myself, but I had to stop by and see how you're doing first."

"You must be exhausted." Jessamine yawned.

"I'm okay, determined to see this through. I'll be running on caffeine today, though."

Jessamine's murky brain was still trying to sort through what Jackson had told her. "But if Naismith just got into town, that confirms what the radio said about him not being the one to murder Victor at the art center opening."

"So, either he had an accomplice, or the fire and the stabbing are two separate crimes."

"It's too big of a coincidence to be two separate crimes."

A knock sounded on the door just then, and a woman in a lab coat walked in.

"Hi, Jessamine. I'm Doctor Howland. Do you remember me from last night? You were pretty exhausted."

Jessamine blinked her eyes a few times and tried to think. She was starting to remember parts of the previous night. She remembered the doctor's blue-rimmed glasses and auburn hair coiled into a tight bun. "I think I remember some things, but most of the night is still pretty hazy in my mind."

"That's perfectly normal. A trauma like what you experienced can do that. Now, how are you feeling?"

Jessamine took her time describing her stinging cough and headache.

"Your voice sounds fine, not hoarse. Any chest pain?"

Jessamine shook her head.

"Your test results all came back, and you're in the clear. Your cough should subside in the next few days, and plenty of sleep and water will get rid of that headache. I'm going to discharge you, but make sure to still take it easy. Do you have someone to drive you home?"

Jackson jumped in before Jessamine could even ask him. "I'll drive her."

The doctor smiled at him and turned back to Jessamine. "Please give me a call in a day or two to let me know how you're feeling. I'll send in a nurse to help you settle things." Doctor Howland left the room.

"Thank you for offering to take me home."

"No problem. I'll help you get settled before heading out to look for Naismith. I can check in again later today."

"That's okay. I'm sure I'll just be resting all day anyway."

Jessamine was sitting on a bench outside the hospital, waiting for Jackson to pull his car around, when someone sat beside her.

"Ms. Rhodes." Howard snapped a picture of her annoyed face. "I didn't think the hospital was going to let the Crazy Art Lady out that quickly. Good thing I got here when I did. Care to share a few words about last night's adventure?"

"How did you hear about it?" Jessamine didn't even bother trying to keep the irritation out of her voice.

"Oh, the fire is all over the local news. They said a woman was trapped in the house when it happened and came out carrying framed paintings. There is only one woman in town I know of who is nutty enough to do something like that. After some investigating, I figured out you were brought here." Howard sat up straight, looking very proud of himself.

"You figured out I was brought to the only hospital in town after suffering from smoke inhalation?"

Howard ignored her condescending question. "So, why were you still at Madeleine's house last night after telling me you were about to leave? Do you know who killed Victor? Did you see who started the fire?"

Jessamine closed her eyes and took in a deep breath. She was about to tell Howard what she really thought about his questions when a car door slammed.

"Get out of here, Howard! Leave Jessamine alone. She's been through enough." Jackson came up to them.

It was probably a good thing he stepped in before she lost it on Howard.

"Okay, okay." Howard put up his hands in defense. "But I still intend to get to the bottom of everything and soon." He snapped another picture of her and walked away.

Jessamine sighed and shook her head as she got into the car. "I don't even know what to say to that guy anymore."

Chapter Twenty-Two

By late afternoon, Jessamine began to feel antsy. Jackson had dropped her off at her home that morning and had stayed long enough to make her a large cup of herbal tea and take Margo out for a quick walk. He promised to swing by sometime in the evening to see how she was doing, with hopefully an update on Naismith. After he left, Jessamine showered, changed into her favorite flannel pajamas, and crawled into bed with her worried beagle curled up beside her. She dozed on and off for several hours before finally getting out of bed around three in the afternoon, feeling much better. *Maybe it's time to stretch my legs and get some fresh air.*

Jessamine noticed she'd missed a dozen text messages from various worried friends and answered them quickly, saying she was feeling fine, before putting on a pair of jeans and an old hoodie. She wrapped a cozy infinity scarf around her neck and leashed up Margo. The dog wagged her tail in excitement, happy her human was alive and well.

The cool, crisp fall air was perfect for clearing her head. The dampness covering the ground and foliage from a morning rain made everything feel fresh in the dim afternoon sun. They walked down to the water, and Jessamine let Margo off her leash. The beagle raced ahead to chase some gulls off their spot on the shore.

Jessamine thought about everything: the case, the fire, her art center, and Carlos and Victor's deaths. Maybe she should back away from the case and leave it to the police. Her life had been put at risk in the fire, and she was still just as far from finding out the truth. She knew Watson Naismith's actions proved he was involved somehow but pursuing that on her own again could potentially lead to something far worse than a house fire. She sighed, feeling defeated at getting off to such a rocky start to her new life in Rose Shore and unsure of what to do next.

Wandering farther down the beach, she found a large piece of driftwood someone had fastened into some sort of bench and sat down. Margo was having a great time running around along the shore, and Jessamine sat and watched her dog for close to an hour, completely lost in thought.

Her thoughts were interrupted by a loud growl. She looked around for a moment before realizing it had come from her stomach. Laughing at herself, Jessamine remembered she hadn't eaten anything since that sad hospital breakfast. "Time to go, Margo. Come here, baby girl."

Margo ran over with a stick in her mouth, her big eyes begging Jessamine to let her keep her newfound treasure.

Jessamine laughed again. "Yes, you can bring that home, silly girl."

After staring aimlessly at her almost bare cupboards for a solid five minutes, Jessamine finally settled on heating up a can of mushroom soup for herself.

While it was warming on the stove, she wrote on a sticky note in large letters "Go Grocery Shopping" and stuck it to the middle of her fridge.

"Well, at least you always have plenty of food." She patted Margo on the head and poured some kibble into the dog's bowl.

Her doorbell rang, and she peeked outside the front bay window and smiled to find Jackson standing on her porch.

He held up a takeout bag from the Secret Garden Tea Shop when she opened the door and grinned. "Hungry?"

She stepped aside to let him in the house. "Yes, very, though I was making myself a fancy dinner of canned mushroom soup."

"Well then, this turkey club sandwich from Emilia's will go nicely with your soup. And I brought some pumpkin cheesecake for dessert." Jackson walked into her kitchen and started setting up the small feast, indicating for her to sit and relax at the table. He was getting to know her cottage and moved around opening cupboards as if they were his own.

Jessamine liked that they were getting so comfortable with each other. *At least moving to Rose Shore gave me a great new circle of friends.*

"So, tell me how you're feeling, honestly." Jackson placed her soup and sandwich on the table in front of her.

"Honestly, I'm fine. Still coughing a bit, but my headache is gone. Margo and I just got back from a walk along the beach, and the fresh air did me some good." Jessamine took a bite out of her sandwich. "How is Emilia, anyway? I hope she wasn't too tired all day after sleeping in that cramped hospital chair last night."

"She wasn't there when I got there. Addison said she went home after the lunch rush to sleep. She also mentioned Emilia wanted to try and swing by this evening as well."

"And how about you? You've been going nonstop for two days now."

"Yeah, I'm starting to feel it now. I'll get some sleep tonight and then be back at it tomorrow morning." Jackson sat beside her with his own sandwich. "Anything new on Watson Naismith or the case?"

"No. I checked out the motel myself, which was a bust. Naismith had checked in for a few nights but checked out yesterday morning. The motel staff was unhelpful. They didn't notice anything strange or unusual about his behavior and had no idea where he went after he checked out."

A swell of disappointment formed in the pit of her stomach. "So, he's still out there."

"It's going to be okay, Jess. He's going to be found. I know he's the number one priority for the Rose Shore police, and the police departments in all surrounding towns are on high alert as well." He reached over and gave her hand a comforting squeeze.

"What about the current owners of the Indigo Art Gallery? Have you found anything on them?"

"Yes, but I doubt they have anything to do with the missing painting. I did some digging and learned they're an elderly couple who retired and moved down to Florida last year. They left the sale and everything up to their realtor. Apparently, Susan is their granddaughter, which could explain why she seems to feel so personally attached to the business."

"So, that's a bust as well." She gave him a tired smile, and they quietly finished their dinner.

"Pumpkin cheesecake?" Jackson got up from the table to clear their dishes.

"I've never had pumpkin cheesecake before, but it sounds good."

Jackson placed two slices of cheesecake onto a pair of dessert plates and brought them back to the table.

Jessamine's eyes grew wide. "Wow! Those are big pieces."

Jackson laughed at her reaction. "I may have sweet-talked Addison into slicing some extra-large pieces for us."

Jessamine took a bite and savored it. "Mmm, so good."

They were finishing up their dessert when the doorbell rang again. Jessamine got up to go answer it, and Emilia, Andrew, and Molly were outside.

"Hey! What are you all doing here?" The surprise of all her friends together made her laugh—truly laugh, and some of her anxiety about the case flittered away.

Andrew stepped forward and gave her a hug. "We were so worried about you. I can't believe you got stuck in a house fire. I want to hear everything!"

"We wanted to make sure you're all right and to assure you to take as much rest as you need. Andrew and I can handle everything at the art center." Molly stepped in to give her a hug as well.

It was a bit awkward, but Jessamine was thankful for the sentiment. "Thanks, Molly, I appreciate it."

Emilia brought up the rear and gave her another hug. "I see the extra pair of shoes by the door. Is Jackson here?" she whispered, and the two friends shared a smile.

"Yes, he brought over some food from your tea shop. So, thank you for dinner." Jessamine looped her arm through Emilia's, and they headed into the kitchen to join everyone else.

"You just missed out on some amazing pumpkin cheesecake," Jessamine said when they entered the kitchen.

Andrew groaned. "From Emilia's? That cheesecake is out of this world."

Emilia reached into her canvas bag and pulled out a shiny blue tin. "I brought some sugar cookies, so hopefully that will satisfy your sweet tooth."

Andrew grinned and grabbed the tin. He opened it immediately and popped a cookie in his mouth. "Thanks, sugar."

Emilia rolled her eyes and headed toward the tea kettle. "I also brought some loose-leaf peppermint tea. It's flavored with rosehips and hibiscus and is supposed to help with stress."

"Thanks, Em. You better make a large pot then." Jackson led everyone into the living room after the tea was made.

"So, has this pyromaniac been caught yet?" Andrew asked as soon as the five friends sat down.

"Not yet." Jackson shook his head. " Hopefully, he hasn't skipped town." He gave everyone a basic rundown of what he'd already told Jessamine about Naismith.

"Do you have a description of him?" Molly asked.

Jackson pulled out his phone and handed it to Molly. "Yeah, I got this off his social media. Hopefully, the local newspapers will run his photo tomorrow to help widen the search."

Molly drew in a sharp breath when she looked at the photo of Watson Naismith.

"What is it?" Jessamine wrinkled her brow.

Molly looked up, her gray eyes wide with fear. "This man was in the art center today."

Chapter Twenty-Three

"What? When?" Jackson's voice rose, and he glared at his phone still in Molly's hand.

"This afternoon. He was in about half an hour before we closed for the day. Do you remember him, Andrew?" Molly handed Andrew the phone.

"Yeah, he definitely was. Quiet guy. He came in and looked through the brochures of classes we have in that stand in the foyer and then left." Andrew handed the phone over to Jessamine and Emilia so they could see Naismith as well.

The picture showed a middle-aged man wearing a pair of crooked glasses with thinning dark gray hair.

"Did he do anything unusual? Did he speak to either of you?" Jackson leaned in close.

"He seemed normal. I just saw him in passing when I was walking back to my office, but I didn't actually talk to him. Did you?" Molly asked Andrew.

"Aside from greeting him and asking if there was anything I could help him with, no. Oh, he did ask me if I knew who killed Victor."

"He asked you that directly?" Jessamine raised her eyebrows.

"No, not directly." Andrew looked thoughtful as if trying to remember exactly how the conversation went. "He asked if the police had found out who killed the local art collector."

"So, he was trying to get information about the case out of you," Jessamine said. "That makes him sound super guilty to me. What did you tell him?"

"I told him I hadn't heard any updates, just that the police were working hard. He didn't say anything after that."

"You didn't tell him your sister is on the force, did you?" Emilia asked.

"No, of course not."

Jessamine voiced the concern that had been in the back of her mind all day, worrying her. "Now I'm sure he knew it was me who was in Madeleine's home last night. It sounds like he's on to me and knows where I work. He might try to harm me again."

Jackson turned to her with a worried look. "We still don't know that, Jess, but I promise I'll keep you safe."

The others all voiced their assurance as well.

"Molly and I will call the police the moment Naismith walks through the art center doors again, if he comes back," Andrew said.

"Having his picture in the paper will help the search," Emilia said. "And I'll stay over tonight to keep you company. I don't mind sleeping on the couch."

"Thanks, Em. I'd like that."

"I'll phone the police and request they have someone sent over here to be stationed outside tonight." Jackson squeezed Jessamine's hand.

She thanked her friends for their kindness. "I really should be heading to bed soon. I'm still tired from yesterday's excitement."

They tidied up the living room, and Molly and Andrew said their goodbyes.

"I'll quickly go home and grab my stuff," Emilia said. "Be back in a few minutes."

"Thank you, and I really do appreciate you staying here overnight. I'm sure I'm just being paranoid."

"No, not at all. I totally understand, and this mess will be behind us soon. Don't you worry." Emilia waved goodbye and followed Molly and Andrew out the front doorway.

"I can stay until Emilia gets back," Jackson offered.

"Are you sure? I know how tired you must be."

"I'm fine, really, and I'd feel much better if I stayed. It's not like I have far to go anyway. I'm going to call the police station right now and get something set up for tonight."

Jessamine loaded up her small dishwasher while Jackson leaned against the counter behind her and made his phone call. As she closed the door and pressed the On button, she gazed outside into the inky darkness and let her thoughts wander over the *whooshing* sounds of the dishwasher.

Something dark in the shadows caught her eye—movement in her backyard.

Jessamine gasped and stumbled backward into Jackson, who had just ended his call.

He reached out an arm to steady her. "What's wrong?"

"I think someone is outside."

"Stay here. I'll look."

Jackson crept up to the back door and slowly opened it. He suddenly flicked on the porch light and flooded the back of the cottage in brightness. "Hello? Anyone out there? Show yourself!" he called out into the night as he walked around the deck in his sock feet and leaned out against the wrought-iron railings.

Jessamine followed him out onto the deck. "No one?"

"Whoever it was is gone now. I'll make sure the officer stationed here tonight knows about this."

"I'm not even positive I saw someone. Maybe my tired eyes were playing tricks on me."

"It's better to be safe. If Emilia hadn't volunteered to spend the night here, I would have. Would you like me to bring Poe over? He's a good guard dog."

"Sure." Jessamine smiled. "I could use an extra furry friend around here."

They headed over to Jackson's house next door to pick up Poe. The dog was almost more excited to see Jessamine than his own human.

"I feel betrayed," Jackson complained, though the laughter in his eyes said he was amused.

"Do you want to spend the night with Margo and me?" she asked Poe in an extra excited voice, rubbing the dog's head.

Poe barked happily in response.

"All right, boy, but you have a job to do. You have to keep everyone safe," Jackson said to Poe with playful sternness, and Poe sat up straight as if ready to take an oath, only to then lean over and scratch his ear.

Jessamine and Jackson laughed.

"I'll gather a few things for Poe." Jackson left Jessamine in the foyer of his home, and she took a moment to look around.

It was laid out like hers, though instead of a front room for an office, the living space was larger and completely open. She noticed an entire shelf of science textbooks near the couch, proof of his taking his high school tutoring seriously.

Jackson came back with a cloth bag filled with food, an extra bowl, and a chew toy for Poe. He also handed her a key. "He's all set. I'll be heading out early in the morning, so bring him over whenever and let yourself in. Just take him for a walk and give him some extra food before leaving him by himself, and he'll be fine."

Jessamine nodded and took the key and bag. She leashed up Poe, and they headed back over to her cottage next door. "Thank you so much for everything. I really appreciate you looking out for me."

"Yeah, no problem. I just want you to stay safe. Naismith will be found, and the painting will be recovered. I'm sure of it."

Emilia pulled into Jessamine's driveway and gave them a wave. She got out of her car with an overnight bag and headed into Jessamine's home.

"Well, I should go and help Emilia get settled. Have a good night."

"Night, Jess."

Inside, Emilia sat on the couch flipping through a magazine. She gave Jessamine a mock look of surprise when she walked in. "I was just getting comfy. I didn't know how long yours and Jackson's goodbyes were going to take."

"Very funny. I was just picking up Poe. I'll get some blankets for you."

While Jessamine gathered extra sheets, blankets, and pillows and set up a bed on the couch, she told Emilia about what happened while Emilia had been picking up her things.

"That's kinda scary."

"I know, though I'm not even sure anyone was out there. But it still made me even more thankful you're staying here tonight, so, again, thank you."

"No problem."

Jessamine headed to bed herself soon after. Despite having slept most of the day, she was still tired from her recovery.

An hour later, Jessamine was still staring straight up at the dark ceiling. Her exhaustion weighed heavily on her, but her mind wouldn't turn off. She kept thinking about the case, and the fact that Naismith had been in her art center only earlier that day was a scary thought.

She could hear Emilia rustling around downstairs and knew her friend wasn't asleep either. Sighing, Jessamine threw back the covers and got out of bed.

"Hey, Em," Jessamine called from the stairs. "Do you want to watch a movie or something? I need to settle my overworked brain."

Emilia looked up from the book she was reading. "Sure. Are you all right?"

"Yes, just a little creeped out that Naismith was in the art center today. And that someone might have been in the backyard. And that I was stuck in a burning building yesterday. I need to think about something else."

Emilia gave a small chuckle. "Sounds like it. What movies do you have?"

Jessamine came downstairs and opened the small cupboard underneath her TV to pull out a basket filled with a variety of Blu-rays. "I have these, or we could watch something on Netflix. I need something lighthearted. A rom-com or a family movie or something." She passed the basket over to Emilia.

Emilia flipped through the small cases, humming and peering closely at the covers. "Aha! This one. I haven't seen this one in years." She pulled out *The Princess Diaries* and handed it over to Jessamine.

Jessamine laughed at her friend's enthusiasm and popped the disc into the player. She curled up against the arm of the couch opposite of Emilia, and both Margo and Poe jumped up to settle in between them. Jessamine leaned into her dog and gave her a cuddle. "This is just the distraction I needed."

Halfway through the movie, the sound of something crashing to the ground rang noisily from outside, and through the frosted window on the front door, the motion detector light suddenly shone through. Jessamine and Emilia both sat up straight on alert, and the dogs began to bark. Poe raced toward the door and growled.

"Someone is outside." Jessamine's hands shook as she reached for the remote to turn off the movie. The dogs stopped barking, and they sat in silence for a moment to listen for any other noise.

More crashes came, though not as loudly as the initial one, but someone was definitely in her driveway. Jessamine was terrified whoever was out there was doing something to her car.

"Should we call the police?" Emilia asked. "Where is that guard Jackson promised?"

"I don't know." Jessamine crept over to the large front window and lifted the blinds slightly to peek outside. "I don't see anyone out there. I feel like it'd be an overreaction to call the police and say 'Hey, my motion detector light came on.'"

"Maybe we should call Jackson instead. He'll want to know, and hopefully, he'll be able to contact the guard directly."

Jessamine grabbed her cell phone and nodded. "You're right."

Jackson answered on the fourth ring, and Jessamine felt a little guilty for waking him up. "Hey, Jess. Is something wrong?" he asked in a sleepy voice.

"I think someone is outside my house again. The front motion lights came on, and we heard something crash."

"Okay. I'm on my way to check it out. Stay on the phone."

Jessamine heard him quickly getting dressed in the background before he came back on the line.

"Did you look outside?"

"Yes, but I couldn't see anyone. The dogs were barking at first, but they've stopped now."

"All right, I'm outside, but I don't see anyone."

Jessamine unlocked her front door and stepped out onto her porch. Jackson was making his way across his front yard toward her. She glanced around her porch and driveway without seeing anyone in the shadows. A police car pulled up just then, and she figured the officer on guard had been doing a lap around the block. He got out of the car when he saw her on the porch, hand to his holster, and slowly approached her house.

She crouched down to look underneath her car and saw a few tin cans, plastic bottles, and other vaguely familiar materials.

These were all items from her recycling bin.

Following the messy trail around the side of her house, she saw that her recycling bin had been knocked over.

A raccoon leaped out from the bin, startling her, before running across the front lawn. At one point, the raccoon was exactly in the middle of Jessamine, Jackson, and the police officer before making its escape down the sidewalk.

"Was that your bandit?" Jackson asked with a laugh, and Jessamine realized she'd forgotten she still held her phone to her ear.

"What's going on? What's all that racket?" a shrill, annoyed voice yelled. "It's after midnight, I'll have you know!"

"Everything's all right, Clara." In the moonlight, Jessamine could just barely make out her neighbor's snowy white hair and irritated face across the driveway. "A raccoon knocked over my recycling. That's all."

"Well, why did you call the police if it was only a raccoon?" Clara demanded.

Jessamine ignored her pestering neighbor and gave a sheepish goodnight wave to Jackson and the police officer before hanging up her phone and scurrying back inside her house.

Chapter Twenty-Four

Jessamine came downstairs the next morning to find Emilia whipping up a big batch of pancakes and her kitchen table cluttered with bowls of diced strawberries, fluffy whipped cream, and various other toppings. There was even already a steaming pot of tea with a teacup just waiting to be filled in her spot. Jessamine tried not to roll her eyes at the tiny teacup; she liked to use extra-large mugs for her morning tea, ones she could wrap her hands around, but she knew dainty teacups were Emilia's favorite.

"Good morning, Jess!" Emilia's chipper voice was hard to concentrate on so early in the morning.

"Hi." Jessamine needed some tea in her first before she could match Emilia's energy. She poured the dark stream of tea into her teacup and breathed in the tangy aroma of Earl Grey. She added a splash of milk and took a long sip, which emptied about half the teacup when she stopped for some air. "Mmm, I needed this."

"Are you ready for some breakfast?" Emilia was already building up a Matterhorn-sized pile of pancakes on a plate for her.

"Yes. That's a huge helping, though. And shouldn't you be off to the tea shop soon?"

"Addison's doing the morning rush, and then I'm going to take over midday. Do you think you'll be going to the art center today?"

"I hope to. I'm getting behind in my work." Jessamine took a bite of the top pancake. "Wow, these are delicious. Thanks for making breakfast."

Emilia sat down and joined her. "No problem."

Jessamine didn't realize how hungry she was until she ate a second huge helping of pancakes. "You must have some sort of secret recipe for these."

Emilia gave a wink in reply, and Jessamine figured her friend had a secret recipe for just about everything. They sat quietly for a few minutes before Emilia started giggling.

"What's so funny?"

"I'm just thinking about that raccoon! I can't believe how freaked out we were about the little critter."

Now it was Jessamine's turn to dissolve into laughter. "You should have seen the look on Clara's face!" she wheezed. "Priceless."

They laughed on and off throughout the rest of breakfast—they only had to look up from their pancakes, meet each other's gazes, and the giggle fits started all over again.

"I should take Margo and Poe out for a walk." Jessamine was finally able to catch her breath. She stood from the table and reached down to give both dogs some ear scratches.

"I already have and gave them their breakfasts as well."

"How long have you been awake?"

"About three hours. I tend to get a lot done before most people are up."

Emilia was already cleaning up the kitchen. "Now, you go relax for a bit, and then I can drop you off at the art center when you're ready."

Jessamine thanked her friend again and went upstairs to take a hot shower. After she got dressed in a warm sweater and leggings, she called Doctor Howland to give her an update about her cough and headache. Since Jessamine was feeling just fine, the doctor gave her the okay to go back to work.

Andrew and Molly greeted Jessamine fondly at the art center and smothered her like she'd returned from months of bed rest.

"I'm fine, really. I appreciate the concern, but I'm eager to get back to work." Jessamine headed to her office and turned on her computer. She started to sort through her emails when one that had been sent the previous morning caught her eye.

"Invitation to Vancouver's Hottest New Art Show" read the subject line. Inside was a list of debut artists showcasing their work at an art show scheduled for the end of November. The email triggered a memory about a similar art show Jessamine had attended earlier that year in San Francisco, where she'd first met Gabriella Everhart. It was the same art show where *Tranquil* had been debuted. She remembered admiring the painting but, at the time, she hadn't known the story behind it about Gabriella's engagement. Her memories of Gabriella's showcase were vague as she'd been at the Bay Area Art Opening to meet with another artist.

But just because Gabriella's revealing of *Tranquil* hadn't been significant to Jessamine at the time, it didn't mean it hadn't been important to someone else. Someone who'd been trying to get his hands on the painting from the beginning.

Jessamine pulled up Gabriella's website on her computer and went to the blog section, scrolling down until she found the posts from the previous spring. Sure enough, Gabriella had written a handful of posts bragging about this amazing piece of art she'd created called *Tranquil*. And there in the photos of the presentation of *Tranquil* was Victor standing nearby. Gabriella had built up so much hype about her new piece that Victor, her biggest fan, had flown all the way down to San Francisco to be one of the first people to see it.

She wasn't sure if this information meant anything, but she decided to let Jackson know anyway. She pulled out her cell phone from her purse and called. After a few rings, she got his voice mail.

"Hey, Jackson, I thought of something that might help us with the case. Call me back when you have a chance. Thanks!"

She didn't have to wait long before Jackson called.

"Hey, Jess. How are you feeling?"

"I'm feeling totally fine, back to normal. Listen, I might have some information for you." Jessamine filled Jackson in on what she remembered from the art show in San Francisco and what she learned from Gabriella's website.

"From what I can figure, Victor went to that art show to persuade Gabriella to sell him *Tranquil*, which she didn't because she and Carlos were still engaged. So, if Naismith had an accomplice, who also wanted to steal *Tranquil* from Victor, the scheming of all this could go back all the way to that art show. Victor was very vocal with wanting that painting." Jessamine could tell by the silence on the other end Jackson didn't completely agree.

"It's a little far-fetched," Jackson said gently. "You should be resting and not investigating, anyway."

"I know, but right now, it's all we've got. I have a hunch about this. If someone wanted to get back at him, then they could have gone to the art show to purchase *Tranquil* out from under him. Gabriella didn't announce she was keeping the piece for herself until the show. Everyone assumed it would be for sale there. I think we should look into it."

"All right. Let's look into this. I'll do some digging on my end and call me back if you remember anyone else of importance who was there."

Jessamine agreed and said goodbye. She racked her brain and tried to remember that art show. *I arrived late due to my flight being delayed. I remember meeting Gabriella a few hours before her showcase started. I'm sure Carlos was there as well, but I don't remember him. Fay would have probably been there also. Oh, these people weren't even on my radar then! I don't recall anything.* Frustration consumed Jessamine, and she unlocked her phone again to look through the old photos she had of the event, hoping something would jog her memory.

She scrolled through them and took a careful look at every small detail, zooming in to look closely at the backgrounds. And on the twelfth or thirteenth photo, she noticed something. Or rather someone.

Watson Naismith.

Their prime suspect was huddled in the back of the photo she took of a display. Jessamine immediately called Jackson back.

"Watson Naismith was at that art show in San Francisco!" she practically yelled into the phone when he picked up on the first ring, not even bothering with a proper greeting. "I have a photo of him. He's in the background of one of my photos."

"Do you think he was trailing Victor?"

"Possibly. Have you come across anything yet?" Jessamine's heart pounded.

"Not yet, but I think I should go talk to Madeleine about this. She's staying at the Rose Shore Resort until the damage from the fire is assessed. I'll go this afternoon."

"I'll come with you."

"Jess, don't you think you should rest?"

"I'll be fine. I think I can handle a trip to a resort and spa."

Jessamine and Jackson went to the Rose Shore Resort & Spa for the second time together in just over a few days.

" Hopefully, we don't find another dead body," Jessamine said.

Jackson gave her a shake of his head. "With you around, I never know what sort of trouble will pop up. Has danger always followed you around?"

"Nope. Only since I got caught up in this investigation."

They went through the same routine at the front desk as Jessamine had done twice already when speaking to Gabriella and Fay. The front desk clerk said someone would be right down to meet them, and Jackson and Jessamine took a seat on a nearby bench.

A few moments later, a woman Jessamine didn't recognize came out of the elevators and walked over to them. She was wearing a navy-blue pencil skirt and a light gray blouse with her black silky hair tied back in a long ponytail.

"Are you here to see Madeleine Carlisle?" she asked.

Jessamine and Jackson stood. "Hi, I'm Jessamine Rhodes, and this is Jackson Yeung."

They shook hands with the woman and she introduced herself as Talia Robson, Victor's former personal curator.

"I flew in this morning to help Madeleine assess the damage done to the art collection, but the fire department hasn't given us the okay to go inside the house yet."

"I don't even want to imagine what those poor paintings look like now."

Talia gave Jessamine a sad smile. "Now I recognize your name. Madeleine mentioned your attempt at trying to save some art."

"Yep, that's me. The Crazy Art Lady."

"Well, I can't say what I would have done in your shoes—I honestly don't know—but I do understand your reasoning behind it, even if it was crazy."

"Completely thoughtless is more like it," Jackson muttered.

"I heard that," Jessamine said.

"I'm just glad you're all right." He grabbed Jessamine's hand and gave it a quick squeeze before turning back to Talia. "Is Madeleine upstairs? We need to talk to her about the fire."

"Yes, of course. Follow me." Talia led them to the elevators and used her hotel key card to access the top floor.

Upstairs, she unlocked the door of a large, penthouse suite, and Jessamine and Jackson followed Talia inside. The suite was beautiful. It opened into a living area complete with couches, armchairs, a coffee table, and a writing desk off to the side. There was a huge television as well as a double-sided gas fireplace that was on, and Jessamine could see the master bedroom on the other side of the dancing flames. Off the living area was a second bedroom as well as a full kitchen, which was where Madeleine sat at a table. Victor's step-brother, Brian, was seated across from her, and dozens of files and papers were scattered around the space between them.

Madeleine looked up at them and smiled. "Jessamine, I'm beginning to think you're growing rather fond of me. And, Jackson, good to see you again." She got up and motioned to the couches. "Please, make yourself comfortable. I apologize I don't have any refreshments to offer you."

"Oh, it's totally fine. We're sorry to barge in when you probably have a lot to deal with," Jessamine said. "We won't take up too much of your time."

"Madeleine, what can you tell us about the Naismith brothers?" Jackson asked.

This seemed to catch Madeleine off guard. She sucked in a breath but didn't say anything.

Talia, who had taken Madeleine's seat at the kitchen table to help Brian, said, "You told me this was about the house fire."

"It is. The house fire is connected to the Naismith brothers. Please, Madeleine, this is important."

"I don't know what to tell you that you don't probably already know. You've heard about my husband's lawsuit from several years ago against Pierce Naismith and the fellow passed away in prison recently?"

They both nodded, and Jessamine said, "Watson Naismith held Victor responsible for what happened to his brother. Do you know if Victor ever received a personal threat from him or anyone else?"

"No, not recently at least."

"What do you mean not recently?" Jackson asked.

Madeleine looked thoughtful. "A few months ago, he traveled to an art show and mentioned something about receiving a threatening note when he called me in the evening. He didn't seem concerned about it, even laughed it off, so I completely forgot about it. But I doubt it's connected to this. That was so long ago and in another city."

"Was it in San Francisco, by chance, at the Bay Area Art Opening?" Jessamine asked.

Madeleine looked at her in surprise. "How did you guess?"

"I was there, and I assumed Victor was as well since that was where *Tranquil* debuted." Jessamine decided to leave out the part of her creeping him on Gabriella's website.

"And Watson Naismith was there as well. Could you please tell us more about the note he found?" Jackson pressed.

"Victor said he found it in his suit pocket after picking it up from coat check at the end of the evening. It wasn't signed and simply read 'Keep close what is precious to you. One day it will be destroyed.'"

"Sounds like a bad fortune cookie," Jessamine said. "Did he keep the note?"

"No, he said he threw it in the trash right after finding it. Like I said, we didn't think too much about it at the time. Do you think Naismith wrote it?"

"It's quite possible. He's our lead suspect at the moment," Jackson said. "I'm going to arrange to have a police officer or hotel security stationed outside your hotel room."

"I would appreciate that. Thank you for looking out for me, Jackson."

"No problem. Let us know if you hear from Naismith or if you remember anything else, and we'll do the same." Jackson stood and shook Madeleine's hand.

"Thank you for stopping by." Madeleine shook Jessamine's hand as well and walked them both to the door of the suite. They said their goodbyes, and Jackson and Jessamine headed toward the elevator.

They rode down to the lobby level, and when the elevator doors opened, Jessamine led the way through the lobby, stopping abruptly when someone caught her attention at the front desk.

Jackson slammed into her back. "You really need to stop doing that." He laughed lightly.

"Sorry," Jessamine whispered, "but doesn't that lady at the front desk look familiar? I can't place her."

The blond woman turned around, and Jessamine recognized her face instantly. "Oh! That's Paula, Maya Leoz's housekeeper."

Jessamine caught Paula's eye, and the other woman reflected a brief flicker of recognition before she ducked her head and headed toward the elevators.

Jessamine hurried after her, with Jackson close behind. "Pardon me! Paula. Hold on."

She turned back to look at them. "Yes? Can I help you?"

Jessamine ignored the fact Paula was pretending not to know them. "Hi, yes. I'm Jessamine, and this is Jackson. We met at Maya's house the other day."

"Oh, yes. I remember. Did you need something?"

"I . . . uh . . . I just wanted to know what you meant when you said you shouldn't have trusted Carlos," Jessamine said awkwardly. "Could we sit down for a moment?"

Paula looked uncomfortable for a moment before slowly nodding her head.

"Thank you. We won't be long." Jessamine led the three of them over to a seating area.

Paula fidgeted with her hands nervously and seemed to be waiting for Jessamine to ask her again before she volunteered any information.

"How about we start at the beginning? When did you meet Carlos?" Jessamine prompted gently.

"I started working for Ms. Leoz about five years ago and had been there for about a year and a half before I met her brother."

"And were you two involved in any way?" Jackson asked.

Paula looked like she was about to cry. "He was so charming. And he always smiled and talked to me. Hardly anyone notices a housekeeper in Ms. Leoz's house. Her friends are all so snobby."

"So, you dated?" Jessamine clarified.

"No," Paula wailed. "He kissed me once and made all sorts of promises, and, like an idiot, I believed him. I had no idea he'd gotten back together with Gabriella until you said so the other day." She practically spat out Gabriella's name. "I hadn't seen him in weeks."

"How come you're here at the resort?" Jackson asked.

"I'm not here to hurt Gabriella, if that's what you're thinking." Paula glared at Jackson. "I'm here on behalf of Ms. Leoz to make some funeral arrangements with her. Don't worry. I'll be on my best behavior." She got up to leave.

"Are you going to be all right?" Jessamine asked and got up as well. "We didn't mean to upset you."

"It's fine. I just need to pull myself together first before heading up to see Ms. Everhart. I don't blame her, not really. Like I said, I should have known better than to trust Carlos." She smiled sadly and left.

"Do you believe her?" Jackson asked.

"Yeah, I do. I think she got in over her head with Carlos, but I don't think she has anything to do with his murder. I just feel bad for her."

Jackson nodded in agreement. "I'm going to hang back and arrange some sort of security for Madeleine. I'll see you later?"

Jessamine smiled. "See you."

Chapter Twenty-Five

On the way back to the art center, Jessamine stopped at Emilia's Secret Garden Tea Shop for a cup of tea to go.

Addison was working the front and greeted Jessamine as she walked through the doorway. "Hey, Jessamine. I can't believe what happened to you. How are you feeling?"

"I'm doing fine. Just needed a day of rest, but I'm back at work today. I love your new hair color, by the way."

"Thanks." Addison spun around to show off the hot-pink highlights streaking through her strawberry blond ponytail. "I'm going to change it back for the wedding, but first, I wanted to have a little bit of fun with it."

"It looks great."

"So, what can I get you? Would you like to try one of our new autumn tea blends? We just released them today." Addison had a touch of pride in her voice as she mentioned the house blends she and Emilia created for each season.

"Sounds enticing. What are you offering?"

"My favorite is the Spiced Cinnamon Chai, a black tea blend with cardamom, ginger, pink peppercorns, and, of course, lots of cinnamon. We also have our Apple Harvest, a white tea with apple and cranberry mixed in, and our Cozy Caramel, a rooibos flavored with bits of caramel." Addison held up a sample of each blend for Jessamine to take in their aromas. Each one made her mouth water.

"I'm impressed, Addison. These all sound and smell delicious. I don't know how you're able to come up with these blends."

Addison blushed slightly at the compliment. "Lots of trial and error at first, and then you learn what goes nicely together and what doesn't."

"Well, I'll definitely want to try all of these at some point soon, but I'll start with the Spiced Cinnamon Chai, with some milk please."

As Addison was getting Jessamine's cup ready to go, she indicated to the national newspaper on the counter beside her. "Did you see you made the paper? The title is something like 'Crazy Art Lady Barely Escapes House Fire with Her Life.'"

Jessamine groaned. "This is so embarrassing. Which page is it on?" She picked up the newspaper and started flipping through it.

"Near the back of the news section, I think, near the obituaries." Addison handed her the cup of tea. "You can keep the paper if you'd like; I'm done with it."

"Thanks, Addison." Jessamine was already scanning through the pages for any mention of her name. *At least I didn't make the front page!*

Jessamine sat in her car in the parking lot and rubbed her temples in frustration.

There it was. Her name was printed in a national newspaper, highlighting her folly at trying to save artwork from a fire as well as mentioning her connection to the missing Gabriella piece. Tears formed in the corners of her eyes, and she quickly wiped them away with her sleeve. This article would surely do more harm to her already-tarnished reputation. It painted her as a complete nutcase who inadvertently destroyed any artwork she encountered.

The newspaper was still spread open on her lap, and her gaze glanced over to the obituaries, feeling thankful her name at least wasn't printed in that section after the fire. Sighing, Jessamine tossed the newspaper onto the passenger seat, causing the pages to fly apart and scatter around the floor and seat of her car.

Now she had to dig through the pages to find her purse for her car keys, which had been left on the floor by the passenger seat. Another newspaper article caught her eye—another one about Pierce and Watson Naismith. It mentioned a lot of what had been said in the radio announcement from the other night, though it gave an update that police knew Watson was currently in Rose Shore and were looking into any known associates of his in the area.

Vague. Though maybe just enough to go on.

Jessamine grabbed her phone instead of her keys and pulled up a Google browser. She sipped on her tea while she searched for Watson Naismith, specifically any connection to Rose Shore. Nothing came up, though, admittedly, she wasn't sure what she was looking for. She really didn't know too much about Watson; she didn't even know what he did for a living. Jessamine tried a broader search instead, just to get any information about him, even if it had nothing to do with Rose Shore.

The best she could find was his name listed amongst the alumni of a small business school in Toronto, having graduated around twenty-five years ago.

Another name jumped out at her from the list of fifty or so students from the same graduating year.

Frank Bates.

She almost spat out her Spiced Cinnamon Chai in response.

"It can't be the *same* Frank Bates!" she said out loud. "It has to be another man with the same name. There's no way Frank and Watson are connected."

Jessamine was in absolute disbelief. She snapped a screenshot of the list and sent it to Jackson.

> **J: Frank and Watson went to the same business school!**
> **JY: What?!**
> **J: New lead? The accomplice we've been looking for?**
> **JY: We need to check this out immediately. Where are you?**
> **J: Just picking up something from Emilia's tea shop.**
> **JY: K, I'll meet you there in 5.**

Jessamine's heart pounded. *Had it been Frank this whole time? Had he even been brought in for questioning?* Jessamine couldn't remember; she could barely think straight. She remembered something about Emilia telling her to go to the police with her suspicions, but then someone had broken into her house, and she forgot. The only thing she knew for sure was she wouldn't be able to concentrate on anything other than the case now; they were so close to solving it.

Instead of driving back to the art center, she went back inside the tea shop to wait for Jackson.

"Jess? What's wrong? You look positively green." Emilia was now behind the front counter when Jessamine walked in.

"It was Frank Bates. I think it was him this whole time," Jessamine said in a low voice. "He's connected to Naismith, and he was at the art center opening. And he has a motive! I can't believe we didn't figure this out sooner."

"Wow, that's awful." Emilia stepped out from behind the counter and led Jessamine to a table in the back corner. "Have you told the police yet?"

"No. I'm waiting for Jackson to get here, and then we're going to figure out what to do. I'm not one hundred percent positive it's Bates, so I don't want to let on that I've been investigating and then be wrong."

"How are you going to find out for certain that it is him?"

"I don't know yet. I'm hoping Jackson has a plan."

"Well, I have an idea," Emilia said slowly.

Jessamine looked at her with surprise, and Emilia wiggled her eyebrows.

"How about a little Jeannie Nelson again?"

Jessamine narrowed her eyes. "Where are you going with this?"

"I call the Indigo Art Gallery again, pretending to be Miss Jeannie Nelson, and get some more information out of that receptionist. At least where he is so we can ask him some questions."

"I don't know."

"Come on, Jess. What do you have to lose? It can't hurt. If we get no info, then we try something else."

Jessamine sighed. "Okay. You're right. I *am* willing to try anything at this point."

Emilia beamed and held out her palm. "Your cell phone, please. Mine's in the back."

Shaking her head at her friend's enthusiasm for trick calls, she dug out her phone from her purse and handed it over.

Emilia was looking up the number for the Indigo Art Gallery when Jackson walked in. Spotting them in the back corner, he hurried over and pulled out a chair for himself. "What's going on?"

He was quickly shushed by Emilia, who held the phone up to her ear as it began to ring.

"Emilia is going to call the Indigo Art Gallery and try to get some info about Bates," Jessamine leaned over and whispered to Jackson.

"How's she planning on doing that?"

"This is Frank Bates' assistant Jeannie Nelson calling," Emilia said into the phone in her fake accent.

Jackson's eyes went wide in disbelief, and he started to laugh. Jessamine quickly slapped a hand over his mouth. "No way anyone is going to fall for that ridiculous accent," he mumbled between her fingers.

"Susan fell for it once before," she hissed. "Now, keep quiet!"

Emilia was completely silent after her introduction, but her facial expressions kept changing. First a look of surprise then embarrassment and then anger. Finally, she grinned triumphantly and handed Jessamine back her phone.

"What happened?" Jessamine asked and looked at her phone to make sure it was off. Susan must have ended the call first.

"Bates is on his way to the bank in Rose Shore right now."

"What—how? What?" Jackson stumbled over his words. "Obviously Susan didn't fall for your little scheme, so why would she tell you Bates is at the bank?"

"She didn't. I heard it from Bates." Emilia was clearly very pleased with herself and having a grand old time keeping them confused.

"Explain, Em," Jessamine said sternly, not in the mood for games.

"All right, all right. So yes, Susan didn't fall for my Jeannie Nelson trick this time," Emilia pouted for a moment, "but as she was lecturing me on 'common decency' and on 'not wasting people's time,' I heard Bates call out in the background that he was heading back to Rose Shore to the bank."

Jackson started laughing again, and Jessamine joined in wholeheartedly. She laughed so hard she had to grab a tissue from her purse to wipe away her tears. "I can't believe you! I can't believe that worked."

Emilia, grinning like a Cheshire cat, stood. "You're welcome. Now, if you'll excuse me, I really should be getting back to work. You two will just have to interrogate him without me. Hopefully, you can manage." She gave them a wink before heading back behind the counter.

Jessamine turned back to Jackson. "Shall we?"

Jackson nodded, and they headed out the doorway.

They arrived at the First Choice Bank only fifteen minutes later. *First Choice? More like the only choice!* It was the only bank in town. At least that made it easy to figure out where Frank was going.

She scanned the parking lot but saw no sign of Frank's car.

"Looks like we beat him. Should we hold a stake out here in the car or in the lobby?" Jessamine asked.

"In the car. That way he doesn't have a chance to run back out the door."

"Good idea. Though he might still be a while if he's coming from Birch Cove."

"Let's brush up on our random trivia while we wait. That way we can beat Andrew next time. I have a fun trivia app on my phone." Jackson got out his phone.

Jessamine laughed and agreed. She was still slightly annoyed Andrew had annihilated them all so easily. They spent the next half hour or so playing the silly trivia game and found they were pretty evenly matched.

Finally, Frank pulled into the parking lot. He parked a few spots away from them and headed inside the bank.

"Ready?" Jackson turned to her. "I have no idea how he'll react. He may get violent. You can stay here if you'd like."

"No way! I want to see this through."

They got out of the car and walked into the bank. Frank stood near the door, looking at a brochure for business insurance.

"Mr. Bates, could we please ask you a few questions about Pierce and

Watson Naismith?" Jackson approached Frank and spoke to him in a soft but firm tone.

"What's going on?" Frank was completely caught off guard, but when he saw Jessamine, he grew angry. "Get outta here, Ms. Rhodes! I don't want anything to do with you."

"We're still trying to get to the bottom of what happened at the opening of the community art center. Can we please ask you a few questions?" Jessamine tried to keep her voice even, despite her rising anger.

Frank glared at the two of them. "Fine, I'll answer a *few* questions, only to get you off my back once and for all. I'm telling you; I have nothing to do with this."

"How about we step outside?" Jackson suggested and held open the door for both Jessamine and Frank. To the left of the bank was a small park, and they sat down at a picnic table. "Mr. Bates, we recently found out you and Watson Naismith went to business school together. Is this correct?" Jessamine asked.

Frank sneered at her. "What are you? A detective now? I don't appreciate you snooping into my past."

"Please just answer the question."

"Again, I can assure you I have nothing to do with any of this. Yes, Watson and I went to business school together. I haven't seen or heard from him in years, though."

"Did you ever meet his brother, Pierce?" Jackson asked.

Frank seemed more willing to answer Jackson's questions than he did Jessamine's. "Yes, both Pierce and Watson were part of a poker club I belonged to."

"Was that what led to his gambling debts?"

Frank nodded grimly.

"Are you aware Watson is in town now?" Jackson asked.

"No, I wasn't. Like I said, I haven't been in contact with him for years." Frank kept a straight face, making it hard for Jessamine to know if he was telling the truth or not.

"He is. And he's currently our prime suspect in the missing painting, the murder of Victor Carlisle, and the fire at his home," Jessamine said.

Frank snorted. "You can't possibly think Watson did all that."

"Funny you should say that," Jessamine said dryly. "We don't, actually. We think he had an accomplice."

"Oh, I see what this is all about. You think I did it." Frank's voice was rising again, and his eyes shot daggers at Jessamine. He pointed angrily at her. "This is all *your* doing because you don't want to be in competition with my art gallery!"

"Oh, you are *not* serious!" Jessamine fired back.

"Yes! You're framing me to get rid of the competition."

"Calm down, both of you," Jackson interjected. "That isn't what's going on here, but we would like to hear your side of the story."

"Well, for your information, I have people who can vouch for me on both occasions," he said in a snarky voice.

"You were at the art center opening. I saw you standing near Victor right after he was stabbed."

"I ran into the foyer after I heard Gabriella screaming, just like everyone else, but I was previously talking to Doctor Charlie Evans from the hospital for most of the evening before Victor was killed. You can ask him."

"And the night of the fire?" Jackson asked.

"I was out for dinner in Birch Cove with someone from the Indigo Art Gallery."

"Who was that?"

"Her name is Susan. She works at the front desk."

Well, now it makes sense why Susan is always so quick to defend Frank.

She has a thing for him. Out loud Jessamine asked, "Can you give us the name of the restaurant?"

Frank did, and Jackson promised he would confirm with Doctor Evans and Susan, as well as the restaurant, about Frank's whereabouts on those two nights.

"One last question. Have you had any contact with Carlos Leoz?"

"No, I'd never even heard of the guy until his death was reported a few days ago."

Jackson nodded. "All right, thank you for cooperating, Mr. Bates."

Frank got up with a humph and walked away. "I better not be late for my appointment."

Jackson turned back to Jessamine after Frank left. "I need to head in for a shift now. Do you want to make these phone calls? Or I can this evening on a break if you aren't able to."

"No, I can. I'll get started right away."

Jessamine pulled up to Victor and Madeleine's house as twilight was setting in. She had hoped to see the house and property in the daylight, but traffic had been slow getting there. *Oh well, I won't be long.*

The rest of her afternoon had been spent making the phone calls to check Frank Bates' stories, and she discovered they all checked out. Doctor Evans had been chatting with Bates right up until the incident, and the manager at the restaurant and Susan had confirmed he'd been out for dinner the night of the fire. Susan had been less than pleasant while speaking to her, and Jessamine sincerely hoped that was the last time she would have to deal with that woman.

So, she was officially out of suspects for Watson's accomplice. Her only choice now was to find Watson, and she hoped the scene of the fire might hold some clues as to where he was hiding. Talia had called Jessamine about an hour ago and said they got the go-ahead to look inside the house, though it would be months before it was liveable again. She thought Jessamine might be interested in seeing how the artwork had fared, and she'd been right.

From the outside, Madeleine's vacation home looked all right. A few scorch marks here and there, but nothing too terrible.

Jessamine walked up to the large entranceway and rang the doorbell. No answer. She tried knocking, but again there was no answer. Figuring she'd beaten Madeleine and Talia there, she walked along the front of the house and peered into the windows. It was too dark to see anything inside. Deciding to investigate around the back of the house for clues to Naismith's whereabouts, she followed the path around the water fountain in the front and into the backyard, feeling a bit like Dorothy following the Yellow Brick Road.

The backyard and patio were set up for entertaining with a cooking show-worthy outdoor kitchen and lagoon-like pool, with a waterfall feature. The back of the house looked similar to the front, covered with large windows and looking safe from the fire.

She heard a car pull up and went back to the front to greet Madeleine and Talia. Poor Madeleine looked like she was about to cry when she stepped out of the car.

"It doesn't look too bad." Jessamine tried to sound encouraging.

She wanted to take back her words the moment the three of them stepped through the front doorway because inside was a whole different story.

The library was completely gone—looking like it had been ground zero for the fire. The walls were completely black, and the furniture and bookshelves were now nothing but skeletons. The kitchen had fared slightly better, with only a harsh smoky smell lingering in the air with a few burn marks up the walls, but the dining room was in similar shape to the library.

Jessamine led the way straight to the art gallery and let out a sob when she reached the doorway. The paintings had all been burned to a crisp. She hadn't realized it the other night, but the library shared a wall with the art gallery. That was probably why she'd smelled the smoke right away.

"Oh, there's hardly anything left." Talia hung her head and covered her mouth. "All mine and Victor's hard work from over the years is gone."

Madeleine wrapped her in a tight hug, each needing the comfort.

Some of the metal frames had made it, but most of the canvases and cartridge papers that once housed beautiful pieces of art were all gone. Jessamine wandered to the back of the art gallery, to where the hidden door had been located. The bookshelf hadn't made it through the fire either, and she carefully stepped through the passageway into the office.

The office reflected the art gallery. Almost everything inside had burned: the desk, the chairs, the shelves, and any artwork that had been on the walls. There didn't seem to be anything there that could aid in her search for Watson Naismith.

Jessamine sighed and headed back into the gallery. *Hopefully, we can catch Naismith tomorrow and solve everything!*

Chapter Twenty-Six

After spending the morning at home researching some more into the Naismith brothers, Jessamine swung by Emilia's Secret Garden Tea Shop for some lunch on her way to the art center for the afternoon to teach a ceramics class. Her online search had come up empty; she'd already read every single article about Pierce Naismith, and there wasn't much more available about Watson. She needed a break, and Emilia had mentioned the tea shop had added some fall favorites to their lunch menu to complement their seasonal teas. Jessamine had been craving a bowl of the chicken and white bean chili. Addison, as well as the sweet aroma of freshly baked cornbread, greeted her when she walked in.

"Hey, Jessamine. Good to see you again. Are you here to try another one of the fall teas?" She began to get a cup ready.

"Sure, but I'm here for some lunch as well."

"What can I get you? We just added some new items to our menu."

"I heard. Emilia was telling me your chicken and white bean chili is a huge hit around here. I think I'll take some of that."

"Good choice." Addison beamed and scooped up some chili to go for Jessamine and placed an enormous cornbread muffin on the side. "And what type of tea would you like?"

"Let's see. I'll try the Cozy Caramel with some milk please."

"Emilia mentioned something about needing to talk to you." Addison poured the freshly steeped Cozy Caramel tea into Jessamine's cup. "Wait here, and I'll go get her." She ducked into the back kitchen area and appeared with Emilia a moment later.

"Hey, Jess, how are you?"

"Hungry. I can't wait to try this chili. It looks and smells delicious."

"It's my perfected recipe and one of our most popular lunch items this time of year," Emilia said. "Anyway, I'm glad you stopped by because I was actually going to call later today about seeing if you wanted to go with me to the Crimson Orchard Spa tomorrow. I thought it'd be the perfect way to thank you for the gift card. And a good way to take your mind off things with the fire and case and, well, everything!" Emilia threw her hands in the air. "You need a break."

Jessamine laughed at her friend's dramatic gesture. "I'd love to, but I insist on paying for myself so you can use the gift card a second time. It was for your birthday, after all."

Emilia grinned. "Deal. How does a pedicure sound?"

Jessamine suddenly remembered the business card Andrew had found outside the front door of the art center shortly after the grand opening. It was for a nail technician who worked at that spa and was the only clue she'd never gotten around to following up on—mostly because she was certain it wouldn't amount to anything. But she was getting desperate. "Sounds great. How about I make the appointment? What time works best for you?"

They settled on a time for the next morning, and Jessamine left to spend the rest of the afternoon at the art center.

"Quick, Jess, let's get inside!" Emilia shouted over the pounding rain as they raced through the Rose Shore Resort parking lot. The balmy autumn weather had taken a miserable turn on Thursday morning, and a heavy rainstorm was violently hitting their little town. Mid-morning felt like dusk under the dark, dreary sky.

Jessamine and Emilia had met in the parking lot of the Rose Shore Resort shortly before their booked appointment at the Crimson Orchard Spa. When Jessamine had called the previous afternoon, it'd been a stroke of luck she was able to book them with Liza Monroe, the same nail technician whose business card was found.

"We look like drowned rats!" Jessamine laughed.

They stopped just inside the lobby to shake out their raincoats before heading down the hall toward the spa. Jessamine held open the door for Emilia and followed her into the peaceful reception area, where the calming smell of sandalwood and sounds of soft music peppered with bird songs welcomed them. The receptionist greeted them warmly and handed them each a glass of ice water infused with watermelon and mint. Other than a small look of surprise, she made no comment on their haggard appearance.

"Mrs. Monroe will be with you shortly. Please, take a seat." The receptionist directed them to a pair of comfy-looking couches in the reception area.

Jessamine and Emilia sat opposite each other.

"I'm looking forward to this. I haven't had a pedicure in years. What color are you going to get?" Emilia asked.

"I'm thinking a dark shade of red, something fall-ish."

"I like it. I'm going to go with purple."

The nail technician came over to greet them. She was warm and friendly and wore a pair of glasses that were a bright shade of pink. "Hello, ladies, I'm Liza Monroe. It's so nice to meet you. Please, follow me." Mrs. Monroe led them to a side room where two pedicure chairs and foot spas waited for them.

"Are you two celebrating anything?" she asked as Jessamine and Emilia sat down to slip off their shoes and socks.

"Just treating ourselves today." Emilia smiled. "Jessamine gave me a gift card for my birthday last week."

"Oh, happy belated birthday! Is this your first time here?"

"It is," Jessamine said. "Crimson Orchard was actually recommended to us by Gabriella Everhart. Have you met her?"

Emilia shot Jessamine a questioning look about the small bluff, which she promptly ignored.

"I have. She's quite the artist. Gabriella is staying right here at the hotel currently, though only for a few more days, I gather. I heard her fiancé died, and she had to extend her stay in Rose Shore. How do you know her?"

"Is that so?" Jessamine pretended like she had no idea. She was glad Liza Monroe was a Chatty Cathy. "I know Gabriella through the art world. I'm the new owner of the Rose Shore Community Art Center."

"Oh, you must have hosted that event Gabriella was in such a hurry to get ready for the other weekend. She kept saying over and over again that she couldn't be late."

This time, Jessamine didn't ignore Emilia's surprised look. They looked right at each other, and Jessamine knew they had the exact same question. Gabriella *had* been late—very late in fact—so why would she have been in such a rush to leave the spa? Where did she go?

"Yes, she was teaching a class there, but are you sure she was getting her nails done for that reason?" Jessamine asked.

"Yes, I'm sure. I remember because she was acting quite strange about it," Mrs. Monroe said. "She booked the earliest appointment available that day and was very upset I wasn't able to come in any earlier. She may very well be a famous artist, but I had to drop my mom off at the airport that day. I'd promised her months earlier to do so, and I couldn't just cancel. And it's not like Mom could have changed her flight simply because it better suited Gabriella. Anyway, Gabriella also made our receptionist and me promise not to mention her early appointment to her assistant, said to say it'd been in the afternoon if she asked. I've never been sworn to secrecy before over a manicure appointment."

"Did she just have a manicure done?" Jessamine asked after the technician was done with her long story.

"Yes, and then she went and chipped a nail right afterward. I had to fix it the very next morning." Mrs. Monroe tsked.

Jessamine thought Gabriella's behavior sounded strange. The artist must have been up to something that afternoon before the watercolor class, and she was sure it had something to do with *Tranquil* disappearing. She quickly stood, surprising both Emilia and Mrs. Monroe. "I'm sorry to say, but we really must get going. Thank you so much for your time."

"But we haven't even started yet!" Mrs. Monroe protested.

"I know, and we'll rebook; I promise." Jessamine quickly put her socks and shoes back on, with Emilia following closely behind. They hurried out of the Crimson Orchard Spa and into the hotel lobby.

"You think it was Gabriella, don't you?" Emilia asked with wide eyes.

Jessamine nodded frantically. "But we need some sort of proof. I doubt Constable Todd will be convinced by a suspicious manicure appointment."

"Well, she's staying here in the hotel, isn't she?"

"What are you getting at?"

"Maybe we could have a little look-see around her room."

"Are you being serious right now?" Jessamine asked with caution.

"Yes."

And Jessamine knew from the look on her friend's face she was being completely serious.

"One problem. Gabriella is staying on the top floor, and we can't even get to that floor without a special key card."

"Well, maybe Fay will let us up. You've stayed in contact with her, right?"

Jessamine nodded. "Well, if—*if* Fay does let us up, and she doesn't like me very much so I don't know if she will, there's a good chance the two sisters are sharing a suite, if it's anything like the one Madeleine is in. So, one of us could distract Fay while the other snoops around Gabriella's room. This could actually work."

Emilia clapped her hands together. "Perfect. Let's do this. Operation Manicure is a go."

"Well, now what do you suggest, Miss Brilliant Detective?" Jessamine asked sarcastically.

They'd asked the front desk clerk to phone Fay, and there'd been no answer from their suite. Jessamine even texted Fay to see if they could meet, and she responded saying she was busy sorting out flowers for Carlos' funeral. Jessamine and Emilia had since plopped themselves on a set of armchairs in the lobby.

"I'm working on it. I'm working on it." Emilia's eyes were tightly closed as if all her concentration was focused on forming a new plan.

"Maybe I should let the police know our suspicions and deal with grouchy Constable Todd. What's the worst he'll do, anyway?" She looked around the crowded lobby and spotted someone she recognized by the elevators. "Wait, Em. You can put that brain of yours to rest before you give yourself a headache. I may have a way to get us up there."

Emilia sprang up out of her chair, ready for action. "What is it?"

"Just follow my lead." Jessamine casually walked over to Ben, Victor's mentee she'd met at the book club. "Hey, Ben! Are you here to visit Madeleine?"

He looked surprised to see her and smiled. "Hey! Jessamine, right? Yeah, I'm here to see her."

"Well, we're on our way up to the top floor to visit a friend of ours. Mind if we ride up with you?"

"No, not at all." Ben led them into the elevator, which had just opened, and he used a fob he had to access the top floor. Jessamine wanted to ask him where he got it but didn't want to seem too suspicious, so she fumbled around in her purse pretending to be looking for one of her own.

Once they reached the top floor, they went their separate ways.

"Say hi to Madeleine for me," Jessamine said.

"Sure thing. See you at the book club tonight?"

Jessamine couldn't believe a whole week had passed since the book club meeting. So much had happened since then. "Possibly. I haven't decided yet. But I'll make it again soon if not."

Once Ben had entered Madeleine's suite, Jessamine and Emilia turned to each other, both with "now what?" expressions on their faces.

"I guess we didn't quite think this through. How do we even figure out which is their suite? And how do we get inside?" Jessamine asked.

A door clicked as it opened and closed, and they quickly ducked around a corner in the hallway. A lady Jessamine didn't recognize walked down the hallway and pressed the button for the elevator. After she stepped inside and disappeared, the two friends came out of hiding.

"This is a bad idea, Em. We could easily get caught. People will know we don't belong up here."

Emilia sighed. "All right. We can head back down."

They headed back toward the elevator when another door opened. On instinct, they scurried back around the corner and peered back toward the footsteps in the hallway.

This time, it was Gabriella leaving a hotel room and making her way to the elevator.

"So, Gabriella *is* here. Why wouldn't she answer the front desk's call to their suite?" Emilia whispered in Jessamine's ear.

Jessamine waited until Gabriella had stepped into the elevator. "I don't know. If she's up to something, she may not want people to know where she is. Or maybe she doesn't want to talk to anyone since her fiancé just died."

"Well, now we at least know which room is hers."

"But we still don't have a way to get in."

"Maybe there's a housekeeping cart around here somewhere."

"Em! That only works in movies. Besides, the housekeepers should have their key cards on them and not on the carts."

"They *should*, but that doesn't mean they always do." Emilia left their hiding spot and walked down the hallway. Jessamine followed, and around one of the far corners, she spotted an unattended housekeeping cart parked inside the open doorway of an empty room. The housekeeper was nowhere in sight, and Emilia marched right up to it and dug through the piles of neatly folded towels and small bottles of shampoo.

"Don't mess it up too much," Jessamine warned.

"Found it." Emilia held up an unmarked white plastic card.

"What?" Jessamine couldn't believe her eyes—or their luck. "Seriously?"

"Yes, and I'm willing to bet this is a generic key card that will get us into any room on this floor."

"Well, we aren't going to try every room to find out. Let's hurry and get into Gabriella's."

Jessamine held her breath as Emilia held up the card to Gabriella's door. The red light turned green, and the door unlocked with a soft click. They crept inside, and Emilia gently closed the door behind them so it didn't make a sound.

"All right, let's make this quick. You start searching, and I'll put the key card back before anyone notices it's gone. I'll knock softly four times when I'm back at the door." The gleam in Emilia's eyes made it obvious just how much she was enjoying the thrill of sneaking around.

"Okay. Hurry up."

The two-bedroom suite was very similar to the one Madeleine had been staying in, and Jessamine began by searching through the cupboards in the kitchen. Soon she heard four quick and quiet knocks on the door.

"So, did you find anything yet?" Emilia asked as soon as Jessamine opened the door.

"No, not yet. Do you want to search the living room area, and I'll take the two bedrooms?"

Emilia nodded and they split up.

It was easy to tell which bedroom belonged to which sister. Gabriella's was a complete mess with designer clothes tossed over every surface and the small vanity covered with beauty products. Even the items related to her profession had no organization. A portfolio was spread wide across the bed, samples of her artwork spilling out from plastic sleeves. Jessamine opened the closet and looked at the dresses stashed in there. Most were piled on the floor, but three were on hangers. She recognized the black one Gabriella had worn to the art center the day *Tranquil* disappeared pressed between a red cocktail dress and a flowery peasant dress.

Disappointed at not finding any evidence to use against the artist, Jessamine slipped into the other bedroom.

This room looked like it hadn't even been used over the past two weeks. She went through the drawers of the dresser and desk and found everything inside neatly folded away. There wasn't much there, though, some clothing, a laptop, and some art magazines.

"Hey, Jess, have you found anything?" Emilia called from the living room.

"No, not yet."

She headed to the closet next. Inside was a wide variety of clothing styles. The more frumpy-looking clothes, like the ones she'd seen Fay wearing the first time they met, were near the front of the closet, but near the back, things got interesting. Each dress she flipped through seemed fancier than the last. Beautiful gowns and sexy halters filled the closet. Jessamine paused when she got to the very last dress. It was a black tunic dress. She'd seen it before—in fact, she'd just seen it a moment ago.

Jessamine grabbed the black dress and raced back to Gabriella's closet. She yanked the other black dress off its hanger and held the two up to each other.

They were the exact same dress. But why would Fay own a copy of her sister's dress? And keep it stuffed at the very back of her closet?

Finally, the small bits and pieces of information Jessamine had been gathering since the afternoon *Tranquil* disappeared began to fit together in her mind like a nearly finished jigsaw puzzle.

Chapter Twenty-Seven

"Hey, Emilia, come look at this."

Emilia wandered into the bedroom and squinted her eyes at what Jessamine held up.

"So? It shouldn't surprise you Gabriella would own two little black dresses."

"But only one is Gabriella's. The other one I found in Fay's closet. And they aren't just any little black dress. They're the exact same one—the one Gabriella wore the day *Tranquil* disappeared."

Emilia's jaw dropped. "Do you think—"

She was cut off by the loud ringing of Jessamine's phone.

"It's Jackson. I should let him know what we've found." Jessamine answered her phone.

"Hey, Jessamine? Where are you?" Jackson's serious tone frightened her, and she sat down on the edge of Gabriella's bed. All thoughts about the dresses slipped away as she clenched the phone tightly to listen to what Jackson had to say next.

"At the Rose Shore Resort. What's going on, Jackson? You're scaring me." Emilia shot her a questioning look.

"I'm getting ready to leave the station. Andrew just called in a nine-one-one from the art center. He's injured and thinks there may have been a break-in."

"Oh no!" She covered her face with her free hand. "Is Andrew all right? Where's Molly?"

"I don't know. All I know is he was conscious when he called in, so I don't think it's too serious, but I don't know where Molly is."

"Okay. I'll meet you there."

"No. You should stay where you are." His voice was filled with intensity. "The police will be on their way soon, and if there was a break-in, it might be dangerous. I don't want you getting hurt again."

"I have to go. I have to make sure Andrew and Molly are all right, and I'm right next door. It'll just take a minute to get there."

"That's my point! I don't want you getting there before the police do."

"I have to, Jackson," Jessamine said softly and hung up the phone.

"What is it? What happened to Andrew?" Emilia looked like she was going to be sick.

"There might have been a break-in at the art center, and Andrew is hurt. I don't really know all the details, but I have to go. I don't even know where Molly is right now. What if she's inside the center?" Jessamine didn't wait for Emilia to give an answer. She raced out of the hotel suite and down the hallway toward the elevators.

"Wait, Jess. Hold on, and think about this for a moment." Emilia was right behind her.

"I have other artwork on display there, and I can't lose another piece. I just can't. What if someone sets another fire?" Jessamine tapped her foot impatiently as they waited for the elevator doors to open.

"How about we head over calmly and wait in the parking lot until the police get there?" Emilia tried to compromise.

"All right. You're right. We should wait for the police."

They rode down to the lobby level in tense silence.

As soon as the doors opened, Emilia headed toward the front desk. "I'm going to check again and see if anyone here knows where Gabriella went."

"Okay. I'll meet you at the art center."

"No, wait—Jessamine!"

Jessamine zipped up her rain jacket, headed out the lobby doors, and raced toward the Rose Shore Community Art Center. Deciding it would be faster to run through the wooded shortcut than to drive between the two buildings, she left her car behind and took off on foot. She was vaguely aware the rain had stopped and the sun was trying to peek through the dark storm clouds as if to cheer her on as she jogged through the trees. The anxiety of what could happen to her friends and business caused another burst of adrenaline to rip through her, and Jessamine arrived at the art center only a few moments later.

She reached the parking lot and noticed neither Jackson nor the police had arrived yet, but the sight of Andrew sitting on the curb near the front doors, holding his arm in intense pain, made Jessamine stop cold in her tracks for a moment. What had happened here? His arm was bleeding heavily through the sleeve of his shirt, and he looked like he was about to pass out.

"Andrew, what happened?" Jessamine's voice was rich with concern. She rushed toward him and pulled off her own jacket to wrap around his arm.

"I forgot my key after coming back from lunch, and Molly didn't answer the door or my texts."

"Where is she?"

"I don't know, but there's a broken window around the side. I leaned in to take a closer look and cut my arm on the broken glass. I think I've lost a lot of blood." He tried to lift his arm up to show Jessamine, only to wince in pain instead. "I called nine-one-one already, and the police and an ambulance are on the way."

"Jackson just called me, and he should be here soon." Jessamine finished wrapping up his arm as best as she could with her jacket. "Do you think anyone is inside?"

"I didn't see or hear anyone when I looked through the broken window. Maybe whoever broke in is gone now. But Molly did mention something about working over her lunch hour today on her new art class project, so I'm surprised she doesn't seem to be around."

The thought sickened Jessamine. "I'm going to take a look inside."

"Okay, but I'm coming with you."

Jessamine shook her head. "You're injured. You stay here to let the police know what's going on when they get here. I have to make sure Molly is all right. I'll be quick. I promise." Jessamine quietly unlocked the front door before Andrew could protest and slipped inside.

The community art center was eerily quiet. Jessamine didn't think her heart could beat any faster, but her pulse quickened. She took in a few deep breaths before doing anything else. The lights were off in the foyer, and every shadow seemed to lunge out at her. Once her eyes adjusted and she'd talked herself into remaining calm, which proved to be quite the challenge, she rationally realized that no one lurked in the foyer. She peered under Andrew's reception desk and behind the chairs.

No one was hiding.

Before going into the rest of the art center, Jessamine looked around for something that could be used as a weapon, just in case someone was still inside. There didn't seem to be any other option as her gaze fell on a forgotten umbrella sitting next to the coat rack. *An umbrella is better than nothing,* she tried to convince herself as she moved on down the hallway toward the classrooms, gripping her new weapon like a baseball bat.

She first went into the large main classroom, the one where *Tranquil* disappeared from, and she suddenly felt very small and alone standing in the empty room. The paintings on display seemed to stare at her as she moved around the room, looking for any signs of an intruder. *Better check the smaller classrooms, too.* Jessamine carefully crept from room to room but didn't find anyone or anything out of place. The only areas left to check were the offices and break room.

Jessamine walked slowly to the back of the art center and opened the door to Molly's office, terrified of finding her friend injured—or worse.

But Molly sat at her desk, rocking out to some loud music coming through her headphones, perfectly fine.

If the situation hadn't been so dire, Jessamine would've laughed at finding out serious and proper Molly was a rock 'n' roll fan.

Jessamine waved frantically and indicated with a finger held up to her mouth to keep quiet. Molly turned off her music and took off her headphones.

"What is it?" Molly whispered.

"Are you alright? There may be an intruder somewhere in the center."

A look of panic spread across Molly's face. "Do the police know?"

"Yes. They're on their way. Now, stay here and keep quiet. I'm going to keep looking around."

Molly nodded, and Jessamine moved next to her own office. No one was in there either, but she did trade out her umbrella weapon for a heavy art-history textbook.

The last place to check was the small break room. Jessamine carefully approached the closed door. She took a deep breath and then swung the door open as quickly as she could, wanting to use the element of surprise to her advantage.

No one.

Something crashed in the main classroom, followed by the sound of hurrying footsteps. It sounded like one of the display easels had been knocked over. Her head swung in that direction, and her arm hairs stood straight up as her senses went on high alert.

Oh, I hope that's just the police arriving. She picked up her pace before cautiously creeping around the corner down the hallway and peering into the classroom.

There she saw Fay scrambling to set a display easel up, the very easel from which *Tranquil* had been stolen. It'd been tucked behind a table in the classroom, just waiting for the missing painting to return. And there, balanced precariously under her arm, was the missing painting.

Chapter Twenty-Eight

Fay must have heard Jessamine coming—in her frantic attempt to place everything back the way it'd been, she knocked the easel down to the ground a second time. As she bent to pick it back up, *Tranquil* slipped out from under her arm, and the metal frame clattered loudly to the floor. Jessamine winced at what that poor painting had been through already and automatically stepped forward to rescue it from any more harm.

Fay countered her reach and lunged toward her. Jessamine quickly realized her mistake. Fay had misinterpreted her reaction as an attack and was defending herself.

"You . . . you shouldn't be here right now! You're supposed to be at the spa. I saw you go in," Fay shouted as she neared Jessamine. Her bloodshot eyes were wild with anger, and her mess of a ponytail, with little frizzy hairs standing out in all directions, matched her smeared makeup. "I warned you to stay out of this."

"Fay, please. Calm down a moment. I don't know what you're talking about."

Fay only continued her advance. "I really didn't want to hurt you, but now I have to silence you, just like I had to silence Carlos." A heavy sob escaped Fay's lips as she said Carlos' name.

Jessamine violently launched the heavy art history textbook in Fay's direction. Her panicked aim missed, but it at least slowed Fay down for a moment.

"Please, Fay, we can talk this through. I know you don't want to hurt anyone again. I know Watson put you up to this." Jessamine tried again to calmly reason with Fay despite having no idea if it had actually been Watson or Fay who initiated everything. The look of madness on Fay's face was terrifying, and Jessamine was willing to say or try anything to get through to her.

Fay was completely sobbing now, and her only response was a wild cry as she picked up *Tranquil* again and attempted to swing it at Jessamine.

"Put that painting down! Please don't ruin it." Her effort at staying calm was failing, and her words came out as a scold.

This only made things worse as Fay made another attempt to swing the painting. It proved to be too heavy for her, and both she and *Tranquil* crumpled down in a heap on the art center floor. Taking advantage of Fay's temporary incapacitation, Jessamine fled in the other direction.

After ducking into one of the dark smaller classrooms, Jessamine crouched down behind a large cabinet filled with art supplies. Fay was still between her and the front doors of the foyer, and Jessamine was running out of options. *Fay has lost it! There's no telling what she'll attempt next.*

"I know you're in here," Fay taunted from the entrance of the classroom. "You aren't going to make it out of this building alive. You know too much. I can't put this all behind me until you're gone."

Fay crept into the dark classroom and paused like she was waiting for her eyes to adjust as she looked anxiously around for Jessamine. Jessamine took a deep breath and counted slowly in her head.

One . . . Two . . . .

On three, she darted out of her hiding spot and pushed past Fay with all her strength, knocking her to the ground. Jessamine kept running down the hallway. She could hear Fay groaning behind her as she got up and quickly followed, soon grabbing Jessamine's arm from behind and shoving her back into the main classroom.

"Fay, please. Don't do this," Jessamine pleaded, feeling desperate. "The police are on their way, and if you cooperate now, it will make things easier for you. It's going to be okay if you just calm down."

Fay's words came out as a blubber. "No. I have to finish this."

"Finish what?" Jessamine backed away from Fay inch by inch. Her back was soon pressed flat against the large glass balcony doors, and a small sense of hope pushed the desperation down inside her. There might actually be a way out of this.

"This! I have to finish this," Fay screamed and leaped toward Jessamine again.

Quickly, Jessamine unlocked the glass door behind her back and stumbled out backward onto the balcony. She hurried to her feet and slammed her body toward the door, fumbling to try and trap Fay inside against her weight.

But Fay was too fast and managed to slip outside onto the balcony after her.

Jessamine, feeling panicked at her failed plan, tried to put as much distance between her and Fay as she could—though suddenly the balcony felt no bigger than her kitchen table. The rain from the morning picked up again, making the balcony floor slick.

Fay swiftly approached with a frightening look of murder. She now blocked Jessamine's only escape back into the building, and the only thing between Jessamine and the cold lake below was a glass railing. She looked down at the thick layer of mist covering the lake. The water beneath the balcony was filled with jagged rocks; it would be too dangerous to try escaping that way.

Fay swung a wild punch at Jessamine, and Jessamine easily ducked out of the way. She realized, through Fay's tears and the rain, her vision was probably becoming limited. Jessamine scurried around Fay and tried to keep out of her direct line of sight, while attempting to make it back to the balcony door. Her plan was to race back inside and lock the door behind her, trapping Fay on the balcony until the police arrived. Jessamine finally heard the sirens pull up to the art center, and a look of panic settled on Fay's face. This was her only chance.

Jessamine ducked under another swinging arm of Fay's and grabbed onto the handle of the door. She shoved it open, just as Fay let out a last cry of desperation and wrapped her arms around Jessamine's waist. She pulled Jessamine back out onto the balcony and knocked them both to the ground. Jessamine struggled to get up, her feet sliding in all directions on the wet surface. Her concentration in trying to find her footing distracted her from Fay's next tackle.

The collision sent them both flying against the balcony railing. The crinkling sound of shattering glass was all around them, and Jessamine knew what was happening before she felt herself fall.

Both Fay and Jessamine crashed into the chilly lake below, with Fay screaming the entire way down. They separated during the fall, and Jessamine hit the water hard. It took her a moment to grasp and be thankful that she'd hit water and not rocks.

Jessamine tried to swim as far away from Fay as she could before coming up for air. As she surfaced and wiped her hair away from her face, she saw Jackson dive off the art center balcony toward her. Molly stood behind him by the broken railing, pointing and shouting in Jessamine's direction, guiding him toward her.

"Jessamine!" Jackson shouted as he neared her in the water. "Are you okay?"

"I'm fine." She tried to tread water, but a sharp pain in her left leg suggested she'd twisted something during the fall. "Where's Fay?"

"Help!"

They looked over to see a bright orange life preserver ring sailing through the air down to Fay. She grabbed on, and two police officers pulled her to the shore underneath the balcony.

Jackson helped Jessamine swim to the rocky shore where they were greeted by a team of paramedics with blankets who immediately looked at Jessamine's leg. She felt slightly embarrassed at recognizing that a few of them had also helped her on the night of the house fire.

Fay was being treated as well but with a squad car waiting nearby.

Constable Todd glared at Jessamine and started to walk over in her direction, only to be stopped by Lauren. They exchanged a few quick words, and he curtly nodded, stepped aside, and let Lauren come over to talk to Jessamine instead.

"What happened in there, Jess? What were you doing inside?" Lauren reached them.

"Is Constable Todd furious with me?"

"Oh, he's just a big old softy. Don't worry about him."

Jessamine was about to answer Lauren's questions when Emilia jogged over to them with Andrew and his bandaged-up arm right behind her. Police officers stopped them a few feet away, but Lauren waved them through.

"Are you alright? I was so worried!" Emilia gave Jessamine an awkward, yet comforting, hug over top of the blanket.

"I'm fine, really." Jessamine smiled to assure her worried friends.

"I should have come with you," Andrew said.

"You were badly hurt."

"What was Fay doing in the art center?" Molly caught up with the rest of them.

"Molly, are you okay?" Jessamine asked.

Molly nodded. "I heard your fight in the main classroom and ran out of the office, but you and Fay were already out on the balcony when I got there, so I ran outside to find help."

Jessamine had lost all sense of time during her scuffle with Fay. She hadn't been able to tell if it had been minutes or hours since she first saw Fay in the main classroom. From Molly's account though, it had apparently been the former.

"So, what was Fay doing here?" Molly asked again.

Jessamine blew out a long breath. "She was returning *Tranquil*."

Chapter Twenty-Nine

Jessamine took a long sip of her steaming Japanese Sencha tea and immediately topped off her empty teacup from the nearby pot. She breathed in the earthy scent before taking another sip. The heat from the nearby fireplace warmed her on the outside as the soothing tea warmed her on the inside.

She'd finished giving her statement at the police station half an hour ago and had stopped by the Secret Garden Tea Shop before heading home. The unexpected fight and swim had given her quite the appetite, and her stomach hadn't been able to stop grumbling during her interview. Second to her need for food and hot tea was putting on her own warm clothes. The police had given her a dry set of pants and a sweatshirt, but Jessamine was very much looking forward to bundling up in her own cozy pajamas when she got home, cuddling with Margo, and finally finishing her rom-com novel.

Emilia walked over to the table, balancing a tray of assorted goodies and sandwiches, with Andrew following behind, carrying a carafe of hot water.

His injured arm was tied up tightly in a proper sling, but he'd actually lost very little blood, thanks to Jessamine's quick actions and now-ruined jacket. Molly sat with Jessamine at the table, enjoying her own cup of silver needle white tea, and Jackson had just texted Jessamine saying he was on his way over. They were expecting Lauren as well with some news about the case.

Jessamine let out a sigh mixed with happiness and exhaustion as Emilia and Andrew sat down.

"What's wrong, Jess?" Andrew gave her a worried look.

"Nothing. Nothing is wrong, and I'm so glad. The case is pretty much solved. All that's left is to find Watson Naismith, and I'm leaving that one to the police." She paused to take a bite out of a raspberry scone. "And I'm so glad to have such amazing friends looking out after me."

Just then Jackson came through the doorway of the tea shop and grabbed the chair beside Jessamine. He put his arm around her in a quick hug before grabbing a chicken salad sandwich and taking a huge bite.

"Hungry?" Jessamine laughed, and Jackson nodded with his face stuffed.

He swallowed and looked at everyone. "So, anything new with anyone?"

"Oh, very funny." Jessamine laughed and nudged his side with her elbow.

The door opened again, and in walked Lauren. She had a huge smile as she walked toward them. She plopped into the seat beside her brother and gave his arm a quick inspection. "How are you feeling?"

"Just dandy, thank you for asking. Now, tell us what your good news is," Andrew said.

"Who said anything about the good news? I just said I had news," she teased.

"Come on, Lauren." Andrew raised his eyebrows at his sister. "You have a huge smile."

"Tell us!" Emilia pressed, and everyone else leaned in closely, eager to soak up all the details of the mystery.

"Okay, okay." Lauren was clearly having a good time keeping them in the dark. "I just found out that Watson has been caught and is already sitting behind bars."

"What? When did this happen?" Jessamine asked.

"A few hours ago. He was picked up in a neighboring town by their local law enforcement. He's already admitted to causing the fire because Fay was suspicious of Jessamine getting too close to figuring out that she killed Victor."

"So, he's been working with Fay this whole time?" Molly asked.

Lauren nodded and turned to Jessamine. "Which means you've been investigating this whole time, haven't you?"

Jessamine took a guilty sip of her tea.

"Jess! You promised."

"Well, technically I didn't . . . anyway, tell us more."

Lauren gave her a look that said she was going to speak to Jessamine about this later. "Anyway, Naismith didn't go into details, but apparently, he and Fay met at an art show in San Francisco and got to talking one night and went out for drinks. There, Fay admitted to being in love with Carlos and said she was planning on destroying *Tranquil* in hopes that it would cool his love for her sister. They then realized their Victor connection because Naismith wanted to get back at Victor, who'd shown outspoken interest in *Tranquil*."

"I think I can take over from here," Jessamine said. "From what I've gathered, Fay was jealous of her sister—and especially of Gabriella's relationship with Carlos. But when Gabriella and Carlos broke up, and Gabriella decided to part with the painting that represented their relationship, Fay decided that was her opportunity to get rid of *Tranquil.* She wanted it gone so it was like Carlos and Gabriella's engagement never happened."

"Talk about a bad case of envy," Emilia said.

"Exactly, so she snuck into the art center and stole the painting. Em and I even found . . ." Jessamine quickly decided it would be best to keep her and Emilia's little break-in at the hotel to themselves. "Never mind. Anyway, Gabriella and Victor were standing too close to her exit, so she turned off the lights so her sister wouldn't recognize her. Victor was still in the way, so she stabbed him to give herself a chance to flee."

"Wait a minute. How did she sneak in?" Andrew asked.

"Oh, Fay was very proud of herself when she answered that." Lauren gave her brother a pointed look. "She dressed up exactly like her sister and waltzed right in. She kept her head low, pretended to be Gabriella, and was in and out so fast, no one realized there were two of them."

No one seemed to notice the knowing look Jessamine and Emilia exchanged. They were all busy looking at Andrew's sheepish expression. "I guess that was my fault for not paying closer attention to the guest list."

Jessamine smiled at him assuredly. "Don't worry about it. Gabriella and Fay look so similar. No one else noticed either."

"And what about Naismith?" Molly asked.

"From what the other police officers have told me, Naismith was planning on helping Fay steal *Tranquil*—to steal the one thing Victor had his sights on for months. He was going to show up at the art center as well but was delayed in Toronto because of his brother's death. Fay also admitted to slipping a threatening note into your purse, Jess. Did you know about this?" Lauren asked.

"Oh, that explains it," Jessamine said out loud to herself.

Everyone looked at her curiously.

"When I went to visit Gabriella the first time at the resort, it took a while for her and Fay to come down. Fay must have been stalling to write that note because she felt nervous I was checking up on them. She must've slipped the note in my bag while we were talking." She gave Lauren a small smile. "And

I decided to keep the note from you because you'd already banned me from the case at that point."

Lauren sighed. "Well, I'll admit you have quite the knack for solving crime, but you still should have told me."

"Okay, so now how does Carlos' death fit into all of this?" Andrew asked. "Did Watson have some sort of grudge against him as well?"

"No, that was all Fay's doing and had nothing to do with Watson. After his breakup with Gabriella, Carlos was using Fay to keep close to Gabriella with the hope of getting back together, and it worked," Jessamine said. "I'm guessing Fay found out and killed him out of jealousy."

"That's right. Carlos was at the resort that night to see Gabriella, and on the way, he ran into Fay. He took Fay out for a walk to explain everything, and he showed her the bracelet he bought Gabriella. Big mistake. Fay was furious, and in her anger, she told Carlos about stealing *Tranquil* out of love for him. Carlos said he was going to go to the police, and she knocked him into the pool in her panic and fled the scene, forgetting the bracelet behind. His head must have hit the side of the deck first, which was why he was unconscious when he drowned," Lauren said.

"Fay confessed all of this to you?" Jessamine asked.

Lauren nodded. "She's trying to cooperate for a lighter sentence. She didn't intend to kill Victor or Carlos. Both were cases of her jealousy getting the best of her. She even admitted she was trying to return *Tranquil* today because she knew she was in over her head. She saw you and Emilia go into the spa and figured that was her chance. She'd stashed the painting in another hotel room she'd booked under a false name since she and Naismith couldn't agree on what to do with it. She wanted to destroy it, but Naismith wanted to sell it and keep the money."

Emilia leaned over to Jessamine and whispered in her ear. "Fay must have left the resort while we were searching their suite."

Jessamine nodded in agreement.

"What are you two whispering about?" Jackson asked.

"Nothing," Jessamine quickly said.

"So, what was she doing breaking into your house that one night?" Emilia asked.

"That, I don't know." Jessamine shrugged. "Did Fay say anything about that to you, Lauren?"

"Well, I did ask, but Fay denied it was her. And I believed her since she was so truthful about everything else. So, I figured it must have been Gabriella. I pulled her back in for questioning, and Gabriella admitted that she broke in that night and she'd lied the first time I asked. She thought Jessamine might have stolen *Tranquil* and was looking for it since she'd gotten back together with Carlos and wanted it back. She also said she was late to the opening class because she'd stopped by to see him on the way."

Jessamine shook her head in disbelief. "Those two sisters are nuts. And I guess they rarely even talk to each other about non-work things if they both thought they were dating Carlos at the same time."

"And what about the person Jessamine thought she saw in her backyard after the fire? Who was that?" Emilia asked.

Everyone looked at Lauren, who shook her head. "Neither of the sisters nor Watson Naismith admitted to that."

"Maybe I really was seeing things," Jessamine said.

"Maybe it was the raccoon!" Emilia's expression was both amused and embarrassed at the memory.

"No, that was me," said a sheepish voice near them.

They all turned.

Howard "Click" McCoy stood nearby, looking extremely self-conscious. "That was me in your backyard the other night."

"And what were you doing there?" Jackson narrowed his eyes at Howard.

"I wanted another interview with Jessamine. I wanted something big for my blog."

"Why were you sneaking around the back?" Jessamine asked.

"I saw all the vehicles in your driveway and wanted to catch you alone. So, I thought if I could get you out to the back deck, I might actually have a shot at a real interview. It was stupid, I know. And then when Jackson came running outside, I got scared and ran."

Jessamine sighed. "It's fine, Howard. Just don't do it again. I promise I'll give you a proper interview tomorrow."

"Well, I must congratulate you on solving the case before I did." Howard stuck out his hand and shook Jessamine's. "But I'll beat you on the next one."

"Oh, I sure hope there isn't another mystery in Rose Shore anytime soon." Jessamine chuckled and smiled at her friends around the table before taking another long, soothing sip of her tea.

Thank you so much for reading *Paint Me a Crime*. If you've enjoyed the book, we would be grateful if you would post a review on the bookseller's website. Just a few words is all it takes!

Acknowledgements

I'm so thankful for TouchPoint Press and their enthusiasm for my cozy mystery series. I'm so glad my characters have found a home with you. Thank you to my agent, Dawn Dowdle, for being my amazing guide through the publishing world. Thank you to my critique group for your wonderful suggestions and to Lisa Bergen and Caity McCaughey for reading the very first draft of this book and telling me it was great. I still don't believe you, but it gave me the encouragement to keep going. A big, giant thank you to my friends and family for all their support, especially to my parents for buying me a ton of Nancy Drew books when I was a kid. And a special huge thanks to my husband, Samuel, for all the love, encouragement, and delicious dinners when I had a deadline. Thank you to Echo and Lillybelle for the distracting cuddles, though this book might have been finished a lot sooner if it weren't for me needing to constantly deal with your shenanigans. And thank you to everyone who picked up a copy of this book. It's crazy that my story is out there in the world, and I hope you enjoy it.

9 781956 851625